AUNT BESSIE'S X-RAY

AN ISLE OF MAN COZY MYSTERY

DIANA XARISSA

D1608047

For Stephen, because it's his turn again.

AUTHOR'S NOTE

X was always going to be a difficult letter for a book title, but I think the title and the story work together. This is the twenty-fourth book in the series and there are only two more titles following this one. After that, I'll be starting a new series with many of the same characters, so don't worry. Bessie will be around for a long time to come.

The stories work best in order, alphabetically by the last word in the title, but they can be read in any order. The characters do change and their relationships develop as the books go along, though.

This is a work of fiction. All of the characters are fictional creations. If any bear a resemblance to any real person, living or dead, that is entirely coincidental. The shops and businesses within the story are also fictional, and the same applies to them. The historical sites on the island are all real, but the events that take place within them in the story are all fictional.

If you've read any of my other books, you'll already know that this book is set on the Isle of Man. It's a truly unique and fascinating place. Situated in the Irish Sea between England and Ireland, this small island is a country in its own right, with its own government, currency, laws, and more. Because of the setting, I use British (and Manx) English throughout the story. There is a short glossary at the back of the book for any terms that might be unfamiliar for readers elsewhere in the world. I've been living in America for more than ten years now and I know that Americanisms are increasingly sneaking into my stories. Please let me know if you find any and I will do my best to correct them.

The photograph on the cover shows the entrance to the Ramsey and District Cottage Hospital as it appears today. The beautiful glass windows and doors are fairly new. The entrance looked somewhat different in Bessie's day, but I don't have any useable pictures from before the new front was installed. The new entrance is pretty, though, and I liked this photo for the cover.

All of my contact information is available in the back of the book. Please don't hesitate to get in touch. I love hearing from readers. You can sign up for my newsletter, all about new releases, on my website. I have a fun and active Facebook page if you want to chat with me and with other readers who enjoy my books. Thank you for coming on another adventure with Bessie.

CHAPTER 1

"I have good news and bad news," Dr. Robins said, grinning at his patient. He was probably forty, with dark brown hair that was starting to recede. His eyes were also brown and his thick glasses had a smudge of something on one lens.

Elizabeth Cubbon, known as Bessie to nearly everyone, frowned. It had been a long morning and she didn't really want to get bad news before lunch. "What's the bad news?" she asked, swallowing a sigh.

"I'm going to need to see you again tomorrow and will probably want to see you again on Thursday," the doctor replied.

"What's the good news?" Bessie felt more hopeful. She'd been certain that he'd been going to tell her that her arm was broken.

"According to the X-ray, you haven't broken any bones. At your age, that's something of a miracle, really."

Bessie bristled at the mention of her age. She'd stopped counting her birthdays once she'd turned sixty. That birthday had given her access to a free bus pass, one that she only used very rarely. The next birthday of note would be her one hundredth, when she would get a card from the Queen. There seemed no point in counting all of the years in between, at least as far as Bessie was concerned. She was still middle-aged, she reckoned, and she didn't need a doctor who was forty years her junior implying otherwise.

"Tell me what happened," he said.

"I've already told the nurse what happened," Bessie replied.

"Did you? She didn't make a note for me. Would you mind terribly repeating yourself?"

Bessie did mind, but maybe not terribly. She actually found the entire incident somewhat embarrassing. "I was out for my morning walk. I walk on Laxey Beach every morning, regardless of the weather."

"Yes," the doctor nodded. "You're in excellent physical condition for your age. I assume keeping active has helped."

Another mention of her age. Bessie wondered if she could request a different doctor. "I was walking along the sand," she continued, choosing to ignore the man's comment. "I got a bit too close to the water's edge and when a large wave suddenly headed towards me, I tried to outrun it, back up the beach."

"And the wave won?"

"No, actually, I did escape the wave, but I tripped over a piece of driftwood that I hadn't seen and fell over."

"Have you had your eyes tested lately?"

"There isn't anything wrong with my eyes," Bessie snapped. "The sun was still coming up and large sections of the beach were in the shadows. I was just below the cliffs."

"Near Thie yn Traie?" he asked, mentioning the large mansion that was perched high on the cliff above the beach.

"Yes, exactly. I'm always very careful of my footing when I walk, but I was distracted by the wave, you see."

Dr. Robins nodded. "You tripped and fell onto the beach, then?"

"Yes, and I think I would have been fine if my arm hadn't landed on a large flat rock. My arm is the only thing that really hurts, at least."

"I should probably X-ray your hip and maybe a few other areas as well, but as long as you aren't in any pain, we'll leave that for today. As

I said, I want to see you again tomorrow. I'll be keeping a very close eye on that arm, just in case."

"Just in case what?" Bessie demanded. "If the bone isn't broken now, surely it won't suddenly break later today, not unless I fall on it again."

"X-rays are useful, but they don't always reveal every fracture. It's possible that you've fractured the bone and that every time you use that arm for something the break will get worse. I want to keep an eye on it. I may order another X-ray tomorrow."

"Does that mean I shouldn't use my arm?" Bessie asked, trying to imagine going through her day without the use of her right arm.

"I would try to do as much as possible with your left arm," the doctor replied. "The injured arm is painful anyway, isn't it?"

"It's very painful," Bessie admitted.

"Try to rest it as much as possible. You can use ice or heat on it if you feel that either helps." He rattled off a number of additional instructions and warnings as Bessie resisted the urge to sigh. It wasn't the doctor's fault that she'd tripped, but she had been hoping that he would be able to offer some sort of treatment that would have quick results. Hearing that it might take months before her arm would be fully back to normal was not good news.

"What about writing?" Bessie asked, thinking about what she'd planned for the day.

"You may be able to write if you support the arm with a pillow or two, but you should stop if it makes the pain worse."

"Thank you," Bessie said, swallowing a sigh. "I'll see you tomorrow, then."

He nodded. "I hope your arm is feeling better by that time."

That makes two of us, Bessie thought but didn't say. She followed the doctor out of the exam room and turned left while he turned right. He was just saying a cheery hello to his next patient as Bessie reached the desk.

"He wants to see you again tomorrow," the receptionist said.

"Yes, I know."

"We have an opening at ten, if that works for you."

"That's fine," Bessie sighed. As she'd never worked and was well past retirement age anyway, many would suggest that she didn't have anything better to do with her time, but Bessie wouldn't agree. She read books, did some historical research for Manx National Heritage, helped out with a few local charities, and mostly simply enjoyed her life on her own terms. Appointments interrupted her normal routine and made her feel out of sorts.

"What did the doctor say?" a concerned voice at her elbow asked.

Bessie looked over at her closest friend, Doona, and shrugged. "My arm isn't broken, but he still wants to see me again tomorrow."

"That's good news," Doona said happily.

"Half of it is good news, anyway," Bessie muttered in reply.

Doona Moore was in her forties, and she and Bessie were unlikely friends. They'd met in a Manx language class some years earlier, while Doona's second marriage had been falling apart. Bessie had helped Doona through the ordeal and the two had been friends ever since.

"What time is your appointment tomorrow?" Doona asked.

"Ten o'clock," the receptionist answered for Bessie.

"I'll see if I can switch shifts so that I can bring you," Doona offered.

"I can get a taxi."

Doona shrugged. "If you don't mind. I may struggle to change things on such short notice."

She took Bessie's left arm and the pair walked together out of the small hospital that served the north of the island. Doona's car was parked right outside.

"Thank you for bringing me," Bessie said as Doona began the drive back to Laxey. "I could have rung for a taxi today as well."

"I have the day off. I was having a lazy morning when Maggie rang me. I was more than happy to bring you here."

Bessie sighed. "Maggie shouldn't have interfered." Maggie Shimmin and her husband, Thomas, owned the row of holiday cottages that ran along the beach between Bessie's home and the stairs to Thie yn Traie. Bessie knew that Maggie was working in the cottages, getting them ready for the first guests of the year, who would be arriving the following month.

"Maggie was worried about you. She saw you fall, and from what she said, the fall looked a good deal worse than it actually was."

"She could have come down and seen how badly hurt I was before she rang you," Bessie complained.

"She rang me on her way down the beach. You're lucky she didn't ring 999. Instead of just me, you could have had an ambulance and a dozen police cars turn up."

Bessie knew that Doona was right. If Maggie had rung 999 the dispatcher would have sent an ambulance and also notified a number of Bessie's friends who were with the police. The last thing she'd have wanted was for police inspector John Rockwell and half the Laxey constabulary to see her as she'd stood on the beach covered in sand and seaweed.

It had been bad enough dealing with Doona, who'd wanted to rush her to Accident and Emergency at Noble's immediately. Bessie had insisted on changing her clothes before she'd rung the Ramsey and District Cottage Hospital to see if she could get an appointment. She'd been relieved that they'd been able to fit her in, as it was a smaller facility and she hoped that going there would mean fewer people would hear about the incident. That was unlikely, as Maggie had no doubt told everyone on the island already, but Bessie was doing her best to hold onto hope that there might be a few people who hadn't heard about what had happened.

Doona stopped her car in the small parking area next to Bessie's cottage. "Do you need any shopping getting in?" she asked.

Bessie shook her head. "I did my usual shop on Friday. I should have everything I need for the week. Assuming we don't end up with another murder to discuss, that is."

Doona laughed. "We do eat rather a lot during murder investigations," she agreed. "Things are very quiet at the station right now. I said to John the other night that it feels as if we're all just waiting for something terrible to happen."

"Maybe the terrible things are done happening for a while. There have been rather a lot of them over the past two years."

Doona nodded. She and Bessie climbed out of the car and walked to the cottage's door. "Next month is the two-year anniversary of the first body you ever found," Doona said. "We'll have to spend the day together."

"I'd like that," Bessie admitted. The anniversary was sure to bring back bad memories, and she'd prefer not to spend the day alone.

She dug out her keys and opened the cottage door, giving the small sign next to the door a pat as she walked into the kitchen. The sign read "Treoghe Bwaane," and it had been in place when she'd purchased the cottage at the age of eighteen. The words were Manx for "Widow's Cottage" and the name had seemed appropriate to the grief-stricken teenager who'd just learned of the death of the man she'd loved. Matthew Saunders had left all of his worldly possessions to Bessie. Her inheritance hadn't amounted to much, but it had been enough to allow her to buy the tiny cottage on the beach. She'd lived there, alone, ever since.

"Let me make you some lunch," Doona said. "What do you fancy?"

Bessie shrugged. "My arm is aching. I'm not really hungry."

"Did the doctor give you anything for the pain?"

"He just said to take some over-the-counter remedy if it got too bad."

"And it's bad enough to be affecting your appetite, so you need to take something."

Bessie thought about arguing, but decided against it. Doona was right. Her arm hurt enough to warrant taking something. After she'd swallowed some tablets, she let Doona heat some soup for her. She ate it under Doona's watchful eye.

"I have to go and collect Amy from school," Doona said reluctantly as Bessie finished eating. "I offered because I was off work today. Obviously, I didn't realise that you were going to need me."

"I don't need you," Bessie said firmly, only just managing not to snap at her friend. She hated being fussed over. "Where is Amy going?"

"She's just started taking piano lessons," Doona explained. "It's something she's always wanted to try, but, well, there were other priorities."

Bessie nodded. John Rockwell was Amy's father. He had been married when he'd first moved to the island two years earlier. His wife, Sue, had disliked the island, and after a year she had taken the children and moved back to Manchester, leaving John on his own. Sue had never stopped loving her first real love, Harvey, and they had been reunited when Harvey had treated Sue's mother for cancer.

Once John and Sue were divorced, Sue and Harvey had married and gone on an extended honeymoon in Africa. Harvey had always dreamed of working in a developing country, helping people in need. At some point during their trip, Sue had developed a fever, and she'd passed away in January. More than a month later, John was adjusting to life as a single parent while the children, Thomas and Amy, were struggling to understand the loss of their mother. Thomas was seventeen and Amy was nearly fifteen, so they were old enough to question everything that John told them about what had happened to Sue.

As far as Bessie knew, the local police where Sue had died had investigated her death. They'd steadfastly refused to release their findings to John, though. Harvey remained in Africa, working in a local hospital. Bessie had even asked a friend, Andrew Cheatham, who was retired from Scotland Yard, to investigate, but he'd been unable to get any additional information from the local authorities. Bessie knew that John wanted Harvey arrested, something that might only happen if the man returned to the United Kingdom.

John was doing his best as a single parent, and Bessie was happy that Doona was doing as much as she could to help. The pair were slowly exploring the idea of turning their friendship into a romantic relationship, but to Bessie it seemed as if they kept taking one step forward before taking two steps back.

Doona had inherited some money when her second husband had died. Was Doona paying for piano lessons for John's daughter? Bessie wondered. There was no doubt in her mind that Doona would be happy to do so, but if John was allowing it, that suggested that the relationship between the pair was becoming more serious.

"Thank you for taking me to hospital today," Bessie said as she walked Doona to the door. "I truly do appreciate your concern, even though I hate it when you fuss."

Doona laughed. "Maybe I'll fuss over you less now that I have the children to fuss over," she teased.

"That would be good."

"Except Thomas and Amy hate being fussed over even more than you do," Doona told her. "It's a constant struggle to be there for them without fussing, except once in a while when they actually want to be fussed over."

"If I can do anything to help, let me know."

"I will do."

Bessie shut the door behind her friend. Doona had insisted on taking care of the washing-up, which meant she had nothing to do. Bessie had been an amateur historian for years. Just recently she'd been sent a collection of letters that had been written over a period of fifty years. The writer, Onnee, had left the island after marrying an American, seemingly almost on impulse. Bessie was slowly transcribing the woman's flowery script and she was fascinated by the story that was emerging. She'd planned to spend her afternoon with Onnee, and now that Doona was gone, she didn't see any reason to change her plans.

In her small office, Bessie rested her arm on a pillow and worked her way through several letters, transcribing them a word at a time. When her eyes began to cross and her head began to ache, she put the copies of the letters aside and read back through her transcriptions.

There had been complications with the birth of Onnee's first child, and doctors had told Onnee that the child would die young, having never managed to meet any of the expected milestones. Onnee proudly wrote to her mother about every little thing that the baby, called Alice, managed to accomplish. At a year old, Alice was crawling, and Onnee wrote that Alice had actually tried pulling herself to her feet once or twice as well. Alice was also babbling happily, and Onnee was convinced that she'd heard the baby call her "mama" more than once.

Onnee also wrote that she suspected she was pregnant again. She told her mother that she was excited, but also mentioned how difficult things were financially for the little family. Her husband, Clarence, was working, but his job didn't pay particularly well. Onnee knew that he would probably be able to find a better job if they moved to a nearby larger city, but Clarence wouldn't hear of moving away from his parents.

Onnee had another reason for wanting them to move, as well. When Clarence had gone travelling, he'd left behind a fiancée, who'd been shocked when he'd returned with his new wife. Faith had been staying with Clarence's parents while he'd been away, and she was still living with them now, more than two years after Clarence and Onnee had arrived. Clarence still spent a great deal of time at his parents' home, sometimes staying with them for a night or two over the weekends. That left Onnee on her own with baby Alice, something that Onnee seemed to feel ambivalent about, really. Bessie put her transcriptions into the folder on her desk and slowly stood up.

Feeling stiff and sore from sitting for so long, and with a dull ache in her arm, she headed back down the stairs, ready for more pain tablets. It only took a few minutes for her to make herself a cup of tea. She washed the tablets down with tea and a biscuit. She was just thinking about finding a book to read when she heard some commotion on the beach outside.

When she looked out the window at the back of her cottage, she could see half a dozen men and women crossing the beach. They seemed to be collecting something, and when Bessie recognised one of the men, she headed for the cottage door.

"Hugh Watterson, what on earth are you doing?" she demanded as she walked up behind the man. Hugh was a constable with the Laxey Constabulary. He'd spent many nights during his teenage years in Bessie's spare bedroom. As she'd never had children of her own, she'd acted as something of an honourary aunt to the boys and girls of Laxey. Hugh's parents hadn't approved of his desire to join the police, which was just one of the reasons why Hugh had preferred Bessie's spare room to his bedroom at home. Bessie's nearly endless supply of biscuits, cakes, and sympathy had also played a part.

Hugh was in his mid-twenties now, but to Bessie he still looked no more than fifteen. He'd married his wonderful wife, Grace, just over a year ago, and the pair had recently welcomed their first child, a little girl who'd been christened Aalish Elizabeth.

Now he spun around and looked at her guiltily. "A few of us were talking, and we thought maybe we could come down and clear away some of the driftwood on the beach," he muttered, looking at the ground.

"Clear away the driftwood?" Bessie echoed. "Why on earth, oh, you can't be serious. You aren't clearing the driftwood because of my fall, are you?"

Hugh flushed. "That may have been part of it, but Grace and I enjoy walking on the beach, too. Driftwood is a problem for everyone."

Grace and Hugh had recently purchased a house on Laxey Beach, but it was some distance from Bessie's cottage. Hugh was going to need a much larger crew of helpers if he truly intended to remove the driftwood from the entire stretch of beach from Bessie's cottage to his home.

"You do realise that the tide will simply bring more driftwood onto the beach later tonight," Bessie said.

"Yes, of course, but, well, we thought it might help."

"You're wasting your time. You should be home with Grace and Aalish. I do appreciate that you're trying to help, but I've been walking on this beach for a very long time and today was the first time I ever tripped over driftwood. I reckon I have another fifty years or so before I have to worry about it happening again."

Hugh looked as if he wanted to argue, but after a second he snapped his mouth shut.

"Call off your helpers. I'm sure you all have better things to do," Bessie told him firmly.

Hugh nodded. "You're right, of course. When I heard about your accident, well, I wanted to do something to help, that's all."

Bessie gave him a hug. "I do appreciate it, but you're fighting a losing battle against Mother Nature out here."

Hugh nodded and then whistled loudly. The other men and women stopped what they were doing, which seemed to have been not much more than strolling along the beach anyway, and gathered around Hugh and Bessie.

"Bessie has sensibly suggested that we give up, as the next tide will probably undo any good we might have managed. Everyone is invited back to my house for hot chocolate and biscuits," Hugh announced.

The little group cheered and then disbursed. Bessie knew nearly all of the young men and women and she was given several hugs as they departed.

"We all worry about you," Hugh said as the last woman hugged Bessie and headed for the parking area.

"You shouldn't. I'm fine and I can take care of myself."

"I know. I'm sorry."

"You'd better get home," Bessie suggested. "Grace is about to get half a dozen guests she isn't expecting."

"She told me to bring everyone back when we're done," he told her. "She hasn't seen anyone for a few days and she's going crazy at home with the baby."

"She can ring me anytime she wants company. I'm only a short walk away."

Hugh nodded. "I'll remind her of that."

Bessie watched as Hugh headed back to his car and then turned and looked at the water. Now that she was outside, the fresh air felt good. A short walk before dinner would clear her head and take her mind off her arm, she decided.

She'd only managed a few paces before she heard her name being called.

"Bessie, oh, Bessie."

She stopped and forced herself to smile as Maggie Shimmin crossed the beach towards her.

"How are you?" Maggie demanded.

"I'm fine."

"Are you certain?"

"I'm quite certain. The doctor took an X-ray and my arm isn't broken."

"I hope he's going to follow up and check it again," Maggie said. "X-rays can miss things sometimes. I had a friend who had a fracture in her wrist and they only managed to spot it on the third X-ray."

"I'm seeing Dr. Robins again tomorrow. He's going to examine it again and maybe take another X-ray."

Maggie nodded. "Please look after yourself, " she said softly.

"How are you?" Bessie asked, bracing herself for the woman's usual litany of complaints.

"Me, oh, I'm fine," Maggie replied. "Thomas wanted to come with me to see how you were, by the way, but he's managed to catch a bad cold. The doctor has him on bed rest for at least a fortnight."

Bessie frowned. Thomas had been struggling with ill health for many months now, including a bout with pneumonia. It was worrying to hear that he was ill again.

"He'll be fine," Maggie said briskly. "I can't live without him, so he has to recover."

Before Bessie could reply, Maggie spun on her heel and walked away.

The air was rapidly getting colder as Bessie continued down the beach. The weather in late February was variable and often included a great deal of rain. Bessie felt fortunate that it was dry, even if it was chilly. When she reached the stairs to Thie yn Traie, she turned around.

When she let herself back inside, the light on her answering machine was blinking frantically. She'd fallen into the habit of turning the ringer on her phone off at night so that she wasn't disturbed by late-night calls from double-glazing salesmen. As she crossed to the phone, she realised that she'd never turned the ringer back on after her accident that morning. She'd missed an entire day of calls, and knowing how the island thrived on skeet, there was no doubt many people had rung once they'd heard about Bessie's accident.

She listened to more than two dozen messages from concerned friends and nosy acquaintances. Feeling as if there was no time like the present, she picked up the phone and started ringing people back. An hour later, she'd spoken to everyone from her advocate to her favourite taxi driver, assuring each one that she was absolutely fine. After making herself some dinner, she curled up with a new cosy mystery by a favourite author and let herself get lost in another world.

The knock on the door surprised her. She'd completely lost track of time, and it took her a minute to even remember where she was as she walked towards the door.

"I'm fine," she told John Rockwell. The handsome man looked better than he had in a long time, Bessie thought. His brown hair had been cut recently and was neatly combed. His green eyes had a smile behind them and he looked as if he'd been eating and sleeping well lately, something that didn't always happen for the busy man.

He chuckled. "I'm sure you are. I just wanted to see for myself."

"My arm is sore, but the doctor assures me it isn't broken," Bessie told him. "But do come in for a cuppa."

"I wish I could, but I'm meant to be doing some grocery shopping. I just stopped here on my way to ShopFast."

Bessie nodded. "I appreciate you taking the time to visit."

He gave Bessie a hug. "Please take care of yourself. There are a lot of people who worry about you."

"I'm absolutely fine and quite capable of taking care of myself," she reminded him.

"I'll try to remember that," he replied before he turned and walked back to his car.

Bessie watched him drive away before she shut the door and locked it behind him. Feeling more tired than she thought she should, she grabbed her book and carried it upstairs. She'd read more once she was in bed, she decided. Except once she was ready for bed, she found that she couldn't keep her eyes open.

Her internal alarm reliably woke her at six every day. She was shocked the next morning to discover that it was ten past seven when she opened her eyes. Frowning, she slowly climbed out of bed, taking care not to bump or use her sore arm. The water from the shower seemed intent on pounding on it, though, which meant Bessie found herself rushing to get finished. Washing her shoulder-length grey bob was also a challenge, but she did her best with her left hand.

Because she felt as if she was behind schedule, she ate a bowl of cereal for a quick breakfast before heading out for her morning walk. While she felt as if she should walk further, she was beginning to get tired by the time she'd reached Thie yn Traie. Turning for home, she promised herself that she'd have another, longer walk later.

When she'd spoken to her favourite taxi driver the previous day, she'd asked him if he could collect her for her doctor's appointment the next morning. Of course Dave had said yes, and Bessie smiled to herself as he pulled his taxi into the parking area in front of her cottage at half nine.

She'd been using the same car service for many years. The original owner had been a friend, and when he'd sold the service to a Douglas-based firm, they'd continued to offer her a generous discount on their services to thank her for her continued loyalty to the company. Increasingly, she found that nearly every time she used them, Dave was the driver who was assigned to her. She wasn't sure if that was his doing or if the dispatcher simply knew of her preference for the man, but Bessie wasn't going to complain.

He was at her side, offering his arm, before Bessie had locked the door behind her.

"I don't need to be fussed over," she reminded him as he escorted her to his car.

"Of course not," he agreed cheerfully as he helped her into the car. He waited until she was buckled into her seat before he carefully shut the door for her.

"How are you today?" the receptionist at the Ramsey hospital asked Bessie a short while later.

"I'm fine. I'm sure my arm is better today." Bessie was being mostly truthful. The arm hurt more than it had the previous day, but Bessie was sure that was simply a sign that it was healing.

"That's good to hear. Dr. Robins will be with you shortly."

"Thank you."

Bessie turned and headed for the small waiting area.

"Miss Cubbon," the receptionist said softly.

"Yes?" Bessie asked, turning back around.

"When you're done with Dr. Robins, could I buy you a cuppa in the coffee shop?"

"I suppose so," Bessie said, feeling puzzled.

"Thank you," the woman said. "I'm hoping you may be able to help me."

"I will if I can. What's wrong?"

The receptionist looked around the crowded waiting room and then leaned closer to Bessie. "My sister was murdered, and the police can't find the killer," she confided.

CHAPTER 2

essie took a seat in the waiting room with the receptionist's words ringing in her ears. She didn't know the woman, although it was possible that she knew her parents. It was clear, however, that the woman knew who Bessie was and knew that Bessie had been involved in a number of murder investigations. Bessie could listen to her story and sympathise, of course, but that was all that she could do. The police were the ones who had to solve the murder.

The more she thought about it, the more curious she became. If the woman's sister had died on the island, the death hadn't been recorded as a murder. Bessie knew firsthand just how much news coverage murder investigations received. Either the death had been ruled something other than murder or the sister had died somewhere other than on the island.

There was no way Bessie would be able to help in any way if the victim had died elsewhere. At least on the island she knew a few police inspectors and constables with whom she could discuss the case. Frowning, she began to doubt the wisdom of agreeing to the meeting.

"Miss Cubbon? The doctor is ready for you now," one of the nurses announced.

Bessie followed the nurse into a small examination room.

"How are you feeling today, then?" the nurse asked brightly.

"I'm sure my arm is much better."

"That's good. Any stiffness or soreness elsewhere after your fall?"

Bessie often had a touch of stiffness, which came with being middle-aged, but today's wasn't any worse than normal. She shook her head.

"The doctor will be in shortly, then," the woman told her. She left the room as Bessie settled into the chair that was next to the small desk in the corner. It was likely that the doctor would want her to move to the exam table when he arrived, but for now she was quite content to sit in a chair.

"Ah, Miss Cubbon, how are you?" Dr. Robins asked as he walked into the room.

Feeling as if she'd done nothing but answer that question for the last twenty-four hours, Bessie swallowed a sigh. "I'm sure my arm is much better," she repeated herself.

"Are you, now? Or are you hoping it's better because you don't want to see me again?" The doctor laughed at his own joke as he sat down in the chair at the desk.

"If I thought I needed to see you again, I wouldn't hesitate to say so, but it seems a shame to take up your valuable time when I'm certain I'm mending."

The doctor took her arm and prodded it gently. "Does that hurt?"

"Yes, some."

After several more pokes and prods, he had her move the arm through a full range of motion, wiggle her fingers, and bend her elbow and wrist.

"Everything seems to be working," he said eventually.

"Yes, I thought so, too."

"Have you been taking tablets for the pain?"

"A few, now and again. I haven't taken any yet today, but I probably will soon."

"Don't suffer unnecessarily. Take tablets when you need them. Obviously, follow the instructions on the bottle. Don't take more than you need, but if you're in pain your body can't focus on healing."

"I'll remember that," Bessie promised.

"Excellent. Make an appointment to come back and see me again on Thursday, please. If you've continued to improve, I shouldn't need to see you again after that."

Bessie thought about arguing. As far as she was concerned, she'd already seen the doctor more than was necessary. Having to come to see him again annoyed her. Before she could complain, though, he turned and left the room. Picking up her bag, Bessie headed for the door.

"Dr. Robins wants to see you again on Thursday," the receptionist told her.

"Yes, and I've no idea why. My arm is fine, just a bit sore."

"Sometimes injuries can be slow to heal. I'm sure the doctor just wants to keep a close eye on you, that's all."

Again Bessie thought about disagreeing, but there seemed little point in doing so with the receptionist. She was just doing her job. Bessie made an appointment for ten on Thursday, silently vowing that it would be the last time she visited Dr. Robins for her arm.

"I get my break in a few minutes. Do you mind terribly waiting?" the receptionist asked as Bessie slid the appointment card into her handbag.

"Not at all," Bessie assured her. She sat back down in the waiting room and idly flipped through a two-year-old copy of the sort of gossip magazine that was one of Bessie's guilty pleasures. It had been some time since she'd purchased any herself, but she was happy to read about the marriages, divorces, and babies of the minor celebrities who filled the pages. For the most part, she had no idea who any of them were, so it didn't matter in the slightest that the news was years out of date.

"I've combined my morning and afternoon break to give us a bit more time," the receptionist said.

Bessie jumped. She'd been so engrossed in a story about wedding disasters that she hadn't noticed the woman's approach. "That was smart," she said as she put the magazine down.

"We still only have half an hour. I'll have to talk quickly. There's a coffee shop in the building. That's probably the best place to go, unless you'd rather go somewhere else."

"I see little point in wasting our valuable time travelling anywhere else," Bessie replied. "Let's just stay here."

The café was small and mostly empty. They sat at the table furthest from the door, and Bessie picked up a menu.

"The menu is limited, but everything is good," the receptionist told her.

"What can I get you?" the waitress who'd wandered over asked.

"Should we share a plate of biscuits?" Bessie asked her companion.

"Yes, you should," the waitress answered for her. "We make them all ourselves. There are half a dozen varieties and every one of them is delicious."

"Perfect, and a cup of tea," Bessie said.

"Tea for me, too," the other woman said.

As the waitress walked away, Bessie smiled encouraging at her companion. "I'm not sure that I'll be able to help in any way. I'm not even sure why you think I might be able to help. I'm always happy to listen, though."

"I've read about you in the papers. You keep finding dead bodies and helping the police solve murders. The police need help. They haven't been able to solve my sister's murder."

Bessie wanted to argue that there was probably very little she could do, but she was too curious to say that to the other woman. "You know who I am, but I don't believe we've ever met," she said instead.

The woman flushed. "I'm sorry. I should have introduced myself. I'm afraid I'm not thinking very clearly. I haven't been since my sister died, really. It's been terrible."

Bessie patted her hand. "I'm sorry for your loss."

"Thank you. I'm Kelly Sutton, before I forget again to tell you. My sister was Kara Sutton. She was twenty-seven when she died. I'm twenty-six, if it matters."

"Did you grow up on the island?"

"Yes, we lived in Douglas. I still live in Douglas. At the moment, I'm living with my parents, actually. After Kara's death, well, we were all so badly shaken that it seemed best if I moved back home. Mum and Dad are very upset, of course."

"Of course."

"Biscuits for two," the waitress announced as she put a large plate in the centre of the table. "And tea for two," she added, handing each woman a teacup. "Anything else?"

"No, thank you," Bessie replied.

"If you need anything, wave or shout," the waitress said with a laugh. "Otherwise, I'll leave you alone."

"What else should I tell you?" Kelly asked after a sip of tea. "My mother is from the island. She met my father at university in Liverpool. Mum insisted on moving back here after they'd both finished school. Dad didn't mind. He works with computers for one of the banks. Mum went back to work once I'd left home. She works as a buyer for ShopFast now."

Time was going to get away from them if she wasn't careful, Bessie thought. Kelly clearly wanted to talk, but she didn't seem to be in any hurry to tell Bessie about her sister's death.

"You only had the one sister?" Bessie asked.

"I forgot to mention Kent," Kelly said with a grin. "He's my older brother. He's going to be thirty soon, something I've been reminding him about for months."

"Does Kent live in Douglas?"

"No, he and his wife, Amelia, have a house in Port Erin. House prices are a bit lower in the south of the island, and Kent and Amelia both work in Castletown, so Port Erin made sense for them."

"What do they do?" Bessie asked, more out of curiosity than because she thought it might be relevant to Kara's death.

"Kent is an advocate and Amelia owns and runs a little café near the castle." Kelly told Bessie the name of the café, and Bessie smiled.

"They have excellent food. I try to eat there whenever I'm in the south of the island."

"Amelia does all of the cooking. Most of the time, she also does all of the waitressing and everything else that goes along with running a café. She loves it, but it's exhausting. I know she and Kent have been talking about either hiring more help or selling the café altogether."

"I'm sure it's terribly hard work."

Kelly nodded. "I help out sometimes on weekends. Amelia is always so grateful. She's hired at least a dozen people in the last few years and none of them have ever lasted for very long. One of them was actually stealing money right out of the till and another walked out with a box full of plates and glasses from the kitchen."

"My goodness."

"Anyway, that's the whole family, well, aside from Cousin Arnold."

"Cousin Arnold?"

"Arnold Stevenson. His mother is my father's sister. The whole family is in Scotland, except for Arnold."

"I get the feeling you don't like Arnold," Bessie said, picking up something from the tone of Kelly's voice.

She shrugged. "He's a little bit odd, that's all."

"Odd in what way?"

"He just has a few quirks." Kelly waved a hand. "I don't think his father is very accepting of his differences, which is why he moved over here. He lives with my parents, too, but he has a good job and he could get his own place if he were unhappy with Mum and Dad."

"What does he do?"

"He works in IT, same as my father, but he does programming for one of the big insurance companies. He's super smart. He just has trouble with social skills and dealing with people."

"We're going to run out of time and you haven't told me about Kara yet," Bessie said gently.

Kelly took a biscuit and nibbled on it slowly. Bessie did the same, enjoying the delicious sugary treat. She was determined not to say anything, leaving it up to Kelly to continue the conversation.

"Kara was two years older than me, and we were pretty much

inseparable when we were small. I still remember when she started school. I was devastated that she was going to be gone all day while I was going to be home. She was mad that she had to go to school and I was desperate to go with her," Kelly said with a shake of her head.

"And your brother is two years older than Kara was?"

"Right around two years older, yes. In my earliest memories, he was already in school, and he seemed almost like another adult rather than a sibling, at least to me when I was small. We're close now, especially since Kara died, but we weren't all that close as children."

"What happened to Kara, then?"

"She went across to university at eighteen. I couldn't wait to follow in her footsteps, but I hated it when I actually got there. Kara earned her degree in three years and I quit after one. That meant we both moved back to the island the same year."

She stopped to take a sip of tea, her mind clearly lost in memories. Bessie finished her own drink and thought about waving for the waitress. More tea sounded good, but she didn't want to interrupt Kelly, not now that she was finally getting to the point.

"Anyway, after a year or two back on the island, Kara started looking for jobs across. She had a good job here, working at the bank where our father works, but she wasn't happy there. She wanted to do something different and she wanted to do it in a big city. About eighteen months ago she moved to Manchester."

"You weren't tempted to go with her?"

"If I'd known what was going to happen next, I would have, but I don't like big cities. That was part of the reason why I didn't like university. I'm afraid the island has spoiled me. The thought of living in a flat in a high-rise fills me with dread, but Kara loved it."

"So she settled in Manchester?"

"She found a flat in the city centre. It was too big for just her, so she advertised somewhere for flatmates. She ended up with three of them."

"Male or female?"

"Oh, all female. Kara wouldn't have wanted to live with a man, not unless she was involved with him, and she wasn't in any hurry to get involved with anyone."

"What was she doing for work in Manchester?"

"She'd found a job with an advertising agency, and she loved it. She was mostly just making coffee and typing letters, but she was sure that she'd be able to move up eventually. She wanted to start writing adverts, and I'm sure she would have been brilliant at it if she'd had the chance."

"You need to tell me what happened to her," Bessie said as gently as she could.

Kelly nodded. "Maybe I could tell you about her flatmates first, though. You need to understand everything."

"You can tell me whatever you like," Bessie said, only just stopping herself from sighing.

"Rachel Curry is a few years older than Kara. She'd been born and raised in Manchester, and she's an athletic trainer at one of the gym clubs in the city. She's pretty, but she's incredibly tough and strong."

"Good for her."

"Brooke Buchanan is the opposite, although I'm not really being fair to Brooke by putting it that way. She's younger, closer to my age, and she's a model who barely makes enough money to survive. That's probably a good thing, because her whole look is based around her appearing as if she hasn't had a good meal in months. She's tiny and far too thin to be healthy, but there are still some people who prefer models to look that way."

"What a shame."

"The thing is, though, Brooke is incredibly sweet, and she does eat. She just never eats biscuits or chocolate or anything else that's nice."

"And the third woman?"

"She's Pamela Ford. She's actually from the island, although Kara had never met her before she answered the advert for the flat. She earned her degree in mechanical engineering and was working for a big company in Manchester when she moved in with Kara."

"That sounds as if she isn't still there," Bessie said.

"Kara's death upset everyone. Pamela was badly shaken, and after a few months she decided to move back to the island. She's working for a company here now that pays her half of what she made in Manchester, but she says she feels a good deal safer, so it's worth it."

"How old is she?"

"She's a few years older. I believe she's already thirty."

"Were any of the women in a serious relationship when Kara died?" Bessie asked.

"No, none of them. Kara always said that they'd agreed that they were all too young to get tied down. They used to go out together quite a lot. I know Kara saw a few different men while she was in Manchester, but I don't think any of them lasted much beyond a second or third date. Kara was focussed on her career and she was planning to keep it that way for at least a few more years. As I understand it, the other three women felt the same way."

"Are any of them in a serious relationship now?"

Kelly shook her head. "I don't really talk to Brooke or Rachel, but I see Pam once in a while. She always shares any news about the other two. The last I knew, all three of them were single and happy that way."

"We only have five more minutes," Bessie pointed out. "What happened to Kara?"

"They were going to have a weekend away," Kelly said, staring down at the table. "The four of them were going to go away together. They'd booked rooms at a bed and breakfast in Glasgow, just for a change of scenery. It was sort of last-minute, too, not something they'd planned for ages or anything. Kara laughed when she told me about it, saying how she loved being able to live so spontaneously."

"Just the four of them?"

"Yes, they'd become good friends by that time. Brooke was the last one to move in, and she'd been there about three months by then. They spent a lot of their free time together, in smaller groups sometimes if someone had to work or was going out, but from what Kara told me, they often went out as a foursome, or just hung around the flat together, talking and maybe sharing a bottle of wine."

"So what happened in Glasgow?"

"I've no idea," Kelly said with a frown. "At the last minute, on the Friday afternoon, Kara's supervisor asked her to work late. The agency had a big presentation to make on Monday and there were a bunch of last-minute changes that needed to be made to it. He offered her a huge bonus if she could get it all done before Monday."

"Was that unusual?"

"The bonus? Yes, I think it was the first time she'd been offered anything like that."

"I mean suddenly having to work over the weekend."

"Oh, that. Not terribly unusual, although this was a much bigger mess than anything that had happened previously. Apparently the creative team had designed an entire campaign around a particular theme and then discovered that the company's competition had used that same theme two years previously. Not only that, the campaign had been a huge flop. Obviously, they had to change everything."

"Was Kara upset about missing the trip to Glasgow?"

"She was disappointed, but she was happy to have a chance to show her supervisor what a hard worker she was. She was happy about the extra money, too. The trip to Glasgow wasn't that big of a deal. It was just meant to be a weekend getaway. The four of them were planning a much bigger trip later in the year. They hadn't decided where they wanted to go yet, but they were thinking about New York City or maybe Australia. Kara was trying to save every penny for that holiday. The trip to Glasgow would have put a dent in her holiday budget, so she might even have been a bit relieved not to be going."

"The other three went without her?"

"Yes, they left as planned on the Friday night. Kara rang me later that evening, from work, just to chat as a short break. She told me that she'd had some trouble convincing the others to go, but that they'd finally agreed. I think the charge for the bed and breakfast was nonrefundable."

"How long were they gone?"

"They got back on Sunday evening. They were meant to get back in the afternoon, but they'd gone in Rachel's car and they'd had car trouble on the way back. They'd had to ring for roadside assistance and then wait while the guy cobbled something together that would let them get home."

Kelly stopped and picked up her teacup. Bessie knew that it was empty, but Kelly put it to her lips anyway. Sighing, she put the cup down and looked at the table.

"I don't want to tell you the rest," she said softly.

"You don't have to tell me the rest."

"I know, but if I don't you won't be able to solve the murder."

"I won't be able to solve the murder anyway," Bessie replied. "I don't know any of the people involved and I know nothing about Manchester."

Kelly nodded. "I thought talking to you about it would help. I never talk about Kara with anyone, but it doesn't seem to be helping."

"You don't have to tell me any more," Bessie said, hoping that she knew enough to track the story down somewhere if Kelly didn't tell her the rest.

"I'm sorry." Kelly took a deep breath and then picked up a biscuit. She ate her way through it while staring at something just behind Bessie's left shoulder. When she was done, Kelly took a deep breath.

"When they got back to the flat, the three women found Kara on the couch, apparently dead of a drug overdose," she said in a rush. "There was an empty wine bottle on the table next to her with a single, empty glass."

Bessie reached over and patted Kelly's hand. "I'm so very sorry."

"They rang the police, of course, and the police treated the flat as a crime scene. They ran all the tests they were meant to run and did all the right things. I'm not complaining about how they handled everything, I'm truly not."

"But?"

"But they decided that Kara had died of an accidental overdose, which simply isn't possible. Kara would never have taken the drugs that were found in her system, not voluntarily. Her flatmates all told the police the same thing that I did, which is that Kara didn't use drugs, not ever."

"So the case isn't officially a murder investigation?"

"I don't know. I doubt it. The official ruling was accidental over-dose. No one seemed to care where the drugs had come from or why Kara had taken them."

"She wasn't suicidal?"

"She was the furthest thing from suicidal that you can be. She was happy and she loved her life. She didn't take drugs because she didn't need artificial highs. I'm not trying to make her out to be a saint or anything. She did drink, especially when she was with her friends, but none of them took drugs. It simply wasn't part of their lives."

"But the police didn't believe you."

"They seemed to think that everyone tries drugs once or twice in their lives. One of the constables I spoke with suggested that she'd been given something by a friend and decided to try it because she was feeling lonely with her friends in Scotland. He told me that it was very easy for someone to overdose accidentally the first time they try a drug."

"That may be true."

"It may be true, but Kara never would have done it. The only way she'd have taken an accidental overdose would be if someone slipped something into her food or a drink and she didn't know she was taking it."

"Is it possible that someone did just that?"

"That has to be what happened, which makes it murder, even if whoever gave her the drugs didn't actually intend to kill her."

"You're suggesting that someone drugged her just for fun?"

"I don't know what I'm suggesting," Kelly sighed. "It's impossible. I still can't quite believe she's even dead, let alone dead in such a horrible way."

"So what do you think happened?"

"I wish I knew. I can almost imagine Kara having a friend come over. She might have been a bit lonely, as I think it was the first time in months that she'd been alone in the flat. Her flatmates all insisted that they didn't know anyone who ever used drugs, but there were some issues at the advertising agency right before Kara was hired.

Several people lost their jobs and a few others went to rehab for a short stint. Kara could have invited a coworker to visit and that coworker might have brought something with him or her."

"And deliberately tricked Kara into taking something?" Bessie tried not to sound as doubtful as she felt.

"Maybe. Whoever it was might have thought it would be funny to get Kara really messed up. Some people find that sort of thing amusing. They could have mixed something up in the wine without telling Kara."

Bessie nodded slowly. "I assume no one has admitted to visiting Kara while the other women were away?"

"Of course not. The coroner reckoned that Kara died on Saturday night. She'd worked late on the Friday and then went back in on Saturday morning for another three hours. Her supervisor took her to lunch on Saturday, after the work was done, to thank her for everything. He then went home to his wife and a houseful of guests who were visiting from Sweden. His alibi is airtight for the rest of the weekend."

"Unless his wife and houseguests all lied."

"It wasn't just them, though. They had a big party on the Saturday night with over fifty people at their house. There were caterers, and they brought in dozens of staff. If Mark had gone out someone would have noticed."

"No chance he gave Kara a bottle of wine to thank her for her work?" Bessie asked.

Kelly shrugged. "If he did, he'll never admit to it."

"Are the police certain that there were drugs in the bottle of wine. Is that how they were administered?"

"That's what the police think, anyway. There were traces of the drug that killed her in the glass on the table, but not in the bottle. According to the coroner, the drugs still could have been in the bottle, as the residue sample he had to test was small."

"But the drugs might have only been in her glass," Bessie said speculatively.

"According to the autopsy, she'd drunk about half a bottle of wine.

I told the police that that proves there was someone there with her, but they didn't agree. According to Kara's flatmates, it wasn't unusual for one of them to drink half of a bottle of wine and then leave the rest for another day."

"Had any of them drunk the first half of the bottle that Kara finished?"

"No, but that doesn't mean that Kara didn't start it on Friday and finish it on Saturday," Kelly sighed.

"So she'd drunk half a bottle of wine. What about food?"

"It seemed as if the last thing she'd eaten was the lunch that she'd had with her supervisor, which is another reason why I'm sure she was murdered. Kara would never have started drinking on an empty stomach. She'd have made herself something for dinner before she'd have opened the bottle of wine."

"Was there food in the flat?"

Kelly frowned. "Not much, actually. Since they were planning to be away for the weekend, none of the women had done any grocery shopping in a few days. Kara complained to me about it, actually, on the Friday night when she rang. She said something about having to have cereal or maybe some canned soup for her meals until she found time to get to the shops."

"But she didn't go shopping on Saturday afternoon?"

"I think, after her lunch, she just wanted to go home and relax. The work she did on Friday night and Saturday was pretty high-pressure stuff. She told me on Friday that she was looking forward to soaking in a hot bath for most of Saturday afternoon."

"And the police never found any evidence that she'd had any company?"

"They couldn't be sure. There were hundreds of fingerprints all over the flat. There is some security in the building, but there aren't any cameras and guests aren't asked to sign in or anything. While there is a security guard in the lobby, anyone can just walk past him and get on the lifts."

"I assume the guard who was working that night didn't notice anything unusual."

29

"Not at all. He did remember Kara coming in from work. She stopped for a quick chat, telling him that she was exhausted and that she needed a long hot bath and a quiet night." Kelly flushed. "As I understand it, Kara and the guard often flirted with one another. He told the police that he'd suggested he could come up and scrub her back for her and she'd laughed and told him to ring her flat when his shift finished. He did ring, but she didn't answer. He just assumed that she'd either gone back out or was simply ignoring the phone."

"Did he leave a message for her?"

"Yes, just in case she didn't know it was him. He just said that he would be at the desk for five more minutes if she wanted to ring back. She didn't."

Bessie sighed. "I'm sorry, but I can't see any way that I can help you."

Kelly nodded, but her eyes filled with tears. "You were my last hope," she said softly. "The police seem to have closed the investigation. My parents won't talk about it anymore. Everyone seems to think that I'm crazy, really. I don't know what else to do."

"I can talk to John Rockwell," Bessie offered. "He used to work in Manchester. He might be able to find out what the police are doing with the case."

"That would be a start, anyway."

"When did all of this happen?" Bessie asked.

"It was exactly a year ago on Monday," Kelly replied.

CHAPTER 3

"*A* year ago?" Bessie repeated Kelly's words.

"I'm not looking forward to Monday. I've taken the day off work and I may just stay in bed and cry."

"I'm sure it will be a difficult day for you, but a year is a very long time in a murder investigation," Bessie tried to explain.

"You think it's impossible, don't you? The police keep telling me that they're doing everything they can, but I can tell they don't even believe me that Kara was murdered. They think it was an accident, or maybe even that she took her own life."

Bessie patted her hand. "I'll talk to Inspector Rockwell. He may be able to speak to someone with the Manchester police. Maybe he'll be able to get more information for you."

"That would help. I just want to feel as if they're doing something." Kelly sighed and shook her head. "That isn't true. I want to know what happened to Kara. I want to know that she was murdered and who did it. I haven't slept properly in the last year and I know I won't sleep well again until her killer is behind bars."

"I'll talk to John tonight," Bessie promised.

Kelly sat back in her seat. "I already feel a little bit better. At least

I'm trying. Maybe if Inspector Rockwell gets involved, the police in Manchester will reopen the investigation."

"I have to see Dr. Robins again on Thursday. Plan on having tea with me again that morning."

Kelly nodded. "I'll try to book some extra time off, like I did today." She glanced at her watch. "Of course, I've gone well over my extra time. I hope I won't be in too much trouble."

She got to her feet and waved at the waitress. "Put everything on my account," she called across the room. "Thank you so much for listening to me," she told Bessie before she rushed out of the café.

"Did you need anything else?" the waitress asked Bessie.

"I'm fine, thank you," Bessie said. Feeling slightly guilty that she'd ordered the biscuits and Kelly had ended up paying for them, she got to her feet.

"Let me put the rest of the biscuits into a bag for you," the waitress said quickly. She was gone before Bessie could object, and then back with a small bag.

Feeling even guiltier, Bessie took the bag and headed for the door. She thought about stopping and dropping the extra biscuits off to Kelly, but she didn't want anyone to think that she was paying a social call on the woman, not after Kelly had taken an extra-long break. Bessie decided that she'd simply have to pay for their tea and biscuits on Thursday to make things right. With that settled in her mind, she walked outside the building and headed for the small taxi rank.

"Where?" the man at the wheel demanded.

"Treoghe Bwaane. It's on Laxey Beach," she explained, wishing she'd thought to ring her regular service before she'd climbed inside this taxi.

"I know how to get to Laxey," the driver said.

"Good, get us to Laxey and I'll give you directions from there."

The route the driver took to Laxey was an unusual one, and Bessie considered complaining about what was sure to be an inflated charge, but he kept her entertained with stories about the two years he'd spent travelling in the US, so she forgave him the circuitous route. When he pulled up in front of her house, he whistled.

"The cottage needs to be torn down, but the land must be worth a fortune."

"I quite like the cottage," Bessie said sharply.

He chuckled. "Sorry, I didn't mean anything. It's just an incredibly beautiful view. If I could afford to buy the cottage and the land, I'd tear down the cottage so that I could just sit and watch the sea."

"If you kept the cottage, you could sit inside it and watch the sea."

The driver laughed heartily. "You're right, of course. I don't know what I'm saying, really. I'm just stunned by the beauty of the scenery. The island is like that in a lot of places, really. I'm often shocked when I drive down a road and then turn a corner and see the sea or the mountains. I've lived all over the world, and this island is definitely the most beautiful place I've ever been."

"I quite agree, although I've not lived all over the world."

"If I owned your cottage, I wouldn't move, not ever."

"I don't intend to move," Bessie told him.

She paid him, adding a generous tip, and then let herself into the cottage. Her answering machine light was blinking, and Bessie listened to two different messages from people who were curious about what she'd been discussing with Kelly Sutton for such a long time that morning.

"It must be something to do with that sister of hers," one of the callers said. "Such a tragedy. She was beautiful, Kara was. Kelly's pretty enough, but Kara was breathtaking. So very young and then to take her own life, it's so sad."

Bessie didn't bother to ring either caller back. She wasn't in the mood for gossip, and she needed to ring John, anyway. That was much more important.

"Laxey Neighbourhood Policing, this is Suzannah. How can I help you?"

Bessie made a face. Suzannah was still fairly new to the job of receptionist at the station, and as far as Bessie was concerned, she wasn't doing her job very well. She nearly always got Bessie's name wrong and had once sent half the Laxey force to Bessie's cottage due to a misunderstanding.

She took a deep breath. "It's Elizabeth Cubbon. I'd like to speak to Inspector John Rockwell, please."

"Certainly, Mrs. Bubble, please hold."

Frowning, Bessie paced back and forth across her kitchen floor as rather loud rock music played in her ear. One song ended and a second, just as cacophonous, began.

"Laxey Neighbourhood Policing, this is Suzannah. How can I help you?"

"I'm holding for Inspector Rockwell," Bessie said tightly.

"Inspector Rockwell? Who's ringing, please?"

"It's Elizabeth Cubbon."

"Mrs. Cluberd, I'm sorry, but Inspector Rockwell is a very busy man. I can take a message and he might ring you back, but as I say, he's very busy."

"It's Elizabeth Cubbon. I believe I'm on the list of people to whom John wishes to speak when they ring."

"I'm not sure who John is or why he has a list. Are you feeling well today, Mrs. Bubbard?"

"John Rockwell," Bessie said through gritted teeth.

"What about him?"

"I believe he has a list of people with whom he wishes to speak."

"If he did, that sort of thing would be classified police information. I'm sure you can understand why I can't reveal the contents of that list."

"I'm not asking you to reveal anything. I just want you to check the list. I'm certain my name is on it."

"I have the list here, or rather I would, if the list exists, which I'm not saying it does. There isn't any Mrs. Evangeline Blubbard on the list, not that there is a list."

"It's Elizabeth Cubbon." Bessie patiently spelled out her surname.

"Please hold," Suzannah said.

This time the music was an American country-western song. Bessie listened as a man sang about losing his dog and his wife and being stuck all alone with only his hamster for company. She shook her head as she decided that she must have misunderstood the lyrics.

"Laxey Neighbourhood Policing, this is Suzannah. How can I help you?"

"You can put me through to John Rockwell," Bessie snapped.

"Inspector Rockwell isn't in his office at the moment. I can take a message and have him ring you back."

"No, never mind. I'll ring his mobile."

"I can't give you his mobile number."

"That's fine. I already have it."

"You do? Civilians aren't meant to have the private numbers of police inspectors."

"John and I are friends."

"Well, if you ask me, it's still wrong. You could ring him up and disturb him when he's right in the middle of something important. I hope you think about that before you bother him."

Bessie winced as the woman put the phone back in its cradle with a bang. As much as Bessie hated to admit it, she tended to agree with Suzannah. She never rang John's mobile unless she felt as if she had no choice. Instead, she decided to ring Doona, who would probably know exactly where John was at the moment.

"Hello?"

"Doona? It's Bessie. I need to talk to John, but Suzannah said he wasn't in the office. I don't want to ring his mobile, in case he's in the middle of something important."

"He was in his office five minutes ago when I rang to ask him about dinner tonight. He was working his way through some paperwork, and I'm sure he'd love to be interrupted again. Go right ahead and ring him. Make sure you complain about Suzannah when you do, too."

"She's just awful."

"John's trying to get her transferred to Castletown. They're shorthanded there, as well, but the chief constable doesn't want to send her there and leave us even worse off. I can't do more hours because I'm doing so much with the children now."

"Yes, we're overdue for a long talk about all of that."

Doona laughed. "We are, actually, now that you mention it. Maybe

I'll come over tonight. John has to run the kids all over the island. I was going to go along for the ride, but I could do with a chat with you, instead."

"You know you're always welcome."

"I'm cooking an early dinner for John and the children, but we should be done by six or half six. I'll be at your cottage by seven and I'll bring something sweet with me to go with our tea."

"That sounds good. See you later."

"John Rockwell." The voice was clipped and Bessie immediately felt certain that she'd interrupted something important.

"It's Bessie. You can ring me back if you're busy. Doona said it wouldn't be a bad time to ring, though."

John chuckled. "Doona was quite right. I'm digging my way through several months of paperwork that should have been dealt with last month, or even the month before. I was just hoping for an interruption."

"I did ring the non-emergency number, but Suzannah kept putting me on hold and then telling me that you were too busy to talk. She also told me that you were not at the station."

John sighed. "I'll talk to her. She's learning, but it's taking time."

"She got my name wrong at least half a dozen times. She simply doesn't listen."

"I hope you didn't just ring to complain about Suzannah?"

"No, although I'm genuinely concerned about her. What if I were ringing with vital evidence in an important case? She'd get it all wrong and no one would know who'd rung because she'd have their name wrong as well."

"I'm working on getting her sent for additional training. It's difficult because we're very short-handed and Doona can't do any extra hours, not with my children's busy schedules, anyway. But what can I do for you?"

"I had an appointment at the Ramsey hospital today. The receptionist there bought me tea and biscuits after I saw the doctor. Her sister was murdered in Manchester a year ago and she doesn't think the police are doing enough to find the killer."

"Oh, dear."

"The thing is, the sister might not have been murdered. It's possible that she died accidentally or even committed suicide. From what Kelly said, the police did everything right, except reach a verdict with which she agrees."

"The police don't reach a verdict. That's the coroner's job."

"Yes, well, apparently he or she ruled it an accidental death."

John sighed. "You'd better give me all of the details. I'll see what I can find out. I still know a few people in Manchester who might be willing to give me an overview of the case."

Bessie told John everything that she could remember from her conversation with Kelly. "A year is a long time in a murder investigation," she said with a sigh.

"Yes, it is," John agreed. "If the official verdict was that it was an accidental overdose, it isn't even a murder investigation. Let me see what I can find out. When will you be seeing Kelly again?"

"Thursday morning."

"Oh, good. I was afraid you were going to say tomorrow. Why don't I plan to come and talk to you tomorrow night? I know you're going to see Doona tonight. She texted me to tell me that I was going to be on my own going here, there, and everywhere tonight."

"I'm sorry about that."

"Don't be. I'll get to have each of the children in the car alone with me for at least twenty minutes. We have our best conversations in the car when I can't actually look at them. While I love having Doona along, sometimes it's good to have one-on-one time with the kids, too."

"Do you want to come for dinner tomorrow, then?" Bessie asked. "Doona is more than welcome, too, and so is Hugh, if he's available."

"Let's do that. I'll bring dinner. The kids both have activities after school. I have to collect Thomas from a friend's house at seven and Amy from the school at half seven. If we meet at five for dinner, we'll be done in plenty of time. I don't think we'll have much to discuss. I can't see my friends in Manchester telling me much, and I probably won't be able to repeat most of what they do tell me, anyway."

"I'll make something for pudding," Bessie said.

"I'll invite the others. Hugh is in the office next to mine, cursing his way though a similar stack of paperwork. I'm sure the prospect of dinner with you tomorrow night will cheer him up considerably."

"I'll make something special for pudding," Bessie promised. "I hope Grace won't mind if he comes, though."

"Maybe she'll send Aalish along with Hugh."

Bessie laughed. "Aalish would be more than welcome, although I don't know what we'd do when she got hungry."

"If I don't talk to you between now and then, I'll see you around five tomorrow," John told her.

Feeling as if she'd done all that she could for Kelly, Bessie made herself a light lunch and then took herself for another walk on the beach. She was nearly home when she heard Maggie's voice.

"Ah, Bessie, there you are," Maggie said, striding across the sand. "I feel responsible, really."

"Responsible for what?"

"I should have warned you about Kelly Sutton as soon as you'd mentioned that you'd gone to the Cottage hospital."

"Warned me about her?"

"I know you spent a very long time talking with her this morning. I'm sure she told you all about her sister's tragic death. The poor woman is rather obsessed with Kara. She always was, though. Kara was the pretty one and the smart one, too. Kelly was left to be the one who stayed home to look after their parents, which is its own tragedy."

"Do her parents need looking after?"

"They didn't, at least not much, before Kara's death. I believe they've both taken their loss quite badly, though."

"That's understandable."

Maggie shrugged. "I hope Kelly didn't try to persuade you that Kara was murdered. The coroner's verdict was accidental death. The case is closed."

"The coroner can make mistakes."

"Yes, I suppose so. In this case, I believe he did, actually."

"Do you?"

"I've always suspected that Kara committed suicide. She was the type."

"What does that mean?" Bessie demanded.

Maggie shrugged again. "She was in a relationship with one of my dearest friends' sons. It didn't end well."

"What happened?"

"He ended things and she got very upset. According to my friend, Kara was devastated. She used to ring him dozens of times a day, begging him to take her back. When he refused, she threatened to kill herself."

"My goodness, how awful. When was this?"

Maggie shrugged. "It was a while ago."

Bessie frowned at the vagueness of the answer. "When?"

"About ten years ago," Maggie said, looking at the ground.

"So Kara would have been seventeen when this happened?"

"She may have been a bit younger, maybe fifteen."

"So we're talking about a teenage romance."

"Yes, well, I mean, I suppose you could say that."

"I hardly think, even if the story is true, that a failed romance at fifteen would leave anyone suicidal at twenty-seven," Bessie said.

"I wasn't suggesting that she was still upset about that failed romance, just that it was a sign of how unstable she was. Ringing someone dozens of times a day in that way isn't normal."

"I assume you've only ever heard one side of the story," Bessie said, determined to ask Kelly about what Maggie had told her.

"Wanda wouldn't have lied to me."

"Perhaps she was just exaggerating."

"Maybe, but even so, Kara was unstable."

"Did you ever hear any other stories about her?"

Maggie frowned. "No, but that doesn't mean there aren't more stories out there. I don't hear about everything that happens on this island. Anyway, Kara moved away. It isn't as if I have sources in Manchester."

"As I understand it, she'd only moved away about six months

before her death. If the romance you're talking about ended when she was fifteen, that means she spent eleven or twelve years on the island without you hearing anything more about her."

"She went away to uni," Maggie said crossly. "Who knows what sort of trouble she got into at uni?"

"But she came home and lived on the island for many years after that."

"Yes, well, whatever, I still think she killed herself. That sister of hers is unstable, too. Imagine trying to convince you, a full year after her sister died, that the woman was murdered. If she really wanted you to investigate, she should have rung you a year ago."

"Except I'm not with the police. I don't investigate anything. Kelly was looking for a sympathetic ear, and I hope she found one with me."

"I'm sure you rang Inspector Rockwell and got him to ring his former police colleagues in Manchester, though. No doubt they'll reopen the investigation now."

"If they do reopen the investigation, it will be for some reason other than my involvement. There's nothing that I can do except listen and sympathise."

"Are you saying you didn't ring John Rockwell?"

"Maggie? Stop bothering Bessie and get back to painting," a voice called down the beach.

Bessie turned and spotted Thomas, Maggie's husband, standing in the door to one of the cottages. "Hello," she shouted at him.

"Hello. I'm not supposed to be out in the cold air," he yelled back. "Otherwise I'd come down and say hello."

"I can come up," Bessie suggested.

Thomas shook his head. "We have to finish this cottage and then I'm going home to bed. We'll talk another day."

Bessie watched as he moved the sliding door back into place and then disappeared into the cottage.

"Don't mind him," Maggie said, blushing. "He truly isn't meant to be outside right now and he has very little energy. He keeps insisting on coming down to help, but he really isn't up to the job."

Bessie had been surprised at how unwell Thomas had looked, but she wasn't about to share that thought with Maggie. Instead, she shrugged. "I'd better let you go and get back to your painting," she said. "Then you can take Thomas home so he can get some rest."

Maggie nodded and then turned and began to walk up the beach. Bessie hurried back to Treoghe Bwaane, afraid that Maggie might remember where the conversation had ended and rush back to ask her the question again.

Safely inside her cottage, Bessie made herself some dinner and then curled up with a book for half an hour. Just before seven, she refilled the kettle with fresh water, ready for Doona's arrival. Doona knocked at one minute after the hour.

"I was afraid I was going to be late," she laughed when Bessie opened the door. "Thomas did the washing-up after dinner, and he's never speedy."

"I wouldn't have minded if you were late."

"I know, but it's incredibly rude."

Bessie nodded. She prided herself on always being on time, something that was occasionally a challenge when she had to rely on buses, taxis, or friends to get her around the island.

"Anyway, I brought fairy cakes," Doona announced. She handed Bessie a bakery box.

"I'll just pop the kettle on and then I'll put these on a plate," Bessie said. "Have a seat."

Doona dropped heavily into a chair, sighing deeply as she did so.

"Is everything okay?" Bessie asked, feeling concerned.

"It's fine. It's just complicated. Or maybe it isn't, maybe I'm just complicating everything."

"You know I don't want to pry, but I'm always happy to listen," Bessie told her.

Doona nodded. "I think I need to talk, but it's sort of scary and weird and I'm not sure what to say."

"It will be easier over tea," Bessie said firmly. She opened the bakery box and smiled with pleasure. There were half a dozen fairy cakes, three with yellow sponge and three with chocolate sponge. They were all covered in thick buttercream icing and, as Bessie moved the cakes onto a plate, she was happy she'd eaten a small dinner.

By the time she'd put the plate on the table and added smaller plates for herself and Doona to eat from, the kettle had boiled. It only took Bessie a few minutes to make the tea.

"Here we are, then," she said brightly as she set Doona's cup on the table. She added her own and then sat down opposite her friend. "We can talk about anything you'd like. The weather, your job, John and the children, anything."

Doona chuckled. "The weather has been quite pleasant for late February, hasn't it?"

"It has, indeed, although there was some chill to the air today. Thomas didn't want to come outside to talk to me because of the chill."

"Thomas Shimmin? I'd heard he'd been quite unwell. How is he?"

"He looks ghastly, probably ten years older than he looked last summer. He's been fighting pneumonia and goodness knows what else. He was helping Maggie paint one of the holiday cottages, but he didn't look up to lifting a paintbrush, really."

"I thought they'd hired someone to take care of the painting."

"Now that you mention it, so did I. I wonder if he quit or was let go."

"Knowing Maggie, he probably quit because she wouldn't stop telling him what to do all the time."

Bessie laughed. "She can be difficult, but she means well, and I do believe she has a good heart."

"But why are we all having dinner here tomorrow night? Don't tell me there was a murder somewhere and I missed it?" Doona asked.

Bessie quickly explained about Kara Sutton's death, including the story that Maggie had told her.

"That's why I don't like Maggie," Doona said when Bessie was done. "I was an idiot at fifteen. I'm sure I rang my first boyfriend at least a dozen times a day when we were together. I ended things, and after that he used to ring my house and say incredibly rude things to me when I answered. By Maggie's standards we were probably both unstable."

"Where is he now?"

"He's a solicitor in London," Doona replied.

Bessie laughed. "I tend to agree that whatever happened when Kara was fifteen has no relevance to her death, but it all helps to build up a picture of her. Not that I expect to be able to do anything to help with the investigation, if there is even an investigation still happening. Kara died nearly a year ago in Manchester. I can't imagine what Kelly thinks I can do."

"I'm sure John will be doing everything he can to find out more about the case."

"I'm sure he will be, too. Kelly could have simply rung him herself, though. She didn't need to involve me."

Doona nodded. "Some people are hesitant to contact the police even if they have a good reason for doing so."

"I'm hesitant, now that I might get Suzannah when I ring."

"Yes, well, that's a different type of problem. I really hope John can get that sorted soon."

"Speaking of John," Bessie said, raising her eyebrows and leaving off the end of the sentence.

Doona flushed. "I'm not sure what to say, really," she said after a moment. "We're, well, I suppose we're trying things out very slowly. We've had several long conversations, mostly about how difficult our being together would be if we were foolish enough to try to have a relationship. Having said that, it seems very much as if we're trying out some sort of relationship now."

Bessie grinned. "I always thought you two would be good together."

"It isn't going to be easy, though," Doona sighed.

"Very little worth having is easy to attain."

Doona stared at her for a minute and then nodded slowly. "That's very true, actually. And John and I are both willing to work hard. We're both just afraid of getting hurt again. The children are a bigger worry, though. I can handle another broken heart, but the kids have been through so much in the past few years. I hate the thought of upsetting them again."

"They have been through a lot," Bessie agreed. "I'm sure moving to the island was a huge upheaval. Only staying here for a year and then moving back to Manchester was another disruption. Of course, dealing with their parents' divorce had to be difficult as well. Sue's death has been the worst blow, though, I'm sure."

"Of course it has, and I feel helpless when it comes to helping them deal with it. I didn't lose my mother until I was thirty-six, and I was still devastated, even at that age. I can't imagine what Amy and Thomas are feeling."

"But we aren't talking about Amy and Thomas," Bessie said. "What are you feeling?"

Doona thought for a minute and then smiled. "John is incredible. He's sweet and kind and funny and I love spending time with him. The kids are busy with lots of different things, so we get odd hours here or there that are just for us. Those are the best times. We talk about everything from local politics and international affairs to why our relationship is probably a mistake and how best to persuade Amy that the dress she wants is too short to wear to a party."

"That's good to hear. How is he feeling now about your money?"

"We haven't really talked about that," Doona said, looking down at the table.

"You haven't talked about the money?"

"Not really. I insisted on paying for piano lessons for Amy. John only agreed because I made it a birthday present for her. Beyond that, though, he won't let me spend any money on the children, or on him."

"And until the estate is finally settled and the court cases are all resolved, you don't even know how much money you have."

Doona's inheritance had come from her second husband. Charles Adams had been a partner in a business that owned hotels, restaurants, and a large holiday park in the UK. One of the other partners was still being investigated for fraud and other crimes, so the entire estate was tangled up in a complicated legal battle. Just recently, Doona had discovered that the solicitor acting on her behalf, Stuart

Stanley, was being paid by another of the partners who was hoping to get Doona to agree to give up her claim to the business.

"My new solicitor doesn't think it's going to take long to get things resolved," Doona told Bessie. "He reckons everything could have been wrapped up a year ago if people hadn't been working behind my back to complicate things."

"What does Doncan think?"

Doncan Quayle was Doona's advocate on the island. He was meant to be overseeing everything, and Bessie knew that he blamed himself for some of the problems that had arisen over the case.

"He's angry that he didn't realise that things were being deliberately delayed, but I've seen the reports he was being sent by my former solicitor and they make for very convincing reading. Stuart sent dozens of reports detailing all of the hard work he was doing on my behalf, even though he wasn't actually doing much of anything."

"Whatever happens with the estate, you need to talk to John about the money."

"I know. We both keep skirting around the issue and then putting it off, but we've agreed that we'll discuss it the next time we're properly alone together. That would have been tonight, actually, if I weren't here."

"So that's why you were so eager to see me tonight."

Doona laughed and then blushed. "You could be right, actually. I won't lie. I love spending time alone with John. We're, well, there's a lot of chemistry between us, let's say. Obviously, we're taking that part of the relationship very slowly as well, but even just holding his hand makes my heart beat faster."

"I'm happy for you both. Let's hope your new solicitor is correct and everything legal can get sorted in the next few months. It would be good for you to have one less thing to worry about."

"You can say that again."

CHAPTER 4

*B*essie spent Wednesday morning with Onnee's letters. Onnee was definitely pregnant again and she talked of hoping for a boy, speculating that Clarence might take more interest in a son than he did in his daughter. Alice was walking confidently now, much to the surprise of her doctors who kept insisting to Onnee that Alice would soon reach the limits of her abilities. Onnee had decided to ignore them and treat her daughter as if she were a perfectly normal baby. Clarence didn't agree, but Onnee didn't seem to care what he thought about the matter.

"Good for you," Bessie muttered as she read a passage about a discussion that Clarence and Onnee had had about Alice's future. Onnee wanted to start a savings account to put money away in case Alice wanted to go to university one day. Clarence had insisted that Alice was never going to be able to do any such thing. In the end, Onnee had persuaded him that, if Alice truly was disabled, they were going to need to have money put aside to pay for her care after they were gone. In the end, Clarence had agreed to the savings account, and Onnee was quietly confident that Alice would one day use the money to pay for a university education, even if she didn't mention the idea to Clarence again.

Clarence had found a better job and they were still looking for a house. Onnee had found one that she liked a great deal, but it was nearly twenty minutes away from Clarence's parents' home, which was further than Clarence was willing to consider.

Bessie put the papers away with a sigh. The letters were fascinating, but reading them was hard work and there were frequently long passages that were about less than interesting subjects. Bessie now knew, in great detail, what every shop in the small town where Onnee was living carried and how much most of the items cost. She also knew the names of the various farmers in the community and which ones had the best vegetables and fruits. None of that was particularly interesting to Bessie, but it seemed likely that a local historian in that part of the US would probably love to have copies of the letters. She'd have to discuss that with Marjorie, she decided as she got up from her desk.

A brisk walk to Thie yn Traie and back cleared Bessie's head. She made herself a sandwich and washed it down with tea. She'd promised John that she'd make pudding, but she hadn't really given the matter much thought. A quick search through her cupboards didn't inspire her. What she really wanted was apple crumble, she decided, knowing that Onnee's long letter about the local apple harvest festival was influencing her. Onnee had written about apple butters, apple cider, apple pies, apple cakes, and a dozen other apple treats that had left Bessie craving them all. Another look through the cupboards revealed that she had everything she needed for the crumble except apples.

Sighing, Bessie slipped on her shoes and pulled on a coat. Making something else would be easier, but it wouldn't be as satisfying, she told herself as she headed for the door. The little shop was at the top of a fairly steep hill and Bessie found herself stopping to catch her breath when she was about halfway through the climb. Clearly the fall and injury to her arm had taken more out of her than she'd realised.

"Ah, good afternoon," the girl behind the till called as Bessie pushed open the shop's door.

"Good afternoon," Bessie replied. Sandra Cook was fairly new to the shop and to the island. Bessie had occasionally lent her some books after Sandra had confessed to being bored in the shop that was often empty of customers.

"I've finished everything you've lent me, but I don't need anything else right now," Sandra said. "I found the library in Douglas and I've taken out a dozen books."

"Douglas has a very good library."

"It was wonderful. When I first went inside, I just went and sat in a corner, just to be surrounded by books. Then I borrowed as many as I could carry. Libraries are almost magical places."

"They are, at that," Bessie agreed.

"But what can I help you with today? We just got the local papers in."

"Oh, I'll have a local paper." Bessie picked up the top copy from the pile and glanced at the headline.

"Local Woman Badly Injured in Beach Fall," the headline screamed at her. Frowning, Bessie turned the paper over. She'd read the article later. For now, she'd simply hope that it was about someone other than her.

"I need apples," she told Sandra.

"We have three different varieties, and I'm afraid I don't know what the differences are between them."

Bessie gave the girl a quick education into some of the various types of apples before selecting a bag to purchase. She waited until she was home, sitting comfortably, to read the paper.

Exactly as she'd feared from the headline, Dan Ross, the paper's most annoying reporter, had written an article about her tumble on the beach.

"'Elizabeth Cubbon, known to everyone as Aunt Bessie, could have been very seriously injured when she stumbled and fell on the beach in Laxey, mere steps from the cottage that she's called home for decades,'" Bessie read aloud.

Dan managed to make her accident sound much worse than it had been, and it included several quotes from a "devastated" and "very concerned" Maggie Shimmin. The last line of the article made Bessie frown.

"'This reporter has made several attempts to contact Miss Cubbon and get an update on her condition. Miss Cubbon is either unable or unwilling to ring me back,'" she read. "Unable? Seriously? Everyone on the island will be ringing me this afternoon, certain that I must be nearly dead."

As if on cue, Bessie's phone began to ring.

"Hello?"

"Ah, Miss Cubbon, it's Dan Ross. I'd appreciate a quote or two for my follow-up article on your sad accident."

"It must be a very slow news day," Bessie said before she put the phone down. If Dan wanted to use that quote in an article, he was welcome to it, she thought as she dug out the pan she wanted for the apple crumble. She set to work, ignoring the phone as it rang repeatedly. It wasn't until the pudding was safely in the oven that she listened to her messages. Only Doona's was worth returning.

"Laxey Neighbourhood Policing, this is Doona. How can I help you?"

"It's Bessie, just ringing you back."

"You're okay, then?"

"I'm fine, why?"

"The article in the local paper made it sound as if you were in quite a bad way."

"You've seen me several times since my accident. You should have known that Dan's article was rubbish."

"Yes, well, I needed to check. We've had several people ring the station to say that they've tried to reach you and were unable to do so."

"I'm not answering my phone right now. Everyone I've ever met is ringing to ask me if I'm okay and I'm not interested in discussing my fall with them."

"If anyone else rings us, I'll assure them that you're fine," Doona said.

"I'll see you at five, then," Bessie replied. The crumble was filling the cottage with the scent of warm apples and cinnamon. While Bessie never ate pudding first, she was tempted to try a bite of the crumble as she removed it from the oven. After having stern words with herself, she moved into the sitting room to get away from temptation. She was lost in a fictional world when someone knocked on her door.

"Doona, John, hello," Bessie said to the pair on her doorstep. "Come in."

John was carrying a large box, which he set on Bessie's counter.

"It smells wonderful. What did you bring?"

"The Indian restaurant across from the station is now a Chinese restaurant under new management. One of the constables went there for lunch yesterday and he said it was much better than the last place had been," John told her.

"I hope it is, and I hope this restaurant stays around. Nothing seems to last in that location for more than a few weeks," Bessie replied.

"There have been some wonderful restaurants there that have been very popular with everyone at the station. I don't know why no one seems to stay in business very long," John said.

"Although we won't miss the Indian place," Doona interjected. "That was one of the worst ones that have been there."

"It wasn't very good," Bessie agreed. "This smells as if it's going to be delicious, anyway."

Bessie put the kettle on while John and Doona arranged white boxes of takeaway food across the counter. As Bessie was getting down plates, Hugh knocked on the door.

"Hello," Bessie called as Doona opened the door and let Hugh into the cottage.

"Hello," he replied. "I'm starving and that smells great."

"It's from the new Chinese restaurant across from the station," Doona told him.

"I've heard good things about that place," Hugh told her.

"That's good news," John said. "Although whatever you'd heard, we have the food now."

Everyone filled plates and then sat down around the table. Bessie poured tea for everyone before she joined them.

"How's Aalish?" she asked Hugh.

"She's wonderful," he replied with a huge smile. "She's really starting to recognise people now and she gives me a big smile every day when I get home from work."

"I remember those days. Enjoy them while you can," John advised. "One day she'll be a teenager and she'll start scowling when she sees you."

"Amy isn't that bad," Doona said.

"Just some days," John amended his words.

"I am enjoying it," Hugh told them. "Grace feels a bit left out, I think, because she doesn't get that many smiles, but she's with Aalish all the time. I offered to bring Aalish with me tonight so that Grace could get a smile when we got back, but Grace wouldn't agree. She didn't want the baby out late."

"It isn't going to be a late night, anyway," John told him. "I have to start collecting the children at seven."

Hugh shrugged. "That's still a long time for Grace to be away from Aalish, in Grace's mind, anyway. Aalish sleeps for hours and hours every day, but Grace won't even leave her during her naps, just in case she wakes up and can't find her mum."

"I'm sure women are biologically programmed to be obsessed with their babies," Doona told him. "It's for the baby's safety, of course. No one loves a screaming, crying infant the same way a mother does."

"I love her just as much as Grace," Hugh protested.

"Even when she's screaming and her nappy needs changing?" Doona teased.

Hugh shrugged. "I love her just as much, but I might not be as eager to cuddle her at those times."

Everyone laughed. A short while later, Bessie served the crumble.

"I was reading about an apple festival in Onnee's letters," she told the others. "That made me want apple crumble."

"What's happening with Onnee, then?" Doona asked.

Bessie had shared some of the details from Onnee's earliest letters with Doona. Now she brought her friend up to date with everything that she'd read thus far.

"That poor woman. I hope Clarence finally wises up and realises how lucky he is to have Onnee. He needs to tell Faith to move back wherever she came from," was Doona's verdict when Bessie was finished.

"I can't quite believe that Faith is still around. Onnee thinks she's having an affair with Clarence, but I don't know if she is or not," Bessie said.

"I hope not. Onnee has enough to deal with," Doona said.

"But we're here to talk about murder," Hugh said in a dramatic voice after Bessie had given him his second helping of crumble.

"Or maybe not," John said. "I've had several conversations with a former colleague in Manchester. The official verdict was accidental death, not murder."

"And your colleague never suspected that it was anything other than an accident?" Bessie asked.

"I didn't say that," John replied, stopping to take a sip of his tea.

"What does that mean?" Bessie demanded as he slowly put his cup down.

John shrugged. "My friend had a bad feeling about the case, that's all. He was the first on the scene and he did everything by the book. No evidence was ever found to suggest that there was anyone else in the flat on the Saturday evening. He still feels that someone was there, though."

"Someone who gave Kara drugs, either with or without her knowledge," Bessie said thoughtfully.

"I hate to interrupt, but I don't know anything about the case," Hugh complained.

"Sorry," Bessie replied. She quickly told him the story that Kelly had told her.

When she was done, Hugh nodded. "There's something off somewhere," he said. "Did your colleague ever find out the source of the drugs that killed the victim?"

John shook his head. "That's part of why the case still bothers him.

He feels as if he should have been able to find the source. Kara was, by all accounts, a perfectly nice woman doing a rather ordinary job. She didn't have a drug supplier easily available. Someone had to have helped her find one or supplied her with the drugs themselves. My colleague feels that if he could find that person, he'd be a lot closer to working out what happened to Kara Sutton."

"No one is going to admit to supplying Kara with drugs, though, are they? I mean, whatever she took was illegal and it killed her," Bessie argued.

"It's unusual, though, in the case of an overdose, to find absolutely no connection to illegal drug use prior to the overdose, not just in the victim's background, but also with all of her friends and family," John explained.

"Did they search the flat?" Hugh asked.

John nodded. "As part of the initial investigation, the flat was searched. There were four bedrooms, one for each woman, and all three of Kara's flatmates agreed to having their bedrooms searched. Nothing was found," John told him.

"What about the advertising agency?" Doona wondered.

"About two months before Kara was hired, one of the agency's senior managers was arrested for trying to buy drugs from an under-cover officer. The entire agency was investigated and a few people lost their jobs. The senior manager went into rehab. When he got out, he instituted several new policies, including random drug testing for all staff. The woman that Kara replaced left because of the new rules," John told her.

"And was Kara being randomly tested?" Bessie asked.

"The company refused to release any information about any one individual's drug testing, but it did confirm that over a hundred different drug tests had been carried out in the six months that Kara had been working there and that every single test had come back negative," John said.

"So she didn't get the drugs from her flatmates or from anyone at work," Hugh said thoughtfully. "What about the men in her life?"

"According to the flatmates, she didn't have anyone special in her life, and hadn't in the six months she'd been in Manchester. She'd seen a few different men for a few weeks here or a month there, but none of the relationships were serious. The police were given the names and they investigated all of them, but didn't find anything to suggest that any of the men were drug users."

"So where did she get drugs?" Doona asked.

John sighed. "That's what's keeping Jacob awake at night, although that's probably an exaggeration. It's more what's annoying him every time he thinks about the case. Officially, it's a closed file, but he can't help but shake the feeling that he missed something."

"Just because he never found the source of the drugs, or is there something more?" Bessie asked.

"Not specifically, but he feels as if there were other things that didn't quite add up. I can't go into any details, but he always felt as if the scene was tidied after Kara died. The flatmates insisted that when they found her they didn't touch anything other than the body, but Jacob felt as if something more was done. Again, I can't give you specifics, and he could be wrong, but it's another thing that bothers him."

"Is he still investigating, then?" Hugh asked.

"Unofficially, he's doing what he can. Mostly, he's still trying to track down the source of the drugs. That he can do legitimately, whatever the verdict on Kara's death."

"So where do we go from here?" Bessie asked, feeling frustrated with the case.

"I'm not sure there's anywhere to go," John told her. "You can tell Kelly that the police are still trying to work out exactly what happened to her sister. While the death has been ruled an accident, the police are still eager to locate whoever supplied Kara with the drugs that took her life. I'm afraid that's all that they can do at this point, though."

"You couldn't think of anything that your friend might have missed?" Bessie wondered.

"Not at all. From what he said, he was very thorough," John replied.

"So where did she get the drugs?" Doona demanded.

"She must have had a friend or a boyfriend about whom her flat-mates knew nothing," Hugh said speculatively. "If this friend or boyfriend was a drug user, that might explain why Kara didn't mention him or her to her other friends."

"Where would she have even met someone like that?" Bessie questioned.

"It was city centre Manchester. She could have met someone in her building; in any restaurant, café, or coffee shop in the city; at the mall; on the street; or in a dozen other places," John told her. "There are very respectable people who are recreational drug users. They see no harm in enjoying themselves on the weekends and probably wouldn't hesitate to introduce a new friend to their favourite high."

Bessie shook her head. "Surely, knowing that she could be tested at work, Kara would have simply refused."

"Possibly. At this point, we simply don't know enough about Kara or her life in Manchester to be certain," John said.

"And we can't learn about those things, either, because she died nearly a year ago," Bessie sighed.

"If Kelly would like to speak to me, I'd be happy to discuss the case with her," John offered. "Maybe she can offer some insight into what Kara was like as a person. If Kara used to spend her weekend volunteering with an organisation that helps the homeless, for example, that might give Jacob another place to look for the drug connection."

"Maybe one of her former boyfriends from the island reconnected with her in Manchester," Doona said. "Get names from Kelly."

Bessie sighed. "It might be easier if I simply tell her that there's nothing further that can be done," she suggested. "We could put in a lot of time and effort trying to work out what happened and get nowhere."

"It's up to you," John assured her. "As I said, I'm happy to speak to Kelly, but I won't go looking for her. If she wants to talk, she can ring my office and set up an appointment. Having talked to Jacob, I'm curious now about what happened, but I'm busy enough without adding Kara Sutton's death to my caseload."

"I'm going to see Kelly tomorrow. I think I'm going to try to persuade her to simply try to move on," Bessie said reluctantly. "I wish your friend hadn't put so many doubts in my head," she told John. "If he'd said it was simply a tragic accident, I would feel better about telling Kelly there was nothing I can do."

"There is nothing you can do," Doona said. "Jacob is still investigating. If Kelly wants to do more, she can talk to John. I'm not sure what she thought you could do from here, anyway."

"I know you're right. I'm just sad that we don't have any answers for her," Bessie replied.

"Deaths related to drug overdoses are very rarely simple," John said. "The circumstances around this one are unusual, but Kara's death still could have been nothing but a tragic accident. Perhaps she bought herself something to try and then overdosed because she was so unfamiliar with taking drugs. That does happen, unfortunately."

Bessie nodded, but her mind was racing. There were too many unanswered questions in the case for her liking. As much as she hated to admit it, it felt to her as if Kara had been murdered. If she told Kelly what she was thinking, though, Kelly would probably want Bessie to do something, and Bessie couldn't imagine what she could do that would help.

"Don't let Kelly talk you into doing anything," John said, voicing Bessie's thoughts. "If she tries, send her to me."

"I'll suggest that she talk to you," Bessie agreed.

"She's going to want you to investigate," Doona said. "You have to make her understand that you can't."

"I'm sure she'll understand that there's nothing I can do," Bessie replied.

"It's getting late," Hugh said. "I should be going."

Bessie had to rush after him to the door in order to get a hug. As she shut the door behind him, she looked at the others.

"He barely said two words tonight. Is there anything wrong at home or work for Hugh?" she asked.

John shook his head. "Not as far as I know."

"He hasn't said anything to me about any problems," Doona added.

"He's been unbelievably happy since the baby came, really."

"He didn't seem particularly happy tonight," Bessie said thoughtfully.

"Maybe he was just missing Grace and Aalish," John said. "He was probably just in a rush to get back to them."

Bessie nodded, but she was worried about Hugh. It wasn't like him to be so distracted during a conversation about an investigation. Leaving early without getting any leftovers to take with him was also out of character.

"I don't think we can do anything more tonight," John said. "It's a little early, but Doona and I can get out of your way so you can get some extra rest. I haven't asked about your arm, but you're clearly favouring the other one, so I'm sure it's bothering you."

Bessie flushed. She thought she'd been doing a good job of acting normally in spite of the pain in her arm. Clearly she'd been less successful than she'd realised. "I'm fine."

"Of course you are. You're seeing your doctor again tomorrow, aren't you?" John asked.

"I am, yes. He may take another X-ray if he doesn't think things are healing properly," Bessie replied.

"Is the pain better or worse than yesterday?" Doona asked.

"I think it's better, but I haven't been taking as many tablets today, so it probably feels worse."

"You should take the tablets," Doona said sternly.

"I simply keep forgetting because I've been busy. I'll take some before bed."

"Promise?"

Bessie frowned. Doona knew her too well. "Yes, okay, I promise," she muttered, remembering that as a small child she'd sometimes lied with her fingers crossed behind her back, which was supposed to make the lie forgivable for some reason. It was too late to include the gesture in the promise, though, and she knew that Doona had her best interests at heart, really.

"On that note, I think we should go," John said, getting to his feet.

"Take the rest of the food home for the children," Bessie suggested.

"I'll never eat all of what's left."

John insisted that Bessie keep a few cartons of her favourites for her lunch the next day, and then packed the rest of the containers back into the larger box. Doona held the door for him as he carried the box back out to his car.

"Send Kelly to me," John said firmly when he returned to give Bessie a hug.

"I'll try," Bessie said, deliberately not making another promise.

"Did you want to take your car home and then ride with me while I collect children from all over the island?" John asked Doona.

"Yes, please," Doona said happily.

Bessie nearly said something to her friend to remind her that she and John were supposed to talk about money, but she bit her tongue. The pair walked to Doona's car and had a short conversation and a longer kiss before Doona climbed in and drove away. John waved at Bessie as he got into his own vehicle and then followed.

Feeling happy for the couple, Bessie went back into the kitchen and did a quick tidy-up. Doona had done the washing-up, so she dried the dishes and put them away, covering the remains of the apple crumble and putting it into the refrigerator. It would go nicely with the leftover Chinese food the next day, she thought.

Time for a good book, she decided as she walked out of the kitchen. The phone dragged her back a moment later.

"Bessie? It's Grace. Can you send that husband of mine home soon or are you having a very important conversation about murder?" the voice on the phone said.

"We aren't even sure if anyone was murdered," Bessie replied, stalling for time to think.

"In that case, you shouldn't need Hugh at all," Grace replied with a laugh.

"Perhaps not," Bessie answered with a small chuckle. "I'll tell him that he's being missed."

"Please do."

Bessie put the phone down and then frowned at it. Hugh had left nearly an hour ago and his house was less than a five-minute drive away. Where had the man gone? She thought about ringing John or Doona, but she didn't want to worry anyone else, not if Hugh had a perfectly good reason for not heading straight home. Refusing to think about possible reasons why Hugh might not have driven right home to his wife and baby, Bessie found her mobile and sent Hugh a text message.

Grace rang to see how much longer you'd be here. I told her I'd let you know that she's missing you. Hope everything is okay.

She pushed send and then began to pace back and forth across the kitchen floor. Two minutes (which felt like twenty) later, Bessie's phone buzzed.

Had to run a few errands on my way home. I'll ring Grace back and let her know that I'll be home soon. Sorry.

Errands? What sort of errands, Bessie wondered. There was no way she could ask, of course, not without seeming incredibly nosy. It was a small island, though. People would soon be talking if Hugh were doing anything he shouldn't have been doing.

Feeling slightly unsettled, Bessie found her book and tried to read. After an hour, knowing that she'd simply read the same paragraph repeatedly for much of that time, she decided to have a very early night. After taking the tablets she'd promised Doona she'd take, she got ready for bed and crawled under the covers.

"It's only half eight," she said loudly. "I'll never get to sleep at this hour."

Seemingly only moments later, she opened her eyes and discovered that it was six o'clock. It felt as if she'd been in the exact same position the entire night. Her body was stiff and several muscles complained as she climbed out of bed. A hot shower soon took care of most of the aches and pains, although her arm still hurt quite badly once she was done.

Tea and toast with honey made for a quick breakfast, and she swallowed two pain tablets with the last of her toast. Still feeling slightly groggy, she headed out for her morning walk. The sun was coming up, and it seemed to be trying to warm the cool air, with little success. Bessie pulled her coat around her more tightly as she headed into a strong wind. She marched across the sand, determined not to stop until she'd reached Thie yn Traie. Turning around would be a relief, as the wind would then push her home.

"Bessie, there you are," a voice called from somewhere over her head, as Bessie reached the stairs to the mansion above the beach.

Looking up, Bessie smiled at Elizabeth Quayle, who was racing down the rickety steps without a care in the world. Elizabeth was the youngest child and only daughter of George and Mary Quayle, the couple who owned Thie yn Traie. Mary and Bessie had become close friends over the years. Elizabeth was in her mid-twenties, and she had dropped out of a number of universities, unable to decide what she wanted to do with her life. Some time back, she'd started a party planning business on the island and, from what Bessie knew, the business was proving to be a great success. She'd planned a few events for Bessie, and Bessie had been thrilled with the results.

"Do be careful," Bessie called.

"It's fine," Elizabeth said carelessly. She jumped off the last step, landing on the beach and then pulling Bessie into a hug.

"Oooh," Bessie exclaimed as her arm was caught in the middle of the squeeze.

"Your arm," Elizabeth exclaimed. "I'm so sorry. That was why I dashed down here this morning. I read all about your accident in the paper and I wanted to make sure you were okay. I was so excited to see you, though, that I forgot all about your arm."

"It's fine," Bessie told her. "And I'm fine."

"You have to come up and have a cuppa with Mum. She's been ever so worried about you. She's been wanting to ring you, but she didn't want to bother you, not if you were seriously injured."

"That hasn't stopped everyone else on the island from ringing," Bessie told her. "She should have rung. I could have assured her that I'm absolutely fine so that she didn't need to worry."

"Never mind. Come and have a cuppa. I'll help you on the stairs."

Bessie hated being fussed over, but she'd once taken a tumble down those stairs, so she let Elizabeth hold her arm and escort her up to Thie yn Traie.

CHAPTER 5

"Aunt Bessie." The formally dressed butler looked delighted to see her. He pulled her into a hug before clearing his throat and taking a step back. "I mean, Miss Cubbon, we were very sorry to hear about your recent accident," he said in his perfectly polished accent.

"You know better than to call me Miss Cubbon," Bessie scolded him. "I've known you far too long for any such nonsense."

The man chuckled. "I was really worried about you," he told her in a low voice, his accent switching to the Manx one that he'd had when he'd lived on the island as a child.

"I'm absolutely fine," Bessie replied.

"I'm awfully glad to hear that," Mary's voice came from the corridor. She rushed into the large entryway and gave Bessie a hug. "I thought about ringing you several times, but I was certain your answering machine would be full of messages from concerned friends."

"It is, but I should have thought to ring you, actually. I am sorry," Bessie told her.

"Never mind that, come and have a cuppa with us," Mary invited.

"Jonathan, tea for three and, for Bessie, we'll have the biscuits and cakes that Andy made, please."

The butler nodded and then bowed before he headed down the corridor. Mary and Elizabeth escorted Bessie into the huge great room with its wall of windows that gave stunning views of the sea below.

"Shall we sit near the windows?" Mary asked. There were half a dozen clusters of chairs and couches scattered around the room. Mary led Bessie to the group that was closest to the windows and waved her into a chair.

"Are you still in much pain?" she asked, nodding towards Bessie's arm.

"Not really. I'm taking tablets when I remember, but I don't always remember, so the pain can't be too bad," Bessie replied.

"Andy wanted to go down and try to remove all of the driftwood from the beach," Elizabeth said. "He actually went as far as walking down to the beach, but Hugh Watterson was there and he told Andy that it was an impossible job."

Bessie nodded. "That's exactly what I told Hugh, actually. Even if he and his mates had managed to clear everything on the beach, the next tide would have brought in more."

Elizabeth nodded. "Andy wants to do something, though. He was thinking of offering to cook you dinner every night while you're recuperating."

"I'm quite capable of cooking my own dinner," Bessie told her. "Andy is more than welcome to visit me and see that for himself."

Mary laughed. "If I were you, I'd be lying on the couch, moaning pathetically, so that Andy would cook for me for days on end. That man is an amazing chef."

"You're right about that. What was I thinking? I can barely manage to lift my arm, let alone cook anything. I'm wasting away, really," Bessie replied with a laugh.

Elizabeth nodded. "I'll confess that I was hoping he might invite me to join you for a meal one night," she said. "He does cook for me sometimes, but it's difficult, as we have a chef here who doesn't really want Andy in her kitchen, and Andy is staying with his mother at the moment. Anne's kitchen is pretty basic. Andy can still turn out amazing meals, but it's a lot more work in that kitchen than it should be."

"I haven't seen him since he finished culinary school. Is he looking for a house on the island now?" Bessie asked.

Andy Caine was a lovely young man whom Bessie had known well in his childhood. He'd had a difficult upbringing, with a mother who'd worked multiple jobs to pay the bills and a stepfather who spent nearly all of his time at the pub. Bessie had been delighted when Andy had discovered that he was heir to a considerable fortune. The unexpected inheritance had allowed him to chase his dream of becoming a chef and owning his own restaurant. After nearly two years at a culinary school in the UK, Andy was back on the island now, and Bessie knew she wasn't the only one looking forward to the restaurant he was going to open at some point.

"He's looking, but he hasn't found the right place yet. There's a lot of new construction going up, but he'd rather have something a little different. Most of what he's found has needed far too much work, though. He wants to focus on the restaurant, but he can't do that if he has to renovate an entire house," Elizabeth replied.

Andy and Elizabeth had started spending time together during his breaks from school. He sometimes provided catering or cakes for the events that Elizabeth planned. Over time, the pair had moved beyond friendship, and Bessie was hopeful that their relationship would continue to grow now that Andy was home for good.

"If I hear of anything coming on the market, I'll let him know," Bessie said. "Does he have a location in mind for the restaurant?"

"He's taking his time, considering his options. Douglas would be the obvious choice, but there's a small cottage for sale in Castletown that appeals to him. It wouldn't hold many tables, but it's a lovely old Manx cottage and there would be room for a state-of-the-art kitchen."

"So he's not even considering Laxey?" Bessie asked.

"Not at the moment. There simply aren't any suitable premises available," Elizabeth said with a sigh. "He'll want a house near the restaurant, because he'll need to be there for so many hours each day, but he isn't finding any houses he likes anywhere."

"Maybe he should buy land and build both a house and a restaurant," Bessie suggested.

Elizabeth shrugged. "That's on the list of possibilities, too. I think maybe he has too many options right now. He's a bit overwhelmed."

"Tell him to come and see me," Bessie suggested. "Maybe I can help him narrow down his choices."

"He's been talking about doing that, but I'm afraid I've been keeping him rather busy," Elizabeth said with a blush. "He's been catering just about every party I've planned since he's been back. He does an amazing job and my clients are always thrilled. I know he'd rather get his restaurant up and running, but I'm really going to miss having him available for my events."

"Maybe he'll still have time to do some of them," Bessie said.

"We'll have to see," Elizabeth replied.

"Here we are," Jonathan announced as he pushed the tea cart into the room. Bessie's mouth began to water when she saw the gorgeous array of biscuits, cakes, and scones. The butler poured them each a cup of tea and then bowed before he left the room.

"He's such a wonderful addition to our lives," Mary said as the trio filled plates with the various treats.

"Jack? I mean, Jonathan?" Bessie asked. Known now as Jonathan, the butler would always be Jack Hooper to Bessie. She could still picture him running on the beach. He'd had ginger hair and freckles in those days, and he'd always seemed to manage to take a tumble at some point, which got him biscuits and sympathy from Bessie. Of course, Jack was just one of the children that Bessie was sure used to fall into the sea entirely on purpose so that they could visit her cottage.

"He's the best butler we've ever employed, and I keep making George increase his salary so that we don't lose him," Mary told her.

"Is that likely?" Bessie asked.

"I hope not. He's very loyal, but I know a few of our friends have made him offers. I'm more concerned that he might get an offer from someone across. George and I can't compete with the salaries that certain families in the UK offer."

"I'm sure he loves the island, though," Bessie said.

"Yes, we're really hoping that never changes," Mary agreed.

"I'm still not sure about sending him on that course," Elizabeth interjected.

Mary shrugged and looked at Bessie. "We're sending Jonathan on a computer course next month. He'll be gone for four weeks. He's going to learn about networking and security and many other things that I don't understand. He's interested in learning it all, and it should be very useful both to him and to us."

"And make him more attractive to other potential employers," Elizabeth added.

"He's eager to learn some new skills, and we're happy to provide him with a chance to do so. George and I both believe that you should never stop learning, and we try to encourage all of our staff to take classes that interest them."

"Maybe you could get the chef to take a few classes in puddings," Elizabeth said in a low voice.

"As Andy is now making all of our puddings for us, I don't think that will be necessary," Mary laughed.

"Andy made all of this, then?" Bessie asked, gesturing towards the tea cart.

"Every last delicious bite," Elizabeth replied. "It was meant to be for a tea party that I was arranging, but that had to be cancelled at the last minute."

"How unfortunate," Bessie said.

"It's all something of a mess, actually," Elizabeth confided. "I've refunded the hostess's deposit and written off the cost of all of the food."

"And now you get to enjoy it yourself," Bessie said.

"This is just a tiny fraction of what Andy made, though. It was meant to be a huge tea party for charity. I donated most of the food to a few local food banks. They were very grateful, anyway."

Bessie frowned. She'd heard rumours about a large charity event being cancelled at the last minute. From what she'd heard, the woman who'd been organising it had discovered that her new husband had been quietly removing large sums of money from their joint bank accounts. The last Bessie had heard, the husband had disappeared with one of the maids, leaving his former wife considerably poorer than she'd been before she'd met him.

"Shall I pour another round of tea?" Jonathan asked as he quietly walked back into the room.

"Yes, please," Mary told him.

"I'm so sorry to interrupt," a voice called from the doorway a moment later.

Bessie looked up at the woman who strode into the room. She appeared to be somewhere around fifty. Her dyed blonde hair concealed any grey and went well with her bright blue eyes. Her casual ponytail suited her, and a dark grey business suit and low heels looked professional, but reasonably comfortable. Feeling certain that she'd never met the woman before, Bessie felt that there was something familiar about her, as well.

"Carolyn? Is there something wrong?" Mary asked, getting to her feet.

"Not at all," the blonde assured her. "George left some papers on his bedside table. At least that's where he thinks he left them. As they're rather important papers, I drove up from Douglas to collect them. I was just going to ask Jonathan to get them for me, but that seemed rude, somehow."

Mary smiled. "It would have been fine, but as I'm here, I'll go and find them for you. Have a cuppa while I'm gone," she added as she headed for the door.

The woman sat down near Bessie and smiled at her. "Miss Cubbon, I'm Carolyn White, George's assistant. We've never been introduced, but knowing the people who are part of George's world is essential in my job."

"It's nice to meet you," Bessie replied. "I thought you looked familiar. I'm sure I've seen you at several events that George and Mary have hosted over the years."

Carolyn nodded. "I probably should have introduced myself at some point over the years, but I always do my best to blend into the background. I'm at events to work, not socialise."

"I can't believe you've never met Aunt Bessie," Elizabeth said. "But let me pour you some tea."

"Oh, no, thank you," Carolyn told her. "I truly can't stay. The missing papers are needed for a meeting that started half an hour ago. I must get back to Douglas as quickly as possible."

Bessie glanced at the clock and then gasped. "I have to be at Ramsey Hospital in less than half an hour," she exclaimed. "I need to get home and ring for a taxi." She started to get up, but Elizabeth held up her hand.

"Have another cuppa. I can have you in Ramsey in ten minutes," she said.

"I don't want to inconvenience you," Bessie protested.

"You aren't doing any such thing," Elizabeth insisted. "I need to get into Ramsey today anyway. I need a few things at the bookshop."

Bessie thought about questioning the girl, but decided not to bother. She'd struggle to make her appointment if she had to rush home and rely on a taxi. Elizabeth's kindness was much appreciated.

Mary was back a moment later, carrying a large file folder. "I hope what you need is in here somewhere," she said as she handed it to Carolyn.

"It is," Carolyn replied after a quick glance inside the folder. "Thank you."

She rushed away, and Bessie and Elizabeth were not far behind. Elizabeth helped Bessie into her little red sports car and they headed off to Ramsey.

"Do you want me to wait for you?" Elizabeth asked as she drove. "You said you had shopping to do."

"I do, but I could take you home first, if your appointment won't take long."

"Actually, I'm meant to be having tea with a friend after my appointment, so thank you, but no thank you. I do appreciate the ride here, though, very much."

"Always happy to help," Elizabeth laughed as she pulled into the car park for the hospital.

"Give Andy my best," Bessie told her as she climbed out of the car.

"I will do," Elizabeth promised. She waited until Bessie waved from the hospital's doors before driving away.

"Miss Cubbon, good morning," Kelly said as Bessie crossed the waiting room. "I'll let the doctor know that you're here. It shouldn't be long."

Bessie nodded. "Are we still having tea after my appointment?" she asked.

Kelly nodded. "Yes, please."

Bessie took a seat and flipped through a five-year-old magazine about gardening. Even after so many years of living on the beach, Bessie still hadn't decided whether she wished she could have had a small garden or not. She'd tried planting a few things on various occasions over the years, but nothing had survived for long, not even when she'd dumped several inches of soil over the sand around the cottage. In the end, she'd decided that the salty air and the windy conditions were probably to blame and she'd given up on the idea. When she read magazines like these, full of glossy photographs of beautiful flowers, she wondered if she should try again, though.

"How's the arm today?" the doctor said as Bessie was escorted into his office a few minutes later.

"Much better," Bessie told him.

He felt up and down her arm and then poked and prodded it in several places. While uncomfortable, it wasn't anywhere near as painful as it had been right after the accident.

"It seems to be healing nicely," the doctor conceded. "Come back and see me on Monday. If it's still the same or better, I won't need to see you again."

Bessie thought about arguing, as she didn't really feel the need to let the doctor poke her arm another time, but she simply nodded. There was a slim chance that her injury was more serious than she thought, and it was best to take the doctor's advice. He was an expert, after all, she reminded herself.

"Ah, I just need five more minutes," Kelly said when Bessie returned to the waiting area.

Bessie sat back down. She was busily planning a huge outdoor garden next to Treoghe Bwaane, when Kelly touched her arm.

"I'm ready now," she said.

"That's good. I was seriously considering buying soil and planting raised beds," Bessie laughed, tossing the magazine aside.

They took seats in the café and ordered the same thing they'd had previously. Bessie felt a bit guilty, eating more biscuits after her lovely tea with Mary and Elizabeth, but it would have been rude not to eat one or two, she told herself.

"I'm paying for today," Bessie told Kelly firmly.

"I should pay. You're trying to help me," Kelly argued.

"You paid last time. It's my turn today or I'll leave before the tea arrives."

Kelly sighed. "I won't argue. I'm already so grateful to you for whatever you've done. I daren't argue with you."

"But I haven't actually done anything."

"You don't think Kara was murdered, then?"

"I didn't say that. I don't know what happened to Kara, but I did ring John Rockwell and ask him to see what he could find out."

"Oh, thank you so much."

"He didn't learn much, though," Bessie warned her. "The case is officially closed, but one of the inspectors is still working to try to find out where Kara got the drugs that killed her."

"If he finds that, he'll find the killer," Kelly said.

"Maybe, or maybe he'll find that she truly accidentally overdosed."

"She didn't. And she didn't kill herself. Someone murdered her, and once the police find out where the drugs came from, they'll have the killer," Kelly said with a smile.

"You mustn't get your hopes up that the case will be solved any time soon," Bessie warned her. "The inspector has several other cases to investigate, and as I understand it, he doesn't have any leads at the moment."

"So we have to find him some."

"I'm not sure what you mean."

"I mean, you need to talk to everyone involved and help me work out all of the possible sources for the drugs."

"Kara could have obtained the drugs from a random stranger or from someone that you don't even know exists. My talking to her friends and family on the island isn't going to help solve the case," Bessie said firmly.

Kelly shook her head and then ran a hand over her eyes. "You're saying it's hopeless, then."

"I'm saying that the police are doing everything they can. You need to let them do their job."

"They've been doing their job for a year and you just said they don't have any leads. How much longer do I have to wait to get justice for my sister?"

Just then the waitress delivered the tea and biscuits, giving Bessie a chance to think about how to word her reply.

"Not all murders are solved," she said carefully. "You may never know what happened to Kara."

Kelly slowly ate a biscuit as tears began to run down her face. "I need to know," she said eventually. "I can't just sit back and wait for the police to solve the case, either. I want to conduct my own investigation. How much do private detectives charge?"

"I've no idea," Bessie said. "I'm sure they aren't inexpensive, though."

"Maybe I can talk my parents into taking out a second mortgage," the woman said thoughtfully. "Or maybe Kent could help. I'm sure he wants to know what happened to Kara almost as much as I do."

"I'm not sure what you think a private detective can do."

"He could talk to everyone in Manchester, Kara's former work colleagues and her former flatmates. Someone must know something. She didn't keep secrets. I thought she told me everything, really."

"I think you'd be wasting your money."

"What else can I do? You won't help and I don't have any idea how to conduct a murder investigation."

The tears were falling more heavily now and Kelly wiped them away with her napkin.

"It isn't that I won't help," Bessie said. "I simply don't think there's anything I can do."

"Will you talk to my parents?"

"Your parents?"

"They spoke to Kara every week. They'll tell you that she never took drugs and that she wasn't suicidal. They'll tell you about all of her friends and the people with whom she worked. Maybe they'll say something that will give you a hint as to where else the police can look for clues. If not, maybe you can help me persuade them that we need to hire a private detective."

"I don't think you need to hire a private detective," Bessie countered.

"Maybe we won't mention that to them, then," Kelly replied, giving Bessie a watery smile. "I'm sorry. I'm desperate and I simply don't know where to turn."

Bessie nodded slowly. "I'll talk to your parents," she said, vowing to discuss their younger daughter's mental health along with everything else.

"You will? Oh, thank goodness," Kelly said, sighing deeply. "What would be best for you? I can bring them to your cottage. I've always wanted to see it, actually. I've read about it in the papers so many times. Or we could meet somewhere else, maybe in a restaurant or a pub? I'd buy lunch or dinner or whatever you wanted if we did that. I'm sure you'd be more than welcome at my parents' house, too, if that sounds better. What would you prefer?"

Bessie bit her tongue before she could reply with the first thought that came into her head. Telling Kelly that she'd prefer to have never met her would be cruel, and the woman was already very upset. "Why don't you bring them to my cottage," she said after a moment. "It's comfortable and private. I'm sure the conversation will be difficult."

Kelly nodded. "Everyone here is used to me crying over my tea. I do it nearly every day, or I have done since Kara died. My parents will be more comfortable talking to you in private, though."

"I thought they might."

"Tonight?" Kelly asked.

Bessie blinked in surprise. "Tonight?" she echoed.

"I mean, I'll have to ring them, but if they're free tonight, would that work for you?"

Feeling as if she might as well get the meeting over with, Bessie nodded. "I don't have plans for tonight."

"Great. Let me ring my mum and see what she and Dad are doing later."

Kelly pulled out her mobile and then walked away as Bessie sipped her tea and nibbled on a biscuit. The girl was back a few minutes later.

"We'll be at your cottage at seven, if that's okay," she said.

"That's fine. John did want me to tell you that you were welcome to talk to him about everything. Maybe that would be a better idea."

Kelly shook her head. "I'm sure he's very nice, but my parents would much rather talk to you than to another police inspector. My father has been ringing someone in Manchester every Monday since Kara died. They never have anything new to report."

"I'm still not sure what you think I'll be able to accomplish."

"You've solved several murders over the past two years or so. How?"

Bessie sat back in her seat and tried to think of how to answer that question. "I'm not sure," she said eventually.

"People talk to you," Kelly said, "and they tell you things that they haven't told the police, because you ask different questions, the right questions."

"I don't know about that."

"I do. I've talked to a few people about you. You have a way of finding some little detail that everyone else has missed that's actually really important. My parents have talked to the police at least a dozen times and I'm certain that they're going to tell you things tonight that they haven't told the police. Maybe none of it will actually matter in the investigation, but maybe it will. As I said, you'll notice it, whatever it is, and that could be the key."

"You're putting far too much faith in me," Bessie said.

"Tell that to Madison Tyler. You worked out who'd killed her brother based on a suspicion that no one else shared."

Bessie thought about arguing, but she knew Kelly was at least partially correct. "I just happened to ask the right questions at the right time," Bessie said after a minute.

"Yes, and you do that regularly. Now I want you to do it for Kara."

"I'll talk to your parents. I can't imagine what they'll tell me that they haven't already told the police, though."

"Neither can they. That's why I want them to talk to you. They think they've told the police everything and I'm sure they know something that might matter."

"Please don't start thinking that I'm going to be able to solve Kara's murder," Bessie said.

"I just want to feel as if I tried everything. I lie awake at night trying to think of something else that I can do. Right now, you're my only hope."

Bessie opened her mouth to protest, but Kelly held up a hand.

"I know, I know. That was a bit overly dramatic, even if that truly is the way that I feel. I know that you're only human and that there's probably nothing that you can do that the police haven't already done, but I'm not exaggerating when I say that I'm desperate. Maybe, if you truly can't find out anything new, then I'll have to admit defeat, but I'm not there yet."

"I'll talk to your parents. That's all I can do."

Kelly nodded and then smiled at Bessie. "I can't thank you enough, really I can't. We'll be at your cottage at seven. Thank you, so much."

"I'll see you at seven," Bessie agreed, swallowing a sigh.

"I need to go and redo my makeup before I go back to work. See you later."

Kelly rushed out of the room, leaving Bessie at the table.

"I'll need the bill when you have a minute," she told the waitress.

"Oh, Miss Sutton already paid the bill," the waitress replied. "I'll just get you a bag for the rest of the biscuits."

There was no point in arguing with the waitress, of course. Bessie took her bag of biscuits and headed out to the taxi rank, determined to have words with Kelly when she arrived at her cottage later in the day. As she walked out the door, a horn beeped and Bessie saw Elizabeth waving from a spot in the car park.

"What are you doing here?" she asked as Elizabeth climbed out of the car.

"I drove back this way after my errands in Ramsey," Elizabeth replied. "I thought, if you were coming out when I got here, I could give you a ride home."

"That's very kind of you," Bessie said, not believing the story for a minute.

They climbed into the car and Elizabeth started the engine. As they exited the car park, she glanced at Bessie. "You've known Andy for a long time," she said. "What sort of girl does he usually go for?"

Bessie hid a smile. This was a side of Elizabeth that she rarely saw. The young woman was usually brimming with self-confidence.

"I don't really know," she said after a moment's thought. "I knew him when he was a teenager. I'm sure he had relationships, but he never talked to me about them. We talked about his difficult life at home, and we did a lot of baking. I don't remember him mentioning girls, at least not often."

"And he never brought a girl over to your cottage?"

"Goodness, no," Bessie exclaimed. "I never encouraged young couples to visit my cottage together. Most of my visitors came because they were having trouble at home. My cottage wasn't the place to talk about their romances."

Elizabeth nodded. "So he might have had a serious girlfriend at some point," she said thoughtfully.

"I'd be surprised to learn that he had," Bessie told her. "Aside from having problems at home, he hated school and went as little as possible. He was something of an outcast, really. I don't think he was popular with girls."

"But he's gorgeous."

"He used to wear his hair really long, and it often looked as if it hadn't been combed in days. His clothes were usually old and tattered, and those things seem to matter a lot to young girls."

Elizabeth sighed. "I'm afraid I wouldn't have looked at him twice if he weren't nearly as rich as my father. I'm sure that makes me a terrible person."

"Not at all. You have to be very careful when getting involved with men. There are a lot of men out there who would be more interested in your father's fortune than in you."

"And I know that isn't the case with Andy. He has oodles of his own money, but he almost seems to not want to spend any of it. He's always looking for bargains and worrying over every penny he spends."

"I'm sure that's all to do with his upbringing. Money was very tight in his house."

"I know. It's just weird to me. I've been trying to talk him into going away for a month, somewhere warm and exotic, but he's really focussed on getting his business started. He said he hasn't earned a holiday yet."

"I can talk to him about that when I see him, but I'm rather inclined to agree with him, really."

Elizabeth laughed. "I knew you'd agree with him. You probably have pots of money tucked away, but you still live frugally in your tiny cottage by the sea."

Bessie was tempted to tell the girl that she was absolutely right. Thanks to her advocate's very careful money management, the tiny sum she'd inherited when Matthew had died was now more than enough for Bessie to live considerably more lavishly than she did. Bessie's only real extravagance was books, and she still considered it a treat when she bought a new hardcover rather than waiting for the paperback version to be released.

"I'll try to get Andy over to see you one day this week," Elizabeth said as she pulled into the small parking area next to Treoghe Bwaane.

"Not tonight," Bessie replied. "I have other visitors coming tonight."

"That sounds ominous somehow."

"I hope not."

Bessie had a light lunch and then forced herself to read a book for the rest of the afternoon. After dinner, she rang John and told him about her conversation with Kelly. He didn't sound very happy with her, but he was busy with the children and Doona, so he didn't argue.

At quarter to seven, Bessie refilled the kettle and then piled the leftover biscuits from the morning onto a plate. She put that in the centre of the kitchen table and then began to pace in circles around the tiny room. The clock ticked slowly as it counted down the minutes. The knock on the door came at six fifty-seven.

CHAPTER 6

$\mathcal{K}$elly looked as if she'd been crying. Bessie stepped back to let her into the house. An older couple followed her inside. They were both frowning.

"Miss Cubbon, these are my parents, Karl and Beverly Sutton," Kelly said.

"It's very nice to meet you both," Bessie replied. "But please, you can all call me Bessie."

"We've met before," Beverly Sutton said flatly. "I'm sure you won't remember."

Bessie stared at her for a moment and then tilted her head as she tried to recognise the face. "I met you at a fundraising event for Manx National Heritage," she said finally. "You were with Peter Marshall, weren't you?"

"You have a very good memory for faces," Beverly told her. "That had to have been fifteen years ago. Peter was a senior manager at the bank where my husband was working at the time. He bought a table at the fundraiser and then invited some of his staff to join him. Karl fell ill at the last minute, but I went along anyway."

"You were wearing a lovely red dress," Bessie remembered.

Beverly smiled. "I loved that dress. It was the first fancy dress I'd bought since we'd had the children. I'd been feeling rather lost in being a mother and for that one night I felt like a person again."

"I'm glad you enjoyed the evening," Bessie said. To her mind it had been a rather tedious affair, but perhaps she'd simply gone to too many similar events to appreciate every one of them.

Beverly nodded. "You may as well know that Karl and I didn't want to come tonight. Our daughter has done something roughly akin to blackmail to get us here."

Bessie swallowed a dozen different replies. "Please, have a seat," she said after an awkward moment. "If you don't want to talk to me, at least have some tea and a biscuit or two. I always enjoy meeting new people. We can talk about whatever you'd like."

Karl and Beverly exchanged glances. Kelly looked as if she wanted to say something, but after a moment she simply crossed to the table and sat down. Bessie switched the kettle on, and by the time she'd made tea, Beverly and Karl had joined their daughter at the table.

"You weren't meant to pay for our tea this morning," Bessie told Kelly.

"Under the circumstances, it was the least I could do," Kelly countered.

"She's been telling you all about Kara, then," Karl said.

"Yes, she has. She doesn't believe that Kara's death was an accident," Bessie replied.

"We've had this conversation a dozen times a week since Kara died," Karl told Bessie. "No one would have murdered Kara. She was just an ordinary woman doing her job and living her life. Murderers have to have motives, and there simply wasn't any motive for anyone to kill her."

"I'm sorry to disagree with you, but I've been involved in a number of murder investigations in the past two years. Many times the motives for the killings have been unthinkable to me," Bessie replied.

Karl shook his head. "I knew talking to you would be a mistake. I knew you'd be eager to convince us that it was murder. You seem to enjoy being involved in these sorts of cases. You've certainly done your best to get mixed up in plenty of them."

Bessie took a deep breath before she replied. "I think it might be best if you did leave," she said in a steady voice. "I agreed to talk with you because Kelly was hopeful that I might be able to find a new angle for the police to consider. You're clearly unwilling to share anything with me. I'd rather not waste everyone's time."

She got to her feet and waited for the others to stand. Beverly put her hand on her husband's arm. When he looked at her, she shook her head slowly.

"Karl and I are both still devastated by Kara's passing," she said in a voice that was barely above a whisper. "We don't like to talk about it or about her."

"I'm sure you've spoken to the police several times. That's all that you need to do," Bessie replied.

"Please, sit back down and let's talk," Beverly said. "Karl can listen."

"Or Karl can leave," the man snapped.

"Of course you can," Beverly agreed. "Kelly and I can get a taxi home."

For a moment, Bessie thought Karl was going to storm out. She watched his face as he seemed to think about the idea. Eventually, he shook his head and sat back in his chair. "I'll listen for now. I may leave at any time."

"Thank you," Kelly said softly.

"Where do you want to start?" Beverly asked Bessie.

"I don't know," Bessie replied. "I told Kelly that the whole thing seems rather hopeless, really, since Kara lived and died in Manchester. I don't know anything about the city or about her friends there."

"I can tell you about her friends," Beverly offered. "Kara and I were very close, maybe too close for a mother and daughter, I don't know. She told me just about everything that was happening in her life. She talked a lot about her friends, too. Her closest friends in Manchester were her flatmates."

"What about her friends on the island?" Bessie asked. "Did she have many friends here?"

Beverly frowned. "Most of her friends left the island for uni at the same time she did. I don't think many of them came back, at least not for long."

"Did she have friends at uni with whom she stayed in touch after she'd finished?" was Bessie's next question.

"Not really," Beverly said. "She made some good friends at uni, but once she came home they all sort of drifted apart. She did have plans to try to meet up with some of them again once she was settled in Manchester, but she never mentioned actually getting around to doing so."

Bessie nodded. "So tell me about her flatmates."

"Rachel is an athletic trainer. She was nice and they had fun together, but Kara told me that she never felt as if she could get close to her. It was like Rachel kept her emotions shut away or something," Beverly said.

"She never told me that," Kelly complained.

"As I said, Kara told me just about everything that was happening in her life. When Rachel first moved in, Kara tried to get to know her better, but they never really got past a rather superficial friendship."

"But they were planning a holiday together," Bessie said.

"And Kara had high hopes of finally getting Rachel to talk about her life on their trip to Glasgow. She didn't really know anything about Rachel's past, aside from the fact that she'd grown up in Manchester."

"What about her family?"

"Kara never met any of Rachel's family. She wasn't even sure if Rachel's parents were still alive or if Rachel had any siblings," Beverly replied.

"That sounds rather odd," Bessie said thoughtfully. "They lived together for six months, didn't they?"

"Yes, although I'm probably making too much of it now," Beverly sighed. "At the time it was just something that Kara mentioned casually. She didn't think that Rachel was hiding any big secrets or anything like that. It was more that the woman was very private. Kara was hoping that Rachel would come to see her as a friend in whom she could confide, that's all."

Bessie nodded. "What about the other women in the flat?"

"Brooke is a model. She's stunning, and Kara admitted to me that sometimes she felt quite insecure when she went places with Brooke. Men would stop and stare, and quite a few would try to get Brooke's number. Kara found it difficult sometimes. Kara was very beautiful, but Brooke is beyond that," Beverly said.

"And Kara was the pretty sister," Kelly muttered.

Karl reached over and patted her hand. "You were the only one who ever thought that," he told her.

Kelly shook her head and then took a sip of tea.

"Did Kara get along well with Brooke, then?" Bessie asked.

"Oh, yes, she and Brooke were very close. Brooke was the opposite of Rachel, really. She told Kara everything about her life, from her difficult childhood to every man she'd ever known. Kara said she sometimes felt as if she knew more about Brooke than she did about herself."

"And the third flatmate?" Bessie wondered.

"That was Pamela. She's a mechanical engineer and she's very smart. Kara was fond of Pamela, but she told me that it was sometimes difficult to talk to her. Pamela's brain just seemed to be on a different wavelength or something. They'd all be chatting about the weather and Pamela would start telling them why a cold front was coming through or exactly how the change in barometric pressure was causing the current rain, that sort of thing. Kara found it exhausting sometimes, trying to follow the conversation and not seem rude."

"So she didn't really care for Pamela?" Bessie tried to clarify.

"Oh, no, she thought Pamela was wonderful. She loved having a really smart friend. She just found it difficult to keep up with her intelligence. Brooke made her feel unattractive and Pamela made her feel stupid," Beverly replied.

"She wasn't stupid," Kelly said.

"No, of course not," Beverly agreed.

"So if Kara had any secrets, she'd have told them to Brooke?" Bessie asked.

Beverly sat back in her chair and frowned. "If Kara had secrets, which she most assuredly did not, she probably would have chosen Brooke to confide in, yes. Rachel worked odd hours at the gym and Pamela worked long hours. Brooke only worked occasionally, when she had a photo shoot or whatever. I remember Kara telling me that whenever she was at the flat, Brooke was there, too. She said something about always being able to rely on Brooke if she needed to talk to someone."

"And did she often need to talk to someone?" was Bessie's next question.

"I don't believe so. The context was to do with how much I worried about her being so far from home. She was simply assuring me that she had people with whom she could talk if she needed them."

Bessie nodded. "What about men in her life?"

"There were a few, but she wasn't ready for anything serious," Beverly said.

"Did she have any steady boyfriends on the island before she went to uni?"

"No, definitely not. She went out a few times with a few different boys, but I wouldn't have let her get into anything serious, not at that age," Beverly said firmly.

"What about boyfriends at uni, then?"

"Again, nothing serious. She knew her studies were important and she gave them priority."

"That just leaves men in Manchester, then. Did she tell you about anyone there?"

"There were a couple men that she mentioned, but no one that she went out with more than a handful of times," Beverly said.

"Did she give you names?" Bessie pushed her.

"One was called Scott Brewer. He was working for the same agency when she first got hired, but then he left to go to work for a different one. He didn't ask her out until he'd moved jobs. The agency frowned on staff getting involved with one another."

"They only went out two or three times," Kelly interjected. "She told me all about him. He was nice enough, but they didn't have any chemistry."

Beverly frowned. "That isn't quite how she put it to me."

"What did she tell you?" Bessie asked.

"Just that things didn't work out. She didn't specify who had ended the relationship, not to me, anyway."

"She told me that she'd ended it," Kelly said.

"Did she mention how he took the news?" Bessie wondered.

"She said he didn't really care. He was seeing other women at the same time and they both knew it was just casual. I don't know if she actually ended it or if she simply stopped texting or ringing him back," Kelly replied.

"Any other men?" Bessie asked, making a mental note to talk to John about Scott.

"Louis Hunter," Beverly said. "He lived in the same building, on the floor above them. He was playing really loud music one night, so Kara went up to ask him to turn it down. He was having a party, and he invited her in. They went out a few times after that, but again, it wasn't serious."

"She said something that made me think that she really liked him," Kelly said. "I got the feeling that he was just having fun, but she was really interested."

"I never got that impression," Beverly said sharply.

Kelly shrugged. "I could be wrong," she said quickly.

"Anyone else?" Bessie asked.

The two women exchanged glances. "Not that I know of," Beverly said after a moment.

"I want to understand the timing of everything," Bessie said. She got up and found a tablet of paper and a pen. "When did Kara move to Manchester?"

"Early October," Kelly said.

Bessie made a note. "And she got the flat right away?"

"Pretty much. It was far too big for one person, though, and she couldn't have afforded it on her own, anyway. She advertised for flat-mates and Rachel moved in within a week or two," Beverly told her.

"Rachel was first, then," Bessie said as she noted the woman's name.

"Yes, and then about a week later, Pamela moved in. Between the three of them, they could afford the rent and the other bills, so Kara stopped looking for anyone else. Brooke rang nearly three months later and practically begged to be allowed to move into the fourth bedroom. She'd been living with another woman and then her flat-mate found a boyfriend, and he'd moved in without warning," Kelly told her.

"How awful," Bessie exclaimed.

"Yeah, apparently, he used to wander around the flat in his pants, and sometimes he wouldn't even bother to put those on," Kelly added.

Bessie felt herself blush. "Where did Brooke find out about the spare bedroom if Kara wasn't advertising anymore?"

Beverly and Kelly exchanged glances.

"I've no idea, but I'm sure she told Kara at the time," Beverly said eventually.

Bessie put a small question mark next to the woman's name. "She moved into the flat in January, then?"

"Actually, it was late December," Kelly told her. "Her parents had decided to spend Christmas in Australia, and Kara ended up staying in Manchester to spend Christmas with Brooke so that she wouldn't be alone."

"I'll never forgive myself for not insisting that she come home," Beverly said softly. "It was her last Christmas."

"She really wanted to stay in Manchester, though," Kelly said. "She ended up working Christmas Eve and Boxing Day and she was sure that her supervisor was impressed by her dedication."

"She should have been here, with us," Beverly said.

Bessie held up a hand. "Tell me where the two boyfriends fit into the timeline," she said.

"She started seeing Louis not long after she'd moved in," Kelly said. "The party she interrupted was on one of the first weekends she was there, probably before Rachel moved in, because if Rachel had been there, I think Kara would have sent her to deal with the noisy neighbour."

Beverly nodded. "I'm sure she would have, actually. They might have gone together, but she wouldn't have gone alone if she'd had a choice."

"And when did they stop seeing one another?" Bessie asked as she added the man's name under the "October" heading.

"They only went out for a week or two," Kelly said. "They went out for dinner the first night. I heard all about that, because he took her to one of the city's finest restaurants. She was very impressed."

"Things went downhill from there," Beverly said dryly. "I believe Louis was disappointed that his expensive evening didn't end with Kara in his bed. He took her out once or twice more, but when she still didn't fall into his bed, he ended things."

Bessie nodded. "And Scott?"

"He switched to his new job on the first of the new year," Kelly explained. "He rang her about a week later and asked her to meet him for dinner. She thought maybe he was going to try to recruit her for the other agency, but it turned out that he was just interested in her personally."

"Was she disappointed by that?" Bessie wondered.

Kelly shrugged. "I think she was excited to think that she might be getting noticed by other agencies, but she loved her job and I don't think she would have moved at that point, not unless it was for a much better opportunity with a lot more money."

"How many times did they go out?"

"Three or four," Kelly said, looking at her mother.

"Probably about that. One week she was talking about him and the next week she wasn't. He wasn't anything special," Beverly said.

Bessie wrote the man's name under January and then looked at the paper. "So she wasn't seeing anyone through all of November and December and she hadn't found anyone else after she'd ended things with Scott?" she questioned.

"As far as I know, that's correct," Beverly said. "She may have had odd nights out with men she met, but if she did, she never mentioned them to me. As I said before, she nearly always told me everything, at least everything that mattered to her."

"She didn't tell me about anyone else, either," Kelly said. "I used to ask every week, too. She usually just laughed and reminded me that she was focussed on her career."

"There was someone in December," Karl interrupted.

All three women turned to look at him.

He shrugged. "I didn't talk to her very often, but she rang one day in December and I was the only one home. She told me she was going to a Christmas party with a new guy she'd just met."

"Did she mention a name?"

"No, and I didn't ask. I didn't want her to think I was prying."

"Can you remember anything else she said?" Bessie asked, feeling oddly as if the conversation was important.

"Just that she'd met a nice guy and that they were going to a Christmas party. I reminded her to be good and she laughed and told me that she was always very good," Karl replied.

"This is all news to me," Beverly said stiffly.

"I told you at the time that she'd rung," Karl said. "You rang her back the next day, I'm sure."

"If I did, she didn't tell me anything about any Christmas party."

"Maybe they didn't end up going," Karl shrugged. "I just assumed, when we talked to the police, that she was talking about either Scott or Louis, as you'd told me about both of them. It wasn't until Bessie made her timeline that I realised that neither of them were in the picture in December."

"I'm not sure that it matters," Beverly said. "A single night out with a random man several months before she died can hardly be relevant, can it?"

"At this point, everything has to be considered relevant," Bessie told her. "Maybe the police can find out the man's name from one of Kara's former flatmates. They may have already given the police his name, of course. He may have already been cleared of any involvement in her death."

"What else can we tell you?" Kelly asked her.

"What do you know about the people with whom she worked?"

"Not a lot," Beverly frowned. "It was, well, it probably still is, a very busy agency. Kara loved the work, but she told me that she never really had any opportunities to get to know the other staff because everyone was always working so hard."

"Her supervisor took her to lunch at least once, didn't he?" Bessie asked, not wanting to add that the lunch had been on the day Kara had died.

"Yes, but as far as I know, it was just that once," Beverly replied. "He was nice, but distant. Kara told me that he was brilliant at advertising copy but not very good with people. She didn't mind, because she had a creative mind, too."

"And she didn't socialise with anyone else?"

"Not that she ever mentioned to me," Beverly replied.

"Me, neither," Kelly said.

They both turned to stare at Karl, who looked surprised. "What? I just said I barely ever spoke to her. I don't remember her ever mentioning anyone from work."

A knock on the door startled Bessie. Perhaps John had come over to see how things were going, she thought as she crossed to the door.

The handsome young man at the door gave Bessie a brilliant smile. "I'm so very sorry to bother you, but I'm looking for Kelly Sutton," he said.

"Jake? What are you doing here?" Kelly said as she stood up and joined Bessie in the doorway.

"I'm so sorry, darling, but I couldn't stop thinking about you. When you cancelled our plans for tonight I was worried that you were upset with me over something. I just couldn't stop worrying that I'd made you angry in some way," Jake explained.

Kelly shook her head. "I told you that my parents and I were visiting Miss Cubbon to talk about Kara. I explained it all to you."

"Yes, I know, but, well, I'm sorry. I'm just a little bit too crazy about you, I suppose," he replied sheepishly.

"Jake, do come in," Beverly called from her seat at the table.

The man beamed. "I don't want to intrude," he said hesitantly.

"You won't be intruding," Beverly insisted. "We were just about done with our conversation, anyway."

Bessie stepped back to let him into the house. His dark brown hair flopped over one eye and he brushed it away almost nervously as he reached for Kelly's hand. His eyes were green, and Bessie guessed that he was probably around thirty years old.

"There are more chairs in the dining room if you'd care to get one for yourself," she told him.

He nodded and then followed Bessie into the next room. Everyone at the table shifted their chairs to make room for one more while Bessie put the kettle on again.

"I'm sorry, Bessie, this is Jake Holt," Kelly said as Bessie made more tea.

"It's nice to meet you," she said politely, even though she thought the young man's appearance at her door was rather odd.

"We've been seeing one another for a few months now," Kelly added.

Jake laughed. "I could tell you the exact number of days, but that might make it seem as if I'm a bit obsessed."

Bessie considered agreeing, but Beverly laughed.

"It's sweet that you care that much," she told Jake.

He shrugged. "I've been looking for a woman like Kelly my entire life."

Bessie handed him his tea and then refilled the rest of the cups. When she sat back down, Jake was studying the sheet of paper she'd left on the table.

"What's all this, then?" he asked.

"We've discovered that my sister went to a Christmas party with an unknown man a few months before she died," Kelly told him.

Jake raised an eyebrow. "And that's going to help the police work out what happened to her how exactly?"

Kelly flushed. "We're hoping Kara might have told one of her flat-mates more about the man."

"Even if she did, you don't think that a man she went out with just the once in early December had anything to do with her death, or do you?"

"We don't know. It's just another piece of the puzzle, that's all," Kelly told him.

He nodded. "My darling, if it makes you happy to have found another piece, then I'm delighted as well. You know I'd do anything to help you work out what really happened so that you can begin to move on with your life."

"She is moving on," Beverly said. "She was moving on, anyway. She'll feel better once the anniversary has come and gone."

"You really shouldn't talk about me as if I'm not here," Kelly protested. "I know you think Jake is wonderful, and I'm rather fond of him myself, but I don't enjoy feeling as if you two are always talking about me behind my back."

"We were talking about you right in front of your face," Jake pointed out. He chuckled and then slid an arm around her. "I'm sorry, darling. Your mother and I both want the same thing, for you to be happy. I know you can't imagine being truly happy again, not without Kara in your life, but I'm prepared to wait however long it takes for you to be ready to let me into your heart."

"Did you know Kara?" Bessie asked Jake.

He blinked and looked surprised. "I never had the pleasure of meeting her," he said after a moment. "I only moved to the island about six months ago. I met Kelly about a week later, after I'd managed to fall down a few steps and break my wrist. I asked her to have dinner with me after every hospital appointment for the next three months. She finally said yes after my very last appointment."

"Three months?" Bessie echoed. "That seems a long time for a break to heal."

"It was a very bad break," Jake told her. "They had to operate, and then I needed a lot of physical therapy to get full use back."

"What do you do for a living? Hopefully not something that requires the full use of both wrists," Bessie said.

Jake laughed. "It was a long three months, both at home and at work. I work for one of the banks, in the lending department. I had to learn to type applications with one hand, which wasn't easy."

"Where were you before the island?" Bessie asked.

"All over the place, really," he replied. "In banking, if you're willing to move around, you can advance a lot faster. I started with the bank in London, moved to Leeds, then to Manchester, then to Coventry, and now here."

Bessie wanted to ask him when he'd been in Manchester, but she felt as if she'd been asking too many rude questions.

Kelly solved the problem for her. "He lived in Manchester about a year before Kara moved there," she told Bessie. "That was one of the first things I asked him when he told me that he'd once lived there. I don't know why it matters, but I wish he'd been there when Kara was there."

"I can't change the past," Jake told her. "If I could, you know exactly what I'd do, anyway."

Kelly nodded. "The same thing I'd do. Save Kara."

Jake leaned over to rest his head on Kelly's. She sighed.

"I think that's quite enough for tonight, then," Karl said. "I'm sure you're very proud of yourself because you've learned something the police don't know," he said to Bessie.

"If it helps the police get to the bottom of what happened to Kara, we'll all owe Bessie a lot," Kelly said.

"That doesn't seem very likely, though, does it?" Jake asked. His tone was gentle, but Kelly still winced at his words.

"At this point, I'm just glad we found something new for the police to investigate. Considering she never mentioned the man again, Kara probably only went out with him once, but maybe one of her flatmates will know more," Kelly said. "More than that, though, it gives me hope that there are other things that the police don't know. If Bessie talks to everyone, maybe she'll be able to find out something even more important."

Bessie held up a hand. "I don't think…" she began.

Karl laughed harshly. "Don't waste our time protesting," he

snapped. "Making Kelly beg before you agree isn't kind. You know you want to talk to everyone else. Interfering is what you do best."

Counting to ten didn't do anything to calm Bessie, so she kept going. When she reached a hundred and six, she took a deep breath. "I'm sorry, Kelly, but I don't think there's any point in my speaking to anyone else," she said firmly. "I'll share everything we discussed tonight with Inspector Rockwell. He'll pass it along to someone in Manchester."

"But you could do so much more," Kelly protested.

"This is really a case for the police in Manchester," Bessie countered.

Kelly opened her mouth to speak again, but Jake interrupted.

"Darling, as much as I hate to say it, I'm afraid I agree with Bessie. I told you earlier today that I couldn't see the point in coming to talk with her about the case."

"Which is why I didn't invite you to come along," Kelly replied.

Jake nodded and then turned to Bessie. "I love Kelly with all my heart. I know we haven't been together for very long, but I know she's the only woman for me. I'm not wealthy, but I have some money put away for a rainy day. If I paid for everything, would you go to Manchester for a few days and speak to Kara's former flatmates and work colleagues there?"

Kelly gasped. "What a brilliant idea."

"I'm sorry, but no," Bessie said firmly. "The police have spoken to all of them, probably multiple times. You would be wasting your money."

"If you change your mind, let me know," Jake said. He got to his feet and held out a hand to Kelly. "Let me take you home," he said. "We can stop for a drink on the way."

"I don't want a drink," she replied as she stood up.

"Then we won't stop," he said easily. "Whatever makes you happy."

Bessie let the pair out and then turned back to Beverly and Karl. "I'm sure this was difficult for you both. I don't believe I told you how sorry I am for your loss."

"Thank you," Beverly said. "At least Kelly has Jake now. He's devoted to her. I know he wants to get married, but she keeps putting him off."

"They haven't known one another for very long," Bessie pointed out.

"But he's felt like part of the family since the day they first met," Beverly replied.

It hadn't seemed to Bessie that Kelly was as enthusiastic about Jake as her mother seemed to be, but she didn't bother to reply. Karl moved the extra chair back into the dining room and then crossed to the door. He looked at Bessie, but didn't speak.

"Thank you for the tea and biscuits," Beverly said awkwardly. "Good night."

"Good night," Bessie replied.

She shut the door behind them and then leaned against it, feeling oddly exhausted from the difficult evening. She needed to ring John and tell him what she'd learned, but she didn't really want to talk about Kara Sutton any more. She was still leaning against the door when someone knocked.

CHAPTER 7

"*I* saw people leaving, so I thought I'd see if you had anything to tell me," John Rockwell said.

"Come in," Bessie replied with a sigh. "I can make you tea or coffee. There are still biscuits on the table."

"You don't sound happy," he remarked.

She shrugged. "It was a long evening, and Karl, Kelly's father, was quite rude to me, really."

"Coffee would be wonderful, if you don't mind. I have to collect Amy from a friend's house in an hour, which is why I was out and about. I often come down and sit in my car and watch the sea when I need to clear my head."

"Is something wrong?" Bessie asked as she started the coffee maker.

"Not really. I rarely get any time alone these days, that's all. I love the kids, but one or the other of them is nearly always at home when I'm there. They leave things all over the house, too, so even when they aren't there, I'm tripping over abandoned trainers or hunting for my things underneath a pile of their schoolwork." He shook his head. "I'm sorry. I never complain."

"You don't, and maybe you should. Not just to me, but to the children. They're old enough to tidy up their shoes and leave their school-work in neat piles."

"I know, but they've been through a lot lately. I don't want to be too hard on them."

"You've been through a lot lately, too, though. I'm sure the divorce was incredibly difficult. I know you missed the children tremendously when they were in Manchester. But you had several months of living on your own and I'm sure you found a routine that worked for you during that time. Having the children to stay for the summer took some adjustment, but you thought they were only going to be here temporarily. Now, as well as mourning the loss of the woman you once loved, you have to deal with getting the children through their grief and the very practical problems that come with having them in your home now for good."

"It isn't for good, though. Every time I get frustrated with them, I remember that Thomas will be off to uni in a year and a half. Amy won't be far behind. I'm going to miss them so much, even though they make me crazy when they're here."

Bessie laughed. "I believe all of this is part and parcel of being a parent."

John nodded. "I shouldn't even complain, as Doona does so much of the work for me, but that's another complication."

"Doona?"

"Yeah," John muttered, flushing.

"If you aren't sure of your feelings for her…" Bessie began.

John's laugh interrupted her. "I'm pretty sure I know how I feel," he said. "She's amazing and I care about her a lot. What I really want to do now is take her away for a week, just the two of us, so that we can really get to know one another. I can't do that to the children, though, not after everything that's happened."

"You simply have to plan things correctly," Bessie said. "Perhaps the children wouldn't mind staying with their grandmother for a week," she suggested. Sue's mother lived in Manchester, and Bessie knew the children had stayed with her before.

"They don't exactly get along well with Sue's mother," John replied.

"She still credits Harvey with saving her life, which means she won't hear a bad word about him. The children blame him for their mother's death. Let's just say it makes for some awkward conversations."

"Thomas and Amy would be more than welcome to stay here for a week," Bessie suggested.

"Thank you, but this isn't the right time. I'm being selfish, wanting to have a holiday with Doona. Right now the children have to be my priority. I'm very fortunate that Doona is willing to make them her priority as well. She's being incredibly understanding about everything."

"I'm happy for you both. I hope it works out."

"Yeah, me, too."

"But you wanted to talk about Kara Sutton," Bessie said.

"Not really, but we probably should. Did you learn anything new from her parents?"

"Some time in December, she mentioned to her father that she was going to a Christmas party with a man she'd never gone out with before. He was never mentioned again, at least not to Kelly or her parents."

John stared at her. "That's it? A single mention of a random man?"

Bessie frowned. "I did my best."

"Of course you did. I wasn't questioning that. I was really hoping for something more. Karl Sutton was not very forthcoming in any of his police interviews, that's all. I was hoping he might open up to you."

"He was almost hostile to me, actually. Aside from telling me about that one night out, he barely spoke when he was here."

"It isn't much, but I'll pass it along to my friend in Manchester. Maybe he can talk to the flatmates again and track down the man in question. What are you going to do next?"

"As far as Kara Sutton's death goes, nothing," Bessie said firmly. "I told Kelly that there was nothing else I can do to help."

"I'm afraid you're probably right about that, actually. All of the witnesses are in Manchester, except for the one flatmate who has moved back to the island. I thought for sure Kelly would talk you into speaking with her."

DIANA XARISSA

"If I thought it might help with the case, I'd consider it, but I'm sure the police will ask her about the mystery man."

"They will."

"Kelly's boyfriend came towards the end of the evening, a young man called Jake Holt. He actually offered to pay for me to travel to Manchester to talk to everyone there."

John shook his head. "I wouldn't recommend sticking your nose into the police investigation over there. The inspectors there don't know you the way that I do."

"I turned him down, of course. The only reason I can sometimes help you is because I know the island and a fair number of its residents. I would be nothing but a nosy, middle-aged woman in Manchester."

John blinked and then swallowed hard. "Manchester is a big city, and Kara died of a drug overdose. Investigations involving drugs are always best left to the police," he said eventually.

"I still can't imagine why they haven't been able to work out from where she obtained the drugs. I wouldn't have the first clue where to get drugs if I wanted any."

John raised an eyebrow. "Really? With all of your connections on the island, I find that hard to believe."

Bessie chuckled. "Okay, you may be right. I could probably find a source if I rang a friend or two. But nothing I've heard about Kara suggests that she had those sorts of connections."

"Maybe she didn't have them in Manchester. Maybe her source was on the island," John said thoughtfully.

"Is that possible?"

"She visited fairly regularly, to see her parents and her siblings. We know she wasn't a habitual user, but if she wanted something, she probably could have found a source here. As much as I'd like to believe that the island doesn't have a problem, drugs are available here and they aren't as difficult for people to find as they should be."

"So there's something for you to investigate," Bessie suggested.

"Indeed. I may ring a few people tomorrow, actually."

"I'll be working on Onnee's letters after my regular Friday trip to the shops in Ramsey," Bessie told him.

He gave her a hug before he left to collect Amy. Bessie tidied the kitchen and did the washing-up. Once everything was back where it belonged, she picked up the sheet of paper that she'd used for the timeline of Kara's months in Manchester. Folding it in half, she slipped it into a drawer in the small desk in the sitting room before she headed up to bed.

The shops in Ramsey were busy the next morning, and Bessie found herself rushing around the large grocery shop in order to get finished in time for her scheduled ride back to Laxey. Of course, the queues at the tills were long, as well.

"Miss Cubbon?" One of the shop's assistant managers spoke to her. "We're just opening till number seven. You can go and start unloading your trolley. Jenna will be right with you."

Bessie walked over to the till and began to fill the conveyor belt. After a minute, she started to feel rather foolish. What if the manager had sent her to the wrong place? Where was this Jenna? With her trolley now empty, Bessie stood behind it, trying to look as if she knew exactly what she was doing.

"Is this till opening?" a woman with two small children and a very full trolley asked her.

"I certainly hope so," Bessie replied "I was told that it was, anyway."

The other woman nodded, but she looked uncertain.

"I'm sorry to have kept you waiting," a voice behind Bessie said.

She turned around and smiled at the young girl who was wearing the shop's unflattering uniform. The shopper with the children sighed happily as she began to unpack her shopping behind Bessie's onto the conveyer belt. Bessie made it out to the car park one minute before her taxi was due.

Her favourite driver, Dave, insisted on carrying her shopping into Treoghe Bwaane for her. She thanked him with a small bag of biscuits and then spent what felt like a long time putting everything away. Soup, with lots of fresh crusty bread from ShopFast's bakery, was her lunch. She was heading for the stairs, eager to get back to Onnee, when someone knocked on her door.

"Ah, good afternoon," the man on the doorstep said, staring at the ground. "I'm very sorry to bother you."

He was probably close to thirty, with thinning brown hair and just a hint of a moustache. He was wearing a dark grey suit, but he'd loosened the tie and unbuttoned his shirt's top button. His shoes had been shined recently, and Bessie guessed he was either selling insurance or double-glazing.

"I'm not interested," she said firmly, taking a step back to shut the door.

The man glanced up and then flushed. "My cousin, Kelly, sent me," he told her. "If you don't want to talk to me, I'll tell her that."

Bessie frowned. "Who are you?"

"I'm Arnold, Arnold Stevenson. Kelly Sutton is my cousin and she wanted me to come and talk to you about Kara. She said you'd give me biscuits."

Sighing, Bessie took another step backwards. "You'd better come in," she said.

Arnold walked into the kitchen and turned in a slow circle, seemingly taking in every inch of the space. "I like it," he announced when he was back to facing Bessie. "It's small, but it's very cosy and it suits you. You've lived here for a long time, haven't you?"

"My entire adult life. I bought the cottage when I was eighteen."

He nodded. "It feels as if it's grown old with you."

Bessie frowned at the word. Before she could reply, he continued.

"I want a little cottage like this one. I live with my aunt and uncle now, and Kelly, too. She's nice, but my aunt and uncle are, well, difficult. I should find a place of my own, really. Do you know of any?"

"You should talk to an estate agent," Bessie suggested.

Arnold nodded slowly. "That's a very good idea." He pulled a small notebook out of his pocket. After flipping it open, he used the attached pen to write himself a note. "I forget everything," he explained as he put the notebook away. "I've been wanting to find my own home for months now, but I keep forgetting to look. If I ring an estate agent, he or she will remind me, won't they?"

"As they only make money when you actually buy something, I'm sure he or she will ring you regularly until you find what you want."

Arnold grinned. "That's exactly what I need."

"Please, have a seat," Bessie offered, waving at the chairs around the kitchen table. "I can make tea or coffee, or I have cold drinks."

"Just water, please. I don't drink hot drinks and I don't really like drinks that are very cold, either."

Bessie filled a glass from the tap and handed it to him. After switching on the kettle, she put biscuits onto a plate and then put the plate on the table. Smaller plates for each of them followed, by which time the kettle had boiled for her tea. Once that was ready, she sat down opposite him and smiled. "Help yourself," she told him, gesturing towards the biscuits.

Arnold studied the plate for a moment and then carefully selected two biscuits. He put them side by side on his plate and then looked up at Bessie. "What do you want to know about Kara?" he asked.

"Not a thing. Kelly has this idea that I'm going to be able to work out what happened to Kara, but I told her last night that I'm not going to get involved. The investigation is in the hands of the police, where it belongs."

"She died of a drug overdose," Arnold said. "I thought Kelly knew that."

"Kelly is concerned about where Kara got the drugs that killed her," Bessie explained.

"Oh." Arnold sat back and looked as if he were trying to think. "I never questioned where the drugs came from. I just assumed she had them for some reason, I suppose. Does Kelly think that someone gave Kara the drugs? Does Kelly think that someone did that to kill Kara?"

"I think Kelly is just looking for answers."

"I watch a lot of telly. People get murdered on telly all the time. There are entire programmes about people getting murdered. I don't know anyone who has been murdered in real life, though. I suppose it must happen, just maybe not as often as it does on telly."

"I'm sure you're right about that," Bessie said, wondering if the last two years of her life would make for interesting television.

"Who would have wanted to kill Kara, though? On telly the victim is always really rich, or obnoxious and mean. Sometimes, though, people get killed because they've seen or heard something they shouldn't have. Maybe that's why Kara got killed. Maybe she witnessed another murder or found out that someone at her office was embezzling money."

"Were you and Kara friends?" Bessie asked.

Arnold frowned. "We were cousins." He shrugged. "I'm not very good at making friends. My parents always told me to try harder, but I have trouble understanding people sometimes. That's why I work with computers. They're much easier to understand."

"Just tell me about Kara, then."

"Tell you what about her?"

"Anything you'd like me to know."

He sat back in his seat, frowning, and clearly thinking hard. After a minute, he picked up and ate one of his biscuits. After a drink of water, he leaned forward.

"She was really pretty, almost as pretty as someone on the telly. She was smart, too. Not as smart as me, but I'm too smart, really. She was smart, but she was also good at dealing with people. Everyone liked her. My whole family, I mean. She came and visited us in Scotland when I lived there and we went lots of places together. One day someone said something mean to me when I was with her, and she shouted at them and told them to go away."

"What did they say?"

Arnold flushed. "I think they thought that Kara and I were together, like boyfriend and girlfriend. This guy came over and started telling her that she could do a lot better than a balding, fat man. I used to be a lot heavier, actually. I've lost about three stone since I moved to the island."

"Congratulations," Bessie said.

He shrugged. "Aunt Beverly doesn't cook for me like my mum did.

I have to get my own meals, mostly. I eat a lot of plain chicken now because it's easy."

"And Kara shouted at the man?"

Arnold stared at her and then shook his head. "Sorry, I forgot what we were talking about. Yes, she told him to mind his own business and that I was smarter than he'd ever be. She was great."

"She sounds wonderful."

"Kelly is nice, too, but she's more quiet. I think she would have just been embarrassed if that had happened when I'd been with her."

"When did all of this happen, then?" Bessie asked.

"Maybe two or three years ago?" He made the answer a question. "I don't really remember. It was before I'd decided to move here and I've been here for just over a year."

"You were on the island when Kara died, then?"

"Yes, although I was still going back and forth a lot. I transferred with my job, but I was still working back in Edinburgh for them a few days a week. I spent most of my first few months here flying back and forth," he explained.

"Did you talk to Kara often when she was in Manchester?"

"I never talked to Kara, really, except when she visited us or we visited the island. My parents and I used to come over for Christmas sometimes. My mum liked to visit here, but my dad always wanted to stay home, so some years we'd come and other years we wouldn't."

"Do you remember the last time you saw her?"

"She came up to Scotland a few weeks after she'd moved to Manchester. She came for a long weekend. I was actually only there for one night before heading to Jersey for a work conference. Anyway, we sat up that night and talked about a lot of things, but nothing that seemed important."

"Did she talk about her flatmates?"

"She mentioned that she'd found a couple. Someone called Rachel and someone called Pamela. She was excited because Pamela was from the island and they were already talking about splitting the cost of travelling back to the island on the ferry for Christmas."

"Doesn't the ferry charge per person?" Bessie asked.

"They have special rates for cars with two passengers," Arnold told her. "If you don't have a car, you have to pay per person."

"Well, now I've learned something new today," Bessie laughed. "Did she tell you anything else about her flatmates or say anything about her work colleagues?"

"She teased me that she was going to hook me up with Rachel, but that was about all. We didn't really talk about work. She'd only just started her job. I don't know that she really knew anyone that well yet."

Bessie took a biscuit and ate it while she tried to think. "She was planning on coming back to the island for Christmas, then," she said eventually.

"I thought she was, anyway. That's what she said when we talked. She didn't come back, though. Aunt Beverly was very upset."

"I wonder why she changed her mind."

Arnold shrugged. "Aunt Beverly said something about her third flatmate not having anyone to spend the holidays with. Kara was probably just too nice to leave her all alone."

"Did she ever tell you anything about the men in her life?"

"We didn't really talk about that sort of thing. Like I said, she teased me about Rachel, but it was just teasing. She would sometimes mention a man's name, but only in passing."

"What do you mean?"

"She'd say something like 'Bob took me to the movies last week. We saw the new superhero film.' And then we'd talk all about the movie. I never asked her about Bob and she never told me anything else."

"Was there a man called Bob, or was that just an example?"

Arnold thought for a minute. "There may have been a man called Bob. I never really kept track."

Bessie nodded and changed the subject. "Did you ever visit Kara in Manchester?"

"No. I'm usually busy with work. I try to visit home sometimes, because my mother complains when I don't, but otherwise I only travel for work."

"Did Kara ring home often?"

"I don't really know. I never answer the telephone at my aunt and uncle's house. I don't feel as if it's my place to do so. Besides, I'd forget to take a message and everyone would get angry at me."

"I'm sure everyone would understand," Bessie replied.

"Uncle Karl wouldn't. He's not very patient with me."

Bessie patted his hand. "He wasn't very patient with me, either," she told him.

Arnold laughed. "Maybe that's just the way Uncle Karl is."

"I suspect you're right."

He ate his second biscuit and then drank the rest of his water. "Was there anything else?" he asked when he was done.

"Is there anything else you can tell me about Kara?"

"I miss her and I wish she hadn't died."

"Did you ever suspect that she might be taking drugs?"

Arnold looked shocked. "Never. She took over-the-counter tablets for headaches, but she never took anything stronger, not that I knew of, anyway."

Bessie sighed. "Thank you for your time. I can't think of anything else to ask you."

"I'll tell Kelly I did my best to help," he said as he got to his feet.

"I'm sure she'll appreciate that you took the time to come to see me."

"I took the afternoon off work, in case it took a long time. The last time I had to talk to the police about Kara it took hours and hours."

Bessie frowned. That seemed unusual, but she wasn't sure why. "I hope you'll go and do something fun with the rest of your afternoon," she told him.

He shrugged. "I may just go back to the office. I was coding a new database interface, and while we've been talking, I've been trying to work out a better way to integrate some of the data points. I have an idea now that just might work."

Bessie nodded, having no real understanding of what Arnold meant. "Well, good luck with that," she said.

Arnold was talking to himself about multiple variable inputs as

Bessie shut the door behind him. As she washed the cups and plates they'd used, she tried to decide if she'd learned anything interesting from the visit. Feeling as if the entire exercise had been a waste of time, she rang the police station anyway.

"Laxey Neighbourhood Policing, this is Suzannah. How can I help you?"

Bessie took a long deep breath. "It's Elizabeth Cubbon. I'd like to speak to John Rockwell, please."

"I'm sorry, but Inspector Rockwell isn't here at the moment. I can connect you to one of the constables or you can leave a message for Inspector Rockwell. If this is an emergency, please hang up and dial 999."

"It isn't an emergency. Please just ask John to ring me back."

"Certainly. I'll see that he gets that message, Mrs. Cubbyhole."

The phone went dead in Bessie's hand before she could correct the woman. Wondering what John would make of a message that asked him to ring Mrs. Cubbyhole, Bessie headed for the stairs. She'd spend an hour or two with Onnee before she tried the station again. Surely Suzannah wouldn't be working all day.

She forced herself to work through five months of letters, transcribing each word one at a time, without paying any attention to the contents, before she stopped. Then, with her sore arm aching, she sat back and read through all five letters.

They mostly detailed what sounded like a very difficult pregnancy. Onnee complained of exhaustion as she struggled to look after a toddler while dealing with a multitude of pregnancy complications. From what Onnee said, Clarence was sympathetic when he was home, which wasn't often. He was working many long hours and, as they needed the money, Onnee couldn't really complain. Indeed, she was hoping that all of his extra overtime would let them consider a somewhat more expensive home, as they'd failed to find anything in their current price range.

The biggest news in the letter was that Faith had seemingly taken an interest in little Alice and was now spending odd afternoons visiting Onnee and the baby. Apparently, Faith was teaching Alice all of the American nursery rhymes with which she'd been raised and that were somewhat different to the ones that Onnee knew. As Bessie put the letters away, she realised that Onnee had sounded happier in the last letter than she had in a very long time. Maybe becoming friends with Faith would finally help her feel more settled in her new home.

Bessie thought about ringing John again, but decided that a walk on the beach would be less frustrating. She marched steadily along the water's edge, taking care to watch the waves. She didn't even pause at the stairs to Thie yn Traie. Feeling as if she'd been sitting for far too long, she kept up her pace until she spotted the new houses on the beach in front of her. On impulse, she kept walking, suddenly eager to see Grace and baby Aalish, if they were at home.

As Bessie walked behind the houses, she glanced into Hugh and Grace's home. Grace was sitting on the floor, waving a toy in front of Aalish. All that Bessie could see of the baby were tiny feet waving in the air.

"Bessie, what a lovely surprise," Grace said when she opened the sliding door that Bessie had tapped on lightly. "Do come in out of the cold."

"It isn't cold, just brisk," Bessie told her. "It's perfect walking weather."

"If you say so. Aalish and I are quite content indoors today."

"I'm sorry to drop in unannounced, but I was reading about Onnee and her baby girl and I thought it would be a real pleasure to see Aalish."

"You are more than welcome anytime. I won't promise the house will always be this tidy, but today you're in luck. You can actually walk across the floor without stumbling over laundry or toys."

Bessie looked around the nearly spotless house. "When do you have time to clean?" she asked as Aalish began to cry.

Grace shrugged. "She's sleeping through the night now and she takes naps. When she's awake, though, she wants my undivided attention."

She picked up the baby and held her up so that she could see

Bessie. "Look, it's Aunt Bessie. She's come to see what a big girl you are now. Stop fussing and smile for Aunt Bessie."

Aalish stared at Bessie, her eyes wide. For a moment, Bessie thought she was going to get a smile, but Aalish clearly had other ideas. She wrinkled up her little face and began to sob as if her little heart was broken.

"My goodness, what on earth is the matter with you?" Grace asked as she turned the baby around and began to rock her gently. "You just ate. I just changed your nappy. You've nothing whatsoever to complain about."

The baby hiccupped a few times and then went quiet, happily cuddled in her mother's arms.

"But how are you?" Bessie asked Grace.

"I'm fine," Grace replied, not looking at Bessie.

"What's wrong?" Bessie demanded.

"Nothing, why would anything be wrong? I have the most beautiful baby in the world. Nothing else matters."

"What did Hugh do?"

Grace looked up at her and chuckled. "I'm too obvious, really. It's fine, though."

"You'll feel better if you tell me what's happened."

"I know I will, but I truly don't want to talk about it. It's probably nothing, anyway."

Bessie nodded. "Well, you know where to find me if you want to talk."

"You're leaving already?"

"Maybe not just yet, but I don't want to overstay my welcome."

"Let's have tea," Grace suggested. "I can put Aalish down for a nap. She clearly needs one."

As if on cue, Aalish began to wiggle in her mother's arms. She began making a series of noises that suggested that she was anything but ready for a nap.

Bessie laughed. "Would you like me to put the kettle on?" she asked.

"That might be helpful."

The large kitchen of the new home had a very functional layout. It only took Bessie a few minutes to make tea for herself and Grace.

"None for you," she told Aalish as she put Grace's cup on the counter.

Aalish gurgled at her while Grace laughed. Bessie thought the laugh sounded a bit strained.

"Biscuits?" Bessie asked after her first sip of tea.

"No, thank you, although you're more than welcome to help yourself. I'm trying to watch what I eat. I'm still carrying a few extra pounds from the baby."

"The baby is only a few months old. Give yourself time."

Grace nodded, but she didn't look convinced. "Thank you for making tea," she said after a moment. She carefully lifted her cup and took a sip, taking care to keep the hot liquid well away from Aalish, who was snuggled up in her arms.

"Do you want to tell me what's bothering you now?" Bessie asked.

Grace shook her head. "I don't, but I will. I think Hugh might be having an affair."

CHAPTER 8

Bessie stared at Grace for a full minute, the words not properly registering in her head. "I'm sorry, but I don't understand," she said eventually.

"Something is going on. I keep trying to think of other explanations, but I can't."

"You aren't trying hard enough. There's no way Hugh is having an affair. He adores you."

Grace shrugged. "I'm so busy with the baby that I don't have a lot of time for him anymore. I'm sure he misses how things were before Aalish arrived."

"He may do, but if you're worried about that, you should talk to him."

"We do talk, sometimes, but usually Aalish interrupts."

"What makes you think that he's cheating, then?" Bessie asked.

"Was he really at your cottage the other night when I rang?" Grace countered.

Bessie flushed. "Why do you think he wasn't?"

"He didn't get home until more than an hour after we spoke. If he was at your cottage, he could have been home in five minutes."

"And because of that you think he's involved with someone else?"

"Yesterday he told me he had to work really early in the morning. He left home at six. When Aalish and I got up, I realised that we were nearly out of nappies so I rang the station to ask him to get some on his way home. He didn't answer his direct line, so I got Suzannah."

"Oh, dear," Bessie exclaimed. "Does she get your name wrong, too?"

Grace chuckled. "Only three times in that conversation. I asked for Hugh, and she told me that he wasn't in the office. That isn't unusual. She always tells everyone that about whomever they're ringing. I simply asked her to ask him to ring me back and she said, 'I'm sorry, Mrs. Waterstone, but Constable Watterson won't be at the station today at all. He has the day off.' I managed to put the phone down before I started to cry."

"She was probably just wrong. I assume you rang Hugh on his mobile as soon as you stopped crying?"

"I never ring his mobile when he's working, but I texted him and asked him to ring me back."

"And what did he say when you asked him about it?"

"He said that she was mistaken. He even offered to hang up and let me ring his desk number so that I could see that he was in his office."

"And did you?"

Grace shook her head. "That seemed, well, as if I don't trust him."

"It sounds very much as if you don't trust him."

"I want to trust him. I'm just afraid to do so. One of my friends found out her husband was cheating when their baby was six months old. He told her that she was too busy with the baby for him so he went out and found someone to give him some attention."

"She's better off without him, then. Babies require a lot of sacrifices from both parents. I'm sure it's difficult for men to adjust, but they were just as much a part of making the baby as the women, and they need to act like adults. Babies get increasingly less demanding as they get older. I'm told teenagers often want nothing to do with their parents."

Grace smiled. "So only thirteen years to go, then. I'm afraid Hugh isn't going to wait that long to have me back, though."

"Whatever is going on with Hugh, I'm certain he isn't cheating on you," Bessie said firmly. "I'll talk to him and see if I can find out what's happening."

"Oh, no, please don't do that," Grace said quickly. "I don't want him to know that I've been talking about him or about our relationship. I really don't want him to think that I don't trust him."

Bessie thought about arguing, but the girl was upset enough. She didn't want to add to Grace's worries. If she couldn't talk to Hugh directly, that didn't mean she couldn't do some quiet investigating, though.

"I already feel better, just for talking to you," Grace said. "You're probably right. It's probably just me. I'm still an emotional wreck from having a baby. I cry at television commercials now and I'm often seized with a mad desire to wrap Aalish in cotton wool and hide her away from the real world."

"I'm often tempted to wrap myself in cotton wool and hide," Bessie said dryly. "The real world can be a scary place."

Grace nodded. "That's why friends are so important. Thank you for being mine."

"The next time you're worried about Hugh, ring me. I'll come over and make tea and we can chat."

"I will," Grace said. "I was going to ring my mother, but she'd just get upset and try to get me to move home. It isn't me she wants home, of course. She's desperate to get her hands on Aalish."

Bessie laughed. "I'm told grandmothers are often that way."

"Maybe I'll find out one day, although that day seems very far away."

Grace seemed a good deal happier when Bessie left a short while later. She gave Bessie a hug at the door and then waved as Bessie headed back down the beach. The walk to Treoghe Bwaane felt long, but Bessie marched resolutely onwards in spite of the cold wind that was blowing. She was always happy to get back to her cottage, but this afternoon it looked extra inviting as she reached it.

The phone was ringing as she opened the door.

"Hello?"

"Bessie? It's Kelly Sutton. I just wanted to thank you for talking to Arnold today."

"I told you that I don't want to be involved in the case," Bessie reminded her.

"Yes, I know, but I was talking to Arnold last night about the conversation that my parents and I had with you and he seemed to be feeling a bit left out because we hadn't included him. I hope you don't mind."

Bessie chose her words carefully. "I don't mind, exactly, but please don't send anyone else to see me unannounced."

Kelly took a deep breath. "That's why I rang, actually. I had a chat with Pamela today. Pamela Ford, Kara's former flatmate. I told her about last night and about what my father remembered. She couldn't remember anything about any men in Kara's life at that time, but we both thought it might be helpful if she talked to you."

"Really?" Bessie said skeptically. She was pretty sure that Kelly had talked Pamela into speaking with her.

"Anyway, she's free tonight, and I thought maybe she could visit you around seven?"

Bessie really wanted to say no, but she felt so sorry for Kelly that she found herself agreeing. "I'll speak to her, but only because she actually lived in Manchester with Kara. She might know something that would be useful."

"And you're just the person to find out what that something is," Kelly said happily. "Thank you so very much."

"I really mean it, though," Bessie told her firmly. "This is the last person with whom I'm going to speak about your sister."

"That's fine. There isn't anyone left, really, not unless you want to go to Manchester. If you're thinking about it, I'll pay your way, though. I don't want Jake paying for anything."

"Why not?"

"We just aren't that serious yet. I like him a lot, but we're still just, well, I don't know what we are, but we aren't serious enough for him to spend a lot of money on me."

"I don't have any intention of visiting Manchester, regardless. I'll talk to Pamela and then I'll report everything I've learned to John Rockwell. That's where my involvement in all of this ends."

"I'll be forever grateful to you for doing that much," Kelly told her. "Pamela will be at your cottage at seven."

Bessie put the phone down and then frowned at it. It was time to try ringing John again, especially in light of the newest development. For once, though, as Bessie dialled the station's number, she found herself hoping that Suzannah would refuse to put her through to John. That would give her the perfect opportunity to talk to Hugh.

"Laxey Neighbourhood Policing, this is Suzannah. How can I help you?"

"It's Elizabeth Cubbon. I'd like to speak to John Rockwell, please."

"One moment, please."

A moment later, John's voice came down the line. "Bessie? Hello."

"Suzannah put me right through," she said in surprise.

"You almost sound disappointed," John laughed.

"No, of course not. I was just surprised. Anyway, I just wanted to let you know about a conversation I had this afternoon and one I'm going to have tonight."

It only took her a few minutes to tell John everything about her chat with Arnold and about what Kelly had planned for the evening.

"So, even though you told Kelly you didn't want to be involved, she keeps sending people to talk to you," John concluded.

"I wish I didn't feel so sorry for her," Bessie sighed. "I should simply refuse to speak to anyone, but I know that Kelly is hurting very badly and that sending people to me makes her feel as if she's doing something."

"I don't like the idea of you being alone with witnesses in a murder investigation."

"Except this isn't a murder investigation. Anyway, Arnold was already living on the island when Kara died, and Pamela was in Glasgow with the other two flatmates."

"None of which precludes either of them from having been the source of the drugs that killed Kara," John pointed out.

"From what Arnold said, he rarely even saw Kara."

"As we've no idea where the drugs came from, we've no idea when or where she got them. Her cousin Arnold could have given them to her for Christmas, for example."

Bessie sighed. "You're more than welcome to come and visit this evening if you want to be here when Pamela is here."

"I don't think I can manage it, but I may send someone else. I'm sure Hugh will want to be at home with the baby, but I'm certain I can find a random constable who would appreciate the overtime."

"What's Doona doing tonight?"

"She's going to be with me."

Bessie wanted to ask for more information, but she bit her tongue. It really isn't any of your concern, she told herself sternly.

"So I'll expect a random constable at some point before seven," she said instead.

"I'll ring you if I can't find someone. Otherwise, ring me if a constable hasn't arrived by quarter to seven."

Bessie put the phone down and then made a face at it. She didn't need babysitting, and it seemed unlikely that Pamela would share much with a police constable sitting in on the conversation. Still, maybe when Pamela told Kelly that the police had been at Bessie's cottage, Kelly would finally realise that Bessie couldn't really help.

With some time to fill before dinner, Bessie baked a cake. She loved to bake, especially when she was entertaining guests. No doubt the police constable would be delighted to be fed while he or she was there.

At half six, someone knocked on the door. Bessie opened it to a constable with whom she had a nodding acquaintance.

"Constable Harrison, come in," she said.

"Miss Cubbon, it's nice to see you again," he replied.

Bessie frowned at his uniform. He looked very much a police constable, where she had been hoping to introduce him to Pamela as a friend who simply happened to work for the police. His dark brown hair was neatly combed and his hazel eyes did a quick survey of the room before he took a seat at Bessie's table with his back to the wall.

"Tea or coffee?" she asked him.

"If you have coffee made, I'll have that. Otherwise, tea is fine, although I wasn't expecting anything," he replied stiffly.

Bessie grinned. Time to get to know the constable a bit better, she thought. She brewed a pot of coffee and put a plate of biscuits on the table.

"We'll have cake when my other guest arrives," she told him as she handed him his drink.

His eyes widened at the word cake. Bessie sat down opposite him and smiled. "Tell me all about yourself," she invited.

Half an hour later, the two were firm friends. The constable, now Harry to Bessie, had told her all about growing up in Castletown. In his teens, he'd been desperate to leave the island and live in a big city. Three years with the police in London had cured him of that desire. It had taken him several more years before he'd finally been able to get a job with the island's force, but now that he was back on the island he didn't plan to leave again.

"I just need to find a nice girl," he sighed over his biscuits. "I'm thirty-two and my mother is starting to worry that I'll never find anyone."

"You're far too young to start worrying about such things," Bessie told him.

He nodded. "Mum hasn't been well. She wants more than anything to be a grandmother, and I'm afraid if I don't find the right woman soon she might not be here by the time her grandchildren finally arrive."

"Be careful that you don't rush into a relationship just to give your mother grandchildren," Bessie cautioned him. "Marriage is for life and children are the ultimate commitment."

He nodded. "It's just difficult because most of the women I meet aren't looking for serious relationships. Most women under thirty seem to be focussed on their careers, which is great for them, but not so great for me."

Bessie took a breath, ready to launch into a string of advice, when someone knocked on the door.

"Miss Cubbon? I'm Pamela Ford. I believe Kelly Sutton told you that I would be coming?"

Bessie nodded. "Please come in," she invited.

Pamela was a pretty brunette with light brown eyes and a warm smile. She was wearing jeans and a sweatshirt, her hair was pulled into a loose ponytail, and Bessie didn't think she was wearing any makeup.

Harry was on his feet as Pamela walked into the room.

"The police?" Pamela said. "Do you think I'm going to confess to something, then?"

Bessie shook her head. "Inspector Rockwell worries far too much about me. He didn't want me meeting with anyone involved in the case on my own."

"So he sent a very handsome man in a smart uniform to take notes?" Pamela asked.

Harry flushed. "Inspector Rockwell didn't ask me to take notes," he said softly.

Pamela laughed. "I'm sure it was an oversight. Maybe you'd better take them, just in case."

The constable shrugged. "I don't think that's really necessary."

Pamela looked him up and down and then looked at Bessie. "It would be too much to ask for him to be single, wouldn't it?"

"I believe he is single," she replied.

"Single as in married but his wife doesn't understand him? Single as in been seeing the same woman for years but won't commit? Single as in married twice so far and divorced twice as well? Single as in involved with another man? Or single as in he still lives with his mother and a dozen cats?"

Bessie and Harry both laughed.

"Single as in I work too hard to meet anyone, and besides, with my job the sorts of women I meet aren't really the sorts of women with whom I want to spend my spare time," he said.

"You'd better take notes, then," Pamela said. "It's Pamela Ford, F-O-R-D." She waited until he'd written it down and then she gave him her address and phone number. "I'm thirty-one and I'm too old to play stupid games. If all you're looking for is a bit of fun, don't bother ringing. I'm not suggesting that we get married and make babies, but that is my long-term goal and I don't waste time on men who aren't prepared to at least consider that in their future."

Harry looked slightly shell-shocked as he put his notebook away. Bessie found herself hoping that he would actually ring the woman and take her out. In an odd way, they seemed as if they might make an interesting couple.

"Tea or coffee?" Bessie asked Pamela.

"You don't have anything stronger?"

"I have some fizzy drinks."

Pamela laughed. "That wasn't what I had in mind, although I suppose I don't dare have a drink, not when I'm driving, not in front of a police constable."

Harry nodded. "I'd really rather you didn't," he said.

"Coffee," Pamela told Bessie.

Bessie poured her a cup of coffee and then topped up her own cup and Harry's. Then she sliced generous slices of the Victoria sponge for each of them. When she finally joined the others at the table, Pamela sat back and smiled.

"Kelly seems to think you're going to solve Kara's murder," she said.

"I hope she doesn't actually believe that," Bessie sighed. "I've told her that there's nothing I can do. I've been able to help the police here a few times with cases because I know the island. I know nothing about Manchester."

"I'm sure it's a lovely city, but my memories of the place will be forever coloured by what happened to Kara," Pamela told her. "I hadn't been particularly happy there, anyway. Kara's death was just the final straw."

"Why didn't you like Manchester?" Harry asked.

Both women looked at him and he flushed. "I was just making conversation," he said. "I forgot I'm just meant to observe."

"We can save that conversation for one night over dinner," Pamela told him with a wink. "Have you ever lived in a big city?"

"I lived in London for several years."

"Then you'll already have some idea why I didn't like Manchester. I believe we're rather spoiled, really, living on the island. Everything I need or want is easily available and nothing is more than a ten-minute car journey away."

"Did Kara like Manchester?" Bessie asked, trying to drag the conversation back to the subject that mattered to her.

"She did, actually. We sometimes discussed it, and she could never quite understand why I wasn't as enamoured with the city as she was."

"And she liked her job?" Bessie asked.

"She loved her job. She was sure that it was just a stepping stone to a fabulous career in advertising. For all I know, she may have been right. My job was boring and tedious, and I was pretty sure it wasn't a stepping stone to anywhere at all, which may also have been a factor in my dissatisfaction with my life in Manchester."

Bessie nodded. "And Kara got along well with all three of her flatmates?"

"Brooke and Kara and I were all fairly new to Manchester. We didn't know a lot of other people, so we tended to stick together. Rachel was from Manchester, but she didn't seem to have any other friends or family around. The four of us went out together most weekends, although sometimes one or the other of us would have a night out with some man we'd met somewhere."

"Tell me about the men in Kara's life, then," Bessie said.

"There were only two who rated more than a single date, at least as far as I knew. Kara had very high standards and if a man didn't meet them on the first date, she'd simply never return his calls or texts again."

"So she went out with more than those two men, but you only know about those two?" Bessie checked.

"Exactly. She met Louis Hunter not long after she'd moved into the flat. He lived above us, and they went out for a fortnight or so. I know they were seeing one another when I first moved in, but it didn't last long after that. I only met him once and he didn't impress me in the slightest."

"And the second man?" Bessie asked.

"Scott Brewer worked with Kara. When he moved to a different agency, they went out a few times. It was just casual, same as it was with Louis, and I don't think he was around as long as Louis had been, actually."

"What can you tell me about the two men?"

Pamela shrugged. "Not very much. If you're asking if either of them could have killed Kara, I simply don't know. Neither seemed murderous or even the slightest bit creepy when I met them, but I'm told murderers often seem perfectly normal."

"That's very true," Bessie confirmed. "Did you suspect either of them of doing drugs?"

"No, not at all. Kara met Louis because he was having a loud party, but we actually discussed how surprised she'd been to find that everyone was pretty drunk but no one was doing anything stronger. We'd both been worried that drugs were going to be everywhere in the big city, but I was never offered any in the time that I lived there, and I'm pretty sure the same was true for Kara."

"And yet she died of an overdose," Bessie said thoughtfully.

Pamela nodded. "I've been over it a million times and I still can't imagine who supplied her with the drugs that killed her."

"If you had to choose between Louis and Scott, which would you say was more likely to have been the source?"

Pamela sat back in her chair and took a sip of her drink. After a full minute, she shook her head. "I can't. Neither of them, either of them, I simply don't know. I only met them each once, and both times it was just a quick introduction. I doubt I said more than ten words to them both combined."

"Kara's father remembers her saying something about going to a Christmas party with a man one night. Do you remember anything about that?"

"I wish I did. Kelly was very excited when she rang me and told me what her father had remembered. She's convinced that somehow that party is the key to everything that happened next. All I can tell you for certain is that at the time it didn't seem important. I don't specifically recall Kara mentioning a Christmas party, but if she did, it was only in passing."

"Do you remember her going out with anyone in December?"

"I was working on a big project through November and December. We had a delivery date of January first and for a long time it looked as if we weren't going to make it. I worked nights and weekends for most of December, and I'm sure I missed a lot of what was going on in all of my friends' lives."

Bessie nodded. While she didn't share Kelly's belief that the Christmas party was significant, she had still been hoping to find out more about it.

"I hate to say it, because I know how Kelly feels, but I can't see what significance one night out three months before her death has to do with anything," Pamela added.

"It probably doesn't have anything to do with anything," Bessie told her. "It was just one little fact that we discovered when I talked to Kelly's parents. Whoever the man was that evening, we've no reason to believe that Kara ever saw him again."

"There were quite a few men that would fall into that category," Pamela said. "Maybe a dozen or more."

"So finding one random one would be like looking for a needle in a haystack," Bessie sighed.

"Maybe not on the island, but certainly in a city the size of Manchester," Pamela agreed.

"Tell me about the men and women who worked with Kara," Bessie said.

"I don't really know much about them. Kara told us all about her job, what she was working on and what new clients the agency had signed, but she didn't talk much about her work colleagues. She mentioned her immediate supervisor occasionally. She really liked him and enjoyed working for him, but they didn't socialise outside of the office. He was married and had a few kids, I think."

"Except he took her to lunch the day she died."

"Yeah, she told me about that, actually. I should say that she texted me about it. She was really pleased because he'd said a lot of nice things about her dedication and hard work over that weekend. She'd even told him that she'd cancelled a planned holiday with her friends and he'd seemed really impressed, apparently."

"No hint of anything romantic there?"

"Not at all. I actually asked her that, and she sent back LOL. She said he wasn't at all that sort of person."

"And he didn't do drugs or offer them to Kara?"

"The whole agency was drug-free, and pretty obsessive about it. There had been issues in the recent past, and they'd done a good job of cleaning house and setting up new rules for their staff. Kara said it was probably the only drug-free ad agency in the whole country, but she was really happy with the policies."

"Did she talk much about her family?" Bessie changed the subject.

"She mentioned them occasionally. She talked about her sister a lot, actually. They were very close, and she missed Kelly. When I came back to the island and met Kelly, I felt as if I already knew her because I'd heard so much about her from Kara."

"What about Kara's brother?"

"She talked about him less. I always got the feeling that she liked her sister-in-law, Amelia, more than her brother, Kent. I've only met him a few times and he's very, well, he's an advocate. I'm not really fond of advocates or used car salesmen."

Bessie chuckled. "I believe I prefer advocates, but only because my own is excellent."

Pamela shrugged. "I should get his or her name from you. I'm buying a house and I need an advocate. I've been thinking of using Kent, actually, but if you have someone you could recommend, I'd love to have the name."

Bessie wrote Doncan's name and office phone number on a sheet of paper and handed it to the woman. "Did Kara ever talk about her parents?" she asked as Pamela slipped the paper into her handbag.

"Not much. I don't think she was terribly close to her father, but she rang her mother at least once a week for a long talk. I know she felt really guilty about not going home for Christmas, and I think her mother did her best to make her feel even worse about it."

Bessie nodded. "But she stayed in Manchester to keep Brooke company?"

"That was what she told everyone, anyway. I thought it was a bit odd, because Brooke had only just moved into the flat. We barely knew her. I'll admit, though, that I was a little annoyed with the situation. Kara and I had talked about splitting the cost of the ferry to the island for Christmas and then she'd decided not to come back. That doubled the expense of my trip home."

"Where was Rachel for Christmas?" Bessie asked as the idea occurred to her. "She was from Manchester, wasn't she?"

"She was, but she'd decided to spend Christmas in Spain with some friend from her university days. As I recall, the friend's mother had recently passed away, leaving her without any family to spend the day with, so she'd begged everyone she knew to join her abroad for the holidays. Rachel was the only one who agreed, I believe."

"And all four of you got along well?" Bessie asked.

"We did. Brooke was the last to move in, some months after the rest of us, but she was a good addition. She's a model and she's gorgeous, but she wasn't weird about it, if you know what I mean. She also didn't waste time trying to persuade me to try makeup or do something with my hair, which some of my female friends have done in the past. I love wearing dresses and heels on special occasions, but even then I don't fuss very much over my hair, and I never wear makeup. It doesn't seem worth the bother."

Bessie nodded. She felt the same way about her appearance, although she did occasionally pat a bit of powder on her nose and apply a coat of lipstick to her lips.

"Is there anything else you can think of that might help the police work out what happened to Kara?" Bessie said.

"I wish I could. I've been trying for an entire year to think of something, anything, that would help. Brooke, Rachel, and I have talked for hours about Kara and what happened to her. Now, after all this time, I have to believe that we'll never know."

"Do you still speak to the other two women?"

"Not very often any longer, but I texted them both to let them know what Kelly was doing, dragging you into the case and trying to get the Manx police involved. I wanted them to know that they might be questioned again."

"They might be, in light of what Kara's father said about that Christmas party."

"Do you want to speak to them?"

Bessie shook her head. "As I said earlier, I've told Kelly that I don't want to be involved. There really isn't anything I can do."

"I'm inclined to agree with you, but I have to say, I feel better for having spoken to you. Kelly told me that every time she talks to you she feels as if she's moved an inch closer to finding out what happened to Kara. I must admit, I feel the same way."

Bessie frowned. The last thing she wanted to do was disappoint the women, but there really wasn't anything else she could do.

"If I ask Brooke and Rachel to ring you, will you speak to them?"

While she wanted to refuse, Bessie found herself nodding reluctantly.

"Give me a minute," Pamela said, pulling out her mobile.

A short while later, everything was arranged. Brooke was going to ring Bessie at ten the next morning, with Rachel following at one in the afternoon.

Feeling as if her Sunday was suddenly going to be rather busier than she'd hoped, Bessie finished the last of her coffee as Pamela put her phone away.

"Thank you," Pamela said as she got to her feet. "I wasn't looking forward to tonight, but it went much better than I'd expected it to go. Your handsome friend was nice to look at, too."

Harry turned bright red. Bessie was sure he was trying to think of an appropriate reply, but Pamela didn't give him the time to recover. She was out the door before he could speak.

"That was interesting," she said to Harry as she closed the door behind the woman.

CHAPTER 9

Bessie rang John while Harry was still at the cottage. She gave him a rundown of everything that Pamela had said, only leaving out the more personal conversation that she'd had with the police constable.

"I don't think there's anything new there," John sighed when she was done.

"I didn't think so either. Maybe I'll have better luck with Brooke or Rachel."

John chuckled. "I thought you didn't want to be involved."

"I really don't, but I feel so sorry for Kelly that I keep agreeing to do just one more thing," Bessie said, feeling cross with herself for being so easily manipulated. "After I speak to the other two flatmates, I'm truly going to be done."

She gave Harry the rest of the Victoria sponge and then, after he'd left, did the washing-up and tidied the kitchen. It was getting late, but she wasn't feeling especially tired. Still feeling annoyed with herself, she paced around the kitchen before going outside to sit on the rock behind the cottage.

For years she'd walked on the beach at all hours of the day and night, but since someone had broken into her cottage some months earlier, she'd been reluctant to leave it empty after dark. Sitting on the rock was a compromise. She could see the doors to the cottage, but she was still able to enjoy the sea air and the night sky.

Half an hour later, feeling more settled, she went back inside and took herself off to bed. When her internal alarm woke her at six, she was vaguely aware of unsettling dreams about walking on the beach while mysterious men appeared and disappeared in the holiday cottages' windows. A hot shower drove most of the uneasiness away. She kept her walk short, stopping at the stairs to Thie yn Traie before returning home. As she opened her door, she admitted to herself that she'd deliberately avoided looking at the holiday cottages while she'd walked.

After breakfast, she curled up with a book and tried not to think about the people who would be ringing her later in the day. When that proved impossible, she gave up on the book and dug out a notebook. It only took her a few minutes to make a list of the questions that she wanted to ask both women. It was still nowhere near ten o'clock, so Bessie dug out a book of logic puzzles and spent a frustrating hour working on one of the puzzles rated as most difficult. No matter what she did, Bessie couldn't make the clues fit together. When the clock stuck ten, she happily shut the book and headed for the kitchen, vowing never to look at that particular puzzle again.

The phone rang a few minutes later.

"Miss Cubbon? This is Brooke Buchanan. Hello."

"Hello. Please call me Bessie."

"Thank you. And you must call me Brooke, of course."

"Thank you. I appreciate you taking the time to speak to me today. I'm trying to help Kelly, Kara's younger sister. She's hoping that someone might remember something new that might help the police work out what happened to Kara."

"I feel so very sad for her. Kara often talked about her. I'm sure she's devastated."

"She is, and very frustrated that the police don't seem any closer to working out what happened than they were a year ago."

"I'm not sure what I can do to help, though. I've spoken to the police at least a dozen times, and Rachel and Pamela and I have talked for hours and hours about everything. We've told the police everything that we know."

"I'm sure you have. When I talked to Kara's parents the other night, though, her father realised that something that Kara had once mentioned to him was something about which no one else was aware."

"Yes, I know. Pamela told us all about the Christmas party mystery date. I wish I could say that I knew more about it, but I didn't even meet Kara until late December. The Christmas party must have been before that, surely."

Bessie sighed. "She never mentioned anything to you about a night out that had gone badly wrong or anything?"

"We talked about disastrous first dates a lot. We'd both had more than our fair share, but I can't tell you for certain if one of her bad dates was that particular Christmas party."

"Tell me about the men she was involved with that you did meet, then."

"I met Scott Brewer once or twice. He and Kara probably only went out three or four times, but that was a lot for Kara, actually. She was usually done with a man after a single night out."

"Really?"

"We all have very high standards, actually, although Kara was especially particular. She'd give a man one chance and she had a checklist of expectations. If they weren't met, she wouldn't see him again."

"A checklist?"

Brooke laughed. "It wasn't a written list or anything, but there was a list."

"What was on it?" Bessie asked, intrigued.

"The man had to come to our door to collect her. He had to have a decent car and it had to be clean. She wasn't bothered about it being expensive or fancy, but it had to be well kept. One guy turned up in a really expensive car but he had fast food wrappers all over the floor in the back. Kara refused to even get into the car."

"I don't blame her."

Brooke laughed. "I thought she was crazy. The guy was gorgeous and he made great money at his job. Kara said that if he didn't treat his car with respect, he wouldn't treat his girlfriend with respect either. I didn't listen to her. I let him take me out a few times. Kara was right."

"What else was on the list?"

"Oh, she wanted to be taken to a nice restaurant the first time they went out. Again, it wasn't about spending a lot of money, she'd even happily pay for her share, but she wanted to go to a proper restaurant and be pampered a bit. She was also a bit obsessed with how her companions treated the restaurant employees. She walked out on a man once when he was rude and demanding with the waitress."

"Good for her."

"It was. I kept telling her that she'd never find a husband if she kept her standards so high, but she kept telling me that she'd rather stay single than accept anything less."

"And she went out with Scott several times?"

"She did. It was still just casual, though. She wasn't really looking for anything serious. Her career was really important to her and that was just starting to take off, or so she'd hoped."

"You can't remember any other men?"

"She went out with Louis, who lived in the flat above us, a few times, but that was before I'd met her. She warned me about him when I first moved in, because he seemed to make a habit of trying to sleep with every woman in the building."

"Oh, dear."

"Yes, well, apparently he was mostly about putting notches in his bedpost rather than anything else, which was why Kara had ended things. She wasn't interested in hopping into bed with a man after one or two nights out and he wasn't interested in going much beyond that."

"Did she ever mention any of the men in her life offering her drugs?"

"No, never, although that was another item on her mental checklist. If a man had suggested anything like that on a night out, she'd have ended things immediately."

Bessie sighed. "Can you tell me anything about the men and women in her office?"

"Not really. We tried not to talk about work. It was a running joke between us, actually. I'd ask her about her day and she'd say that she'd spent it typing and filing, and then she'd ask about mine and I'd tell her that I'd spent it standing in front of a camera, pretending to smile. Then we'd talk about other things."

"She liked her job?"

"She loved her job. She got along with everyone at the office and she thought her immediate supervisor was wonderful."

"But she didn't socialise with her colleagues outside of the office?"

"They worked long hours together. I think they were happy to get away from one another after hours. Maybe some of them did spend time together after work. I don't really know. By the time I'd moved into the flat, Kara, Rachel, and Pamela were firm friends. They spent their weekends together, nearly every weekend. That was one of the things that made me want to move in there, actually."

"How did you get Kara's number?"

"What do you mean?" Brooke sounded confused.

"Kelly told me that Kara advertised for flatmates when she first moved to Manchester, but that she stopped advertising once Pamela and Rachel moved in. Where did you get her number three months later?"

"I found it in a newspaper. I was staying with some friends, another model, actually, and she had a bunch of old newspapers. She had a pet bird and she used them to line the cage. That was just one of the reasons why I was so eager to move out. Anyway, I didn't check the date on the papers, I just skimmed the ads in several of them before they went into the cage." She stopped and laughed. "Until you pointed it out, I hadn't actually thought about the fact that they were old papers," she said. "I rang at least half a dozen different people and I got quite annoyed because every one of them told me that the room they'd advertised was no longer available. At the time, I just thought that such things moved very quickly in Manchester."

"But Kara still had a room available."

"She did, and I was thrilled, especially once I'd met her and the other women."

"Where are you living now?"

"I moved in with a different friend from the modelling world. He's gay, but I do feel a tiny bit safer living with a man. I never worried about safety before Kara's death, but now I often have trouble sleeping at night. Every strange noise worries me."

"I appreciate you taking the time to talk to me. Can you think of anything else that might help?"

Brooke sighed. "I wish I could. I wish I'd paid a lot more attention to the men in Kara's life. I wish I'd made her come with us to Glasgow. I wish I'd rung her that Saturday night. We were out, dancing and drinking and flirting with handsome Scottish men, while our friend was dying alone."

If she was alone, Bessie thought, but didn't say.

"If you do think of anything, please ring me back, or ring the police in Manchester and share it with them," she said instead.

"I will. I promise. I'd do anything to bring Kara back. She was a wonderful person and I miss her terribly."

Bessie put the phone down and sat back in her chair, feeling sad. While she still didn't think there was anything she could do, she desperately wanted to find answers for Kelly and for all of the people who'd known and loved Kara.

She knew her mind was elsewhere when she took her hot soup out of the microwave and then discovered that she'd put bread into the toaster but had forgotten to slide down the lever to turn the toaster on. Sighing, she pushed it down and then ate half her bowl of soup while she waited for her toast. A short walk on the beach after lunch didn't do much to clear her head. Something was nagging at her, but she couldn't work out what it was.

Sitting on the rock behind her cottage helped improve her mood, and she might have stayed there for hours if she hadn't been expecting

Rachel to ring. Bessie was back in her kitchen, pacing anxiously, at quarter to one. The phone rang ten minutes later.

"I know I'm a bit early, sorry," the voice on the other end of the line said.

"It's not a problem. I assume this is Rachel Curry?"

The woman laughed. "I'm doing this all wrong. I was so nervous about speaking with you that I got myself into a bit of a state, I'm afraid. Yes, this is Rachel Curry. Please call me Rachel. I assume this is Miss Cubbon."

"It is, but you must call me Bessie."

"Bessie? Is that short for Elizabeth?"

"It is, yes."

"I'm ever so jealous of you, really. I've always wanted a nickname, but there isn't much you can do with Rachel."

Bessie thought for a minute. "No, I suppose there isn't really, is there?" she said eventually.

Rachel sighed. "I've tried them all. One former boyfriend used to call me Rach, leaving off the second syllable, but it was mostly just lazy rather than affectionate. Anyway, my middle name is Marie, and there aren't any nicknames for that, either. But I didn't ring you to complain about my name. As I said, I'm in a bit of a state. I'm not even sure why I agreed to speak with you, really."

"I'm sure you've spoken to the police many times already."

"I have, dozens, probably. I only agreed to talk to you because Kelly is convinced that you'll be able to work out what happened to Kara. I feel as if I haven't slept properly since she died. I hate not knowing what happened."

"I'm sure all of her friends and family feel the same way."

"We do. Which is why we're all rallying behind Kelly and her quest to find answers. Nothing will bring Kara back, but if we can find out who gave her the drugs that killed her, at least that person can be punished. I'm expecting that to make us all feel better."

"You don't know of anyone who was in Kara's life who could have supplied the drugs?"

"I know some people who could have supplied them. I could have, if Kara had asked. I don't touch them myself. I'm a personal trainer and I try to take excellent care of my body. I would never put anything into it that might harm it. But that doesn't mean that I don't know where to go to get drugs if I did want them. Manchester is a big city. I'm pretty sure most people who live here could find a connection pretty easily."

Bessie sighed. "So the drugs could have come from anywhere."

"Except Kara wouldn't have gone looking for them. She didn't take drugs. She was almost as fanatical as I am, really. I mean, she ate more chocolate and drank more wine than I do, but otherwise she was really focussed on looking after herself. She was even talking about joining the gym where I work. I told her I would work with her for free if she was a member."

"That was kind of you."

"We were friends."

"And were you also friends with your other two flatmates?"

"Yes, of course. We all got on really well, actually. It was surprising, really. I've had lots of flatmates over the years and, for the most part, we've done best by keeping to ourselves. Living with Kara was different. The four of us became very close."

"Tell me about the other women in the flat."

"Pamela moved in not long after I did. It was Kara's flat, and she'd advertised for flatmates in a few local newspapers. I was looking for something closer to my work, which is why I moved in. Anyway, Pamela is great. She's super smart, and sometimes she'd talk about things and I wouldn't understand anything she'd said, but she usually realised when she was talking over our heads. The good thing was, she could repeat herself in simpler language so that we'd all understand and she never seemed to mind doing so."

"And she didn't use drugs?"

"Oh, goodness, no. She's too smart to do anything like that."

"And Brooke?"

"Brooke is just sweet and kind and much too nice to be a model. She's, I don't know, almost vulnerable. Maybe she just seems that way because she's so tiny. She looks as if a slight breeze might blow her away."

"She was the last to move in, wasn't she?"

"Yes, just before Christmas. When we found out that she was going to be alone for Christmas, we were all upset. I'd booked a trip away with a friend, but I offered to cancel. Kara ended up staying with her in the end, though."

"Why?"

There was a short silence on the phone. "I'm sorry, I'm trying to remember how it all worked out. Brooke told us over dinner one night that her parents were going to Australia for Christmas. It may have even been over the welcome dinner that we had for her when she moved into the flat. A few days later, once I'd had a chance to get to know Brooke a bit better, I offered to change my plans. She told me that Kara had beaten me to it."

"I see."

"That's how I remember it now, anyway."

"That's fine," Bessie said. "Anything else about the flatmates?"

"We talk once in a while, the three of us, or just two at a time. We've been over Kara's death a million times. We all wish we could go back in time and stay home that weekend. We never should have left Kara home alone."

"You couldn't possibly have known that she'd be in any danger."

"Of course not. I think we'd nearly all spent a night or two alone in the flat by that point. Brooke travelled for work sometimes, just a few days away here or there, but she wasn't always at home. I went to fitness shows at least every other month. Pamela went on training courses and sometimes spent time at her company's offices near London. We were all in and out all the time and we never worried about the others."

"Kara was always there, though? She didn't travel?"

"She did, actually. She went back to the island once in a while, and she went to visit family in Scotland at least once, too. Her family was near Edinburgh, though, not Glasgow. We chose Glasgow for our weekend getaway because none of us had ever been there."

"And Kara was planning to go with you until the very last minute?"

"Exactly that. She had her bags packed, and then her supervisor asked her to work on Friday night and Saturday and she really couldn't say no."

Bessie wondered if she was missing something about that weekend. Was there some significance to it that she hadn't picked up on? "What about the men in her life?" Bessie asked.

Rachel told her about Louis and Scott, nearly parroting everything that Bessie had already heard about the two men. "Those were the only two men that I remember her going out with more than once," Rachel said in the end.

"I'm sure Kelly told you about what her father remembered."

"Yes, that odd Christmas party some time in December. I've been trying to remember everything I can about that, but it's all a bit of a blur."

"Pamela said she was working a lot of extra hours in December."

"I do remember that," Rachel laughed. "Kara and I joked about renting out her room to someone else and seeing how long it took her to notice. It wasn't really that bad, but she was often getting home as we were heading to bed and she was usually away in the mornings before my alarm went off. I was extra busy, too, of course. We always get a rush of clients in November who want to lose twenty pounds before Christmas."

"In a month?"

"Exactly. We tell them that it isn't healthy to lose weight that quickly, but that we can help them tone up their problem areas, which can make them look slimmer, anyway."

"Can you make much difference in a month?"

"Not a lot," Rachel admitted. "We do try, though, and what we do is a lot healthier for our clients than any fad diet they might try."

"So you were working overtime in December," Bessie sighed.

"I probably did more in November than December," Rachel replied thoughtfully. "Most of our clients only book a session or two with a trainer and then carry on by themselves. If they haven't started by early December, they're never going to be in better shape by Christmas."

"Did you and Kara talk about the men in her life?"

"All the time," Rachel laughed. "We both used to complain about men pretty much constantly. Kara only gave men a single chance. She'd let them take her out once and if they didn't meet her standards, she'd never speak to them again. I'm making it sound harsh or rude, but it was simply Kara. She didn't want to waste her time on men who weren't potential life partners."

"Did she go out often?"

"Probably once every other weekend or so. I know men used to ask her out everywhere she went. She was very pretty, but she also had a bubbly quality that made her very attractive to men. Actually, it made her attractive to everyone. We became close friends almost as soon as we'd met."

"Tell me about the various men she went out with, then. What horror stories, did she share?"

Rachel took a deep breath. "She rarely mentioned names. I suppose that's how I knew that the relationship with Scott was more serious than the others. She told me his name after she came home from her first dinner with him. Mostly, she gave the men nicknames."

"What sort of nicknames?"

"Things like 'Tall, Blond, and Thick' or 'Going to be a Creepy Stalker One Day.' That sort of thing."

"'Going to be a Creepy Stalker One Day?'" Bessie echoed.

Rachel laughed. "It was some guy that she'd met in the queue at the local bookshop. He was nice, and cute, too, but he was a bit obsessive, that's all. She said she worried about anyone who went out with him more than once or twice because he seemed as if he'd become a creepy stalker before long."

"You're sure she never saw him again?"

"She did see him again, as in see him visually, but she never went out with him again. She used to bump into him at the bookshop once in a while. She bought him a coffee one day at the shop's café. They were friendly, but she was clear that she didn't want to get romantically involved."

"Because she was afraid that he'd stalk her."

"When you put it that way, it sounds terrible, but she wasn't actually afraid of him. She just thought he was the type who might develop an obsession with the woman in his life. Some women love that, though."

"There's a very fine line between being in love and being obsessed."

"Exactly. I very nearly got married once. I can't believe I'm telling you this. I never even told Kara this story. When I was eighteen, I met this amazing guy. He was a few years older, but not so much so that it was odd. Anyway, he was my first real boyfriend and we quickly became inseparable. We did everything together, and I was more than a little obsessed with him. He was totally obsessed with me and I thought it was wonderful."

She fell silent, leaving Bessie to wonder what happened next. After a long pause, Bessie demanded to hear the rest.

"Oh, sorry. We went ring shopping, and I wanted this really expensive ring and he wanted to buy me something much cheaper. Then he said that we had to save as much money as we could, because once we were married I'd be quitting work to stay home and look after him. I laughed, because I was sure he couldn't possibly be serious, but he was. I ended things that afternoon in the jewellery shop."

"My goodness."

"That's when things got weird," Rachel continued. "He started ringing my house at all hours of the day and night. He used to drive by the house really slowly at odd times, too. I was still living with my parents at that point, and one night my father went out and spoke to him. I don't know what he said, but the guy stopped harassing me. I went away to uni a few months later and I've never seen the man again."

"You don't remember when Kara went out with the man she thought might turn into a stalker, do you?"

"Not really. It was before Brooke moved in. I'm sure of that because after Brooke moved in she joined in the conversations, too, and I know she wasn't there for that one. He might even have been the man with whom she went to that Christmas party. I simply don't recall."

"Do you know how many times she saw him again after their one night out?"

"Just a few, or, at least, Kara only mentioned seeing him a few times. It wasn't a big thing, though. They both loved that little bookshop and I'm pretty sure he lived somewhere nearby."

"I think you should tell the police about the man," Bessie said.

"I can, but I don't know what they can do with the information. I can't imagine how they'd ever find him. He was just a random man Kara went out with once."

"She never described him to you or gave you a name?"

"She said he was very attractive. I remember that because I teased her that I wouldn't mind being stalked if he was cute enough. She actually offered to introduce me to him, but I'd just met someone that I thought had real potential, so I turned her down."

"She wouldn't have offered if she'd actually thought he was dangerous," Bessie said thoughtfully.

"She didn't think he was dangerous. The nickname was just a joke, really. She called another one 'Big Ego, Small, um, Man Bits.' She never got anywhere near close enough to actually be certain about the second half of that, but that didn't stop her from giving him that nickname. The names were just for fun when we were talking."

Bessie swallowed a sigh. She spent several more minutes talking to the woman, discussing Kara's family and her work colleagues. Rachel didn't say anything else noteworthy.

"I'm going to ring the local police inspector who has been talking with Kelly and the family," Bessie said in the end. "I'm going to tell him everything that you told me. An inspector from Manchester may get in touch."

"About the Creepy Stalker guy," Rachel sighed. "They'll never find him. I'm sure the bookshop has hundreds of customers every day."

"They might, but they might not have all that many regular customers," Bessie countered. "It's a new lead, even if it goes nowhere.

They may find the man easily enough and then discover that he's now happily married and living in Leeds or something."

"I just hope the police can finally find some sort of solution. Not knowing what happened is very difficult."

Bessie put the phone down and then frowned at it. Feeling as if she'd spent far too much of her day using it, she was reluctant to pick it back up to ring John. The information from Rachel felt too important for her to wait, though.

"Laxey Neighbourhood Policing, this is Suzannah. How can I help you?"

"It's Elizabeth Cubbon. I'd like to speak to John Rockwell, please."

"I'm sorry, Mrs. Bubbles, but Inspector Rockwell isn't available right now. I can put you through to the constable on duty, if you'd like."

"Who is the constable on duty?" Bessie asked.

"It's Constable Watterson."

"Oh, yes, I'll talk to him," Bessie replied eagerly.

"Certainly, Mrs. Cublay."

"Hugh Watterson." The voice was clipped and professional.

"It's Bessie. How are you?"

There was a short pause. "I'm fine, why?"

Bessie laughed. "No special reason," she said, bending the truth slightly. "I was actually ringing to talk to John, but Suzannah said he wasn't in his office."

"No, he's out dealing with a burglary in Lonan. It's going to be a quick one to wrap up, but it needed an inspector to oversee everything."

Bessie wanted to ask a dozen questions, but she swallowed them all. "I was just ringing to tell John about a few things that I was told by some of Kara Sutton's friends," she explained.

"Is any of it urgent?"

"As Kelly has been dead for almost a year, I think it can wait a few more hours."

"I'll tell John to ring you back. Knowing him, he'll probably stop to see you later today."

"That would be fine. I'll be here. You're more than welcome as well."

"Ah, thanks, but I'm a bit busy tonight."

"I saw Grace on Saturday. Aalish is getting big quite quickly."

"She is, yes. I'll let John know that you rang. Is there anything else?"

Bessie frowned at the receiver. It wasn't at all like Hugh to rush off the phone with her. "No, nothing else," she replied.

The clattering noise made Bessie think that Hugh had dropped the phone back into its cradle. Frowning, she got to her feet and began to pace around her kitchen. As if she didn't have enough to worry about, there was clearly something wrong with Hugh.

CHAPTER 10

*B*essie was heading for the stairs, going to work on Onnee's letters to try to get her mind off of Hugh, when someone knocked on her door. There was no way that John could have arrived from Lonan that quickly, she thought as she turned around.

"Ah, good afternoon," the tall and handsome man on the doorstep said. "I'm Kent Sutton. I wasn't certain that you'd be home, so I left my wife in the car. Let me get her."

He turned and walked away before Bessie could reply. She watched as he opened the passenger door to the expensive-looking black car in the parking area next to Bessie's cottage. The woman who climbed out was a very pretty blonde. She said something to Kent, who shook his head before leading her to Bessie's door.

"Good afternoon," the woman said. "I'm Amelia Sutton. Kent was supposed to apologise profusely for disturbing you in this way. We would never normally visit someone unannounced, but the circumstances seemed to warrant it just this once."

Bessie smiled at her. "I never mind visitors, unannounced or otherwise. Please come in."

"Thank you so much," Amelia beamed, and then followed Bessie into the cottage. Kent followed, a small scowl on his face.

"I can make tea or coffee," Bessie offered.

"Oh, I'd love a cuppa," Amelia said quickly. "We had an early lunch before we drove up here. Kent was worried about finding you. We've never been to Laxey Beach before, you see. It's incredibly beautiful."

"Thank you. I never get tired of my view."

"I can't imagine looking out at that every day," Amelia sighed. "We have distant sea views from our home. Imagine living right on the water," she said to Kent.

"Maybe one day," he replied.

Amelia shrugged. "I don't want to move, actually. I love our house and we've finally managed to get everything just the way we want it."

Bessie filled the kettle while the pair sat down at the kitchen table. While she waited for the water to boil, she piled biscuits onto a plate and put it in the centre of the table. A few minutes later, she served everyone tea and then joined the couple.

"What can I do for you, then?" she asked, certain that Kelly had sent them.

"For a start, please don't tell my sister that we were here," Kent surprised her by replying.

"You don't want Kelly to know you were here?" Bessie asked.

"I'd rather she didn't, although I'm sure she'll find out sooner or later," he said. "We know that she's dragged you into the investigation surrounding Kara's death. We also know that she's had many of Kara's friends speak to you about the case. She's deliberately excluded us from the conversation, mostly because she knows that we don't approve of what she's doing."

"Why not?" Bessie asked bluntly.

Kent and Amelia exchanged glances. "It's been a very long year," Kent said slowly. "Kara's death was a horrible shock, and we're still reeling from the loss. I'm certain that the police have done everything in their power to work out what happened to her, but Kelly won't be satisfied until she has someone to blame for Kara's death. I think she's wasting a lot of time and energy looking for someone who simply doesn't exist."

"Someone gave Kara the drugs that killed her," Bessie pointed out.

"Gave them to her or sold them to her," he countered. "I'm sure Kelly has told you what a saint Kara was and how she'd never have taken anything illegal, but the truth of the matter is that none of us had seen Kara in months. She chose not to come home for Christmas, which wasn't at all in character for her. It pains me to say it, but Kara could well have started taking drugs in the last few months of her life. Maybe it wasn't yet a habit, but we've no idea what she may or may not have tried."

Bessie frowned. Kent was the first person to suggest that Kara might have deliberately taken the drugs that had killed her.

"I don't think Kent is being entirely fair," Amelia said. "He's still angry that Kara didn't come home for Christmas. It was a miserable holiday because his mother was so upset about her absence. Her decision to remain in Manchester to keep her flatmate company was very much a Kara thing to do, though."

"She should have brought her flatmate to the island with her," Kent said.

"Why didn't she?" Bessie asked.

"We aren't sure," Amelia answered. "Beverly suggested it, but nothing came of the idea. It's possible that Kara's flatmate didn't want to come here or that Kara decided against it. I spoke to Kara a couple of times a month, but after she'd decided not to come home, we both seemed to avoid the subject of Christmas altogether, both before and after December. It was a difficult subject, really."

"Where would she have found herself a source for drugs?" Bessie asked.

Kent laughed harshly. "She was in Manchester. Her flat was in a fairly nice area, but I'm sure there were people in her building who could have supplied her with anything she wanted. She even mentioned to me once that she thought she'd walked through a drug deal in her foyer without realising it."

"How awful."

He shrugged. "It's part of living in a big city. If you mind your own business, you should be fine."

"You said that you spoke to her regularly," Bessie said, turning to Amelia. "Did she ever tell you about seeing drug deals?"

"She sometimes told me that she thought maybe she'd seen something," Amelia replied. "It didn't happen very often, but it did happen from time to time. As much as I hate to agree with Kent on the subject, I do think that, if Kara had decided that she wanted to try something, she wouldn't have had any trouble finding what she wanted."

"Why do you hate to agree with Kent?" Bessie asked.

Amelia laughed and patted her husband's hand. "I don't think Kara took anything deliberately. I think someone either tricked her into trying something or gave her something without her knowledge. Kent thinks that I'm being unrealistic and sentimental."

"She is," he snapped. "She's like Kelly. They want to remember Kara as perfect. She was a wonderful person and I loved her dearly, but she wasn't perfect."

Bessie nodded. "When you spoke to Kara, did she tell you about the men in her life?" she asked Amelia.

"Sometimes. She used to tell me about her disastrous dates and then I'd complain about how boring it was being married." She glanced at Kent and then blushed. "She used to tease me that I was only bored because I'd married her dull brother."

Kent stared at his wife for a moment and then swallowed hard. "She would," he said with a hint of emotion in his voice.

"One of her flatmates said that she often gave the men she went out with nicknames," Bessie continued.

"Oh, yes, she loved doing that," Amelia laughed. "One man was called 'Loves His Car' and another was 'Lives With His Mother,' even though he didn't really live with his mother. He was just the type, if that makes sense."

"Can you remember any of the others?" Bessie asked.

Amelia flushed. "There was 'Big Ego, Small, er, Other Thing' and one she called the 'Creepy Stalker,' although he'd never stalked her or anything like that."

"Are you sure of that?"

"What are you suggesting?" Kent demanded.

"I'm not suggesting anything," Bessie replied. "It worries me that Kara went out with a man who she believed might turn into a stalker, that's all."

"They only went out once," Amelia told her. "I'm sure she never saw him again after that."

"She did see him again, though," Bessie countered. "According to one of her flatmates, she occasionally saw him in the local bookshop."

"Now that you mention it, I do remember her telling me that she'd seen the man again," Amelia said. "She said something about seeing him across a room and giving him a wave or something, and then a few weeks later, she said that she'd seen him again and that they'd had coffee together. I seem to remember her saying that she was trying to find him a nice girl, because he was sweet, just a bit intense."

"Do you remember when she first met him?" Bessie asked.

Amelia shrugged. "It's all something of a blur now. Let me think." She sat back in her seat and took a sip of her tea.

Bessie picked up a biscuit and nibbled on it so that she wouldn't be tempted to speak. Kent ate two biscuits while he stared at his wife.

"It was before Christmas," she said eventually. "She used to ring more regularly before Christmas, maybe once a week. After Christmas, when she knew that Kent was upset with her, she started ringing less frequently."

"I had every right to be upset with her," Kent said.

"Of course you did," Amelia agreed. She looked at Bessie. "As I said before, last Christmas was pretty miserable."

"Did either of you ever visit her in Manchester?" Bessie asked.

Kent shook his head. "We're both very busy. I'm a partner in a very successful law firm and Amelia has her own business. While we both know we should try to find the time to take a holiday now and again, I'm afraid neither of us ever manages it."

"I'd take one, if I could find reliable staff," Amelia sighed. "My café is my baby and I've worked really hard to build its reputation. I took one day off last month and the man who was supposed to be my manager decided it would be fine to substitute half of my homemade menu items with stuff from the grocery shop because it was easier."

Her voice had risen as she'd spoken, and Kent was already rubbing her back by the time she'd finished. "It's all fine now," he said soothingly.

"It isn't, though. I don't know if I'll ever trust anyone with my café again," she said sadly.

"So maybe it's time to take that break we've been talking about," he said.

She stared at him and then shrugged. "I know you want children soon, and so do I, really, but the thought of giving up the café, well, I just don't know."

The pair stared at each other until Kent cleared his throat. "Bessie doesn't want to hear about all of our domestic issues," he said. "We came to talk about Kara, after all."

"I miss her a lot," Amelia said. "Every time the phone rings, I hope it's her, just the same as when she was alive. We used to talk for hours about nothing at all."

"What do you think happened to her?" Bessie asked.

Amelia took a deep breath. "Honestly? I think someone she thought she could trust slipped her something that killed her. She was alone in the flat. If a friend or a work colleague came by and suggested that they have a drink together, she would have agreed."

"Can you name any of her friends in Manchester, then?" was Bessie's next question.

"Really, I think her only friends there were her flatmates," Amelia answered with a frown. "She talked about some of her work colleagues once in a while. They were friendly, but not truly friends. Having said that, I'm sure she wouldn't have sent any of them away if one of them turned up on her doorstep with a bottle of wine."

"Can you give me any names?"

"I think there was a woman called Maggie or Megan, and her supervisor was called Mark. She didn't really talk about the people she worked with much, although she did tell me about the various campaigns that they did."

"Did she ever mention any names to you?" Bessie asked Kent.

He shook his head. "I rarely spoke to her. She and Amelia enjoyed talking for hours and I was happy to leave them to it."

"Who else might she have trusted?" Bessie asked. "Do you think she'd have let the man she called the Creepy Stalker into her flat?"

Amelia looked at Kent and then shrugged. "She was pretty careful when it came to men, but I think she felt as if she knew him pretty well. As you reminded me before, she used to see him in the bookshop every once in a while and she was trying to find him a nice girl. She may well have invited him in for a drink if she was feeling a bit lonely that night."

"What about any of the other men she'd been out with once?"

"Again, maybe, but probably not. She usually had really good reasons for not seeing a man a second time, reasons that would keep her from wanting to spend any additional time with the guy. I don't think she felt that way about Creepy Stalker. It's a terrible nickname, and it sounds as if she was afraid of him or something, but she just used it to mean that she thought he might turn out that way if she encouraged him."

"And having coffee with him wasn't encouraging him?"

"No, because she'd spent the whole time talking about other women he might like to meet. I believe she ended up trying to arrange a night out for him and one of the women from her office, actually, although I don't know if it ever happened."

Bessie sighed. It was just possible that she was getting slightly obsessed with the man Kara had called Creepy Stalker. There was nothing to suggest that he'd had anything to do with her death, though. A knock on the door interrupted her thought process.

"Hello," John Rockwell said when Bessie opened it.

"Hello," she replied. "I have company."

John raised an eyebrow and then followed Bessie into the cottage.

"Kent and Amelia Sutton, this is Inspector John Rockwell with the Laxey Constabulary."

Kent frowned. "We've already spoken to the police."

"I'm here to see Bessie, not you. I didn't even know you were here," he replied. "I can come back later, though."

"No, no, that's fine," Kent replied, getting to his feet. "Amelia and I have other things to do this afternoon."

"We do?" Amelia asked, winking at Bessie.

"Yes, we do," Kent said firmly. He was halfway to the door before Amelia stood up.

"If you think of anything else that you think might help with the investigation, please ring me or the Manchester police," Bessie told the pair.

"We will, of course," Kent replied. "Obviously, we want to know what happened to Kara, as much as anyone."

Amelia held out a hand to Bessie. "Thank you so much for your time," she said. "I really hope that Creepy Stalker didn't have anything to do with Kara's death. Now that we've discussed him, I feel as if I should have warned Kara about him, but I truly didn't feel that way at the time."

Bessie gave her hand a squeeze. "I understand. I'm sure he seemed harmless. There's a very good chance he was harmless."

Amelia nodded, but she didn't look convinced. Kent opened the cottage door and then stepped back to let Amelia out first. She gave Bessie a quick smile and then rushed out.

"As I said before, I'd rather you didn't mention our visit to my sister," Kent said before bowing slightly and then turning and walking out of the cottage.

Bessie shut the door behind the pair and then looked over at John.

He raised an eyebrow. "Creepy Stalker? What have you learned now?"

"Let me put the kettle on," Bessie replied. "This may take a while."

She refilled the biscuit plate and then poured tea for them both. While she was busy with that, John cleared away Kent's and Amelia's plates and teacups. It wasn't long before the pair were sitting together with tea and biscuits.

"Where should I start?" Bessie asked.

"First, to whom have you spoken since we last talked?"

"Just about everyone," Bessie sighed. "Let me start with yesterday, then."

An hour and three cups of tea later, Bessie finally sat back in her seat with a biscuit. John had taken several pages of notes and now he flipped back through them with a frown on his face.

"I understand that it was just a nickname, but this Creepy Stalker worries me. What worries me the most is that she saw him occasionally after their night out but never seemed to think that maybe that was because he was already stalking her."

"That was my thought, too," Bessie told him. "I didn't want to say that to anyone else, though. Her friends and family will feel terrible if it turns out that he's the one who killed her."

"Kara herself didn't seem worried about him, though," John pointed out. "She was even trying to find him a girlfriend, which suggests that she thought he was a nice guy."

"She may have badly misjudged him."

"Exactly. I'm going to give all of this to my colleagues in Manchester. I'm hoping someone at the bookshop might have some idea who the man might be, although it's a long shot. It's been a year, as well. The man may have moved or simply stopped shopping there."

A loud ringing noise made Bessie jump. She picked up the telephone.

"Hello?"

"It's Kelly, Kelly Sutton," the voice came down the line. "I was just hoping you might have an update for me now that you've spoken to all of Kara's flatmates."

Bessie made a face. "I have company right now. Can I ring you back in half an hour?"

"Oh, I mean, I suppose so. Jake will be here, but that doesn't matter. We're going to dinner, but he won't mind waiting for a short while."

"I'll ring you back as soon as I can," Bessie promised. She put the phone down and looked at John. "What do I tell her?"

"You may as well tell her everything. She's probably going to ring the other flatmates anyway. It's up to you whether you tell her about Kent and Amelia's visit."

Bessie thought for a minute. "I don't want her upset with Kent," she said eventually. "I'll try to leave them out of it, if I can."

"Do you want me to stay and listen in to the conversation?"

"No, it's probably best if you don't. I'd have to tell her that you were here and that might complicate things. She's going to want the police to find that man and question him immediately. I'll tell her that I've spoken to you and that you're going to speak to the Manchester police. Hopefully that will keep her happy for tonight."

"Let's hope. Tomorrow is the anniversary of Kara's death. I'm sure she's not looking forward to that."

"No, it's going to be a difficult day for her," Bessie agreed.

She let John out and then picked up the phone. Kelly answered on the first ring. "Hello?"

"It's Bessie. I don't think I've learned anything particularly useful, but I have given John Rockwell one thing for the Manchester police to look into."

"What?" Kelly demanded eagerly.

Bessie told the woman what Rachel had said about nicknames and then told her about the man Kara had called Creepy Stalker. When she was done, Kelly was silent for a minute.

"Are you okay?" Bessie asked eventually.

"Bessie? It's Jake. Kelly's very upset at the moment. I'm not sure what you told her, but it's really upset her. She can't talk right now."

"Yes, I can," Bessie heard in the background. After what sounded like a brief scuffle, Kelly's voice came back down the line.

"Kara was always giving men silly nicknames. We used to laugh about them, but I never paid much attention. Do you really think the man she called Creepy Stalker killed her?"

"Not at all," Bessie said quickly. "I just suggested to the police that they might want to investigate the man, that's all. If nothing else, he might be able to give them a different perspective on Kara, since they went out once and then were friendly afterwards."

"Yes, I suppose that makes sense. I was hoping you thought he'd killed her. I was hoping you'd solved her murder."

"We don't know that it was murder," Bessie pointed out gently.

"Now you're talking the way Kent does," Kelly sighed. "I have to go. Jake and I are going out for dinner. He's trying his best to distract me because of tomorrow."

"That's very kind of him."

"Yes, it is. I've decided to work tomorrow morning. I thought it would be best to try to pretend that it's just a normal day. You're seeing Dr. Robins in the morning, aren't you?"

"I am, yes, at ten."

"So I'll see you then," Kelly said. "Maybe I can take my break when you're done and we can get tea and talk. I'm going to try to remember what I can about Creepy Stalker, as I'm sure Kara mentioned him to me at least once."

"I'll see you tomorrow, then," Bessie said. "Take care."

"Yes, thank you," Kelly replied.

Bessie put the phone down and sighed. The poor woman was going to have a difficult day tomorrow. Perhaps she should have taken the day off work, but maybe she would be better off keeping busy. Everyone dealt with grief differently.

After too many biscuits and far too much tea, Bessie wasn't at all hungry when five o'clock came around. Instead of sitting down to dinner, she went for a long walk on the beach. Walking as far as the new houses was tempting, but Bessie wasn't eager to see Grace again, not until she'd worked out what was going on with Hugh. With that in mind, she stopped as soon as the houses came into view, turning back and walking briskly towards home. She was nearly at her cottage door when she heard her name being shouted down the beach.

"Bessie, Bessie, hello," Maggie Shimmin yelled.

"How's Thomas?" Bessie asked as soon as Maggie reached her.

"Thomas? He's better, or at least I hope he's better. He was meant to be on bed rest, but he kept insisting on coming to help with the painting. Now the doctor has put him in Noble's and he can't get underfoot here."

"He's in hospital?" Bessie gasped.

"He's managed to turn another cold into pneumonia," Maggie sighed. "I don't know how he does it, but he's been doing so quite regularly this year. I've no idea how I'm going to manage to get all of the cottages ready by myself."

"I thought you'd hired someone to do some of the work."

"He did one cottage and then took a job across. I haven't been able to find anyone else who's willing to do the work, not at a fair rate of pay, anyway."

Bessie wondered what Maggie considered a fair rate of pay. With the difficulty she was having finding anyone to do the work, it seemed likely that it wasn't very generous. "Well, good luck. If I hear of anyone looking for work, I'll send them your way."

"Thomas suggested that we hire a few teenagers. They may not do a very professional job, but they wouldn't cost what a professional would cost, either. To be honest, they'd probably do as good a job as I am. I'm not very good at painting."

Bessie grinned. "I'm terrible at it. I want to repaint my bedroom, but it's such a chore that I keep putting it off. Maybe one day."

"I was surprised to hear that you're still investigating Kara Sutton's death. I can't imagine you've learned anything new, not after all this time."

"I'm not investigating anything," Bessie said.

"No? Kent and Amelia Sutton just came to your cottage to say hello, then? And Pamela Ford? Was she just in the neighbourhood?"

"I didn't realise you were watching my cottage with such interest," Bessie said coolly.

Maggie flushed. "I'm not watching your cottage. I'm painting. I'm always painting. I do think it's quite neighbourly of me to notice who goes in and out of your cottage, though. You did have a break-in recently, after all. I'd hate for anything like that to happen again."

"I would as well. Have you finished putting in the new security systems in the holiday cottages?"

"We've had to put that project on hold," Maggie said with a sigh. "They put an alarm on the last cottage, and we were woken up every night for an entire week because the alarm kept going off. I kept ringing the police, but they never found anything wrong. The alarm company said that the strong winds on the beach might be setting things off, so we've switched the system off and told them not to bother installing any more. Imagine if we had a dozen alarms going off at once, just because of the wind." Maggie shook her head.

"Maybe I won't rush to have anything similar put into my cottage, then," Bessie said.

A burst of music suddenly came from Maggie's pocket. She pulled out her mobile and frowned at it.

"Hello?"

"Yes, okay. I'll be there."

"Is something wrong?" Bessie asked as Maggie put her phone away.

"Thomas is just bored. He wants me to come and visit, that's all." She opened her mouth again and then shut it.

Bessie was surprised to see her blinking back tears. "I'm sorry," she said softly.

"I just don't know what to do. He can't seem to get well again. He's lost so much weight and he can't seem to gain it back. I buy him everything he likes. We've a houseful of biscuits and cakes, but he doesn't fancy anything. I end up eating them so they won't go to waste. I've gained over a stone, but he's lost much more than that." She shook her head. "The doctors are doing everything they can, but he isn't getting better."

Bessie pulled the woman into an awkward hug. "Maybe he needs to spend some time somewhere sunny and warm," she suggested. "I know how hard you both work. Maybe you both need a holiday."

Maggie took a deep breath and then took a step backwards. "We might try that, if the doctors will give him permission to go." She turned and walked up the beach without a backwards glance.

Feeling as if she was worrying about far too many people at the moment, Bessie let herself into her cottage. She made herself an evening meal on automatic pilot, her brain jumping from Kelly to Hugh and Grace to Thomas and Maggie and then back again. After dinner, she forced herself to read a book, even though she knew she wasn't actually comprehending what she was reading.

"Tomorrow is another day," she told her reflection in the bedroom mirror before she crawled into bed. When she opened her eyes at two minutes past six, she felt as if she'd barely slept. Dragging herself out of bed, she showered and pulled on clothes before she went down to the kitchen and started a pot of coffee. For once, she waited until she'd had her first cup before she went out for her walk.

Still feeling out of sorts, she rang for her taxi a bit early. Pacing around her cottage wasn't improving her mood. The waiting room at the Ramsey hospital would at least be a change of scenery. When she walked into the foyer of the building a short while later, there was a stranger behind the reception desk.

"Can I help you?" the woman asked.

"I'm Elizabeth Cubbon. I have a ten o'clock appointment."

"I've been trying to ring you," she was told. "We're rescheduling whenever possible. The regular receptionist didn't turn up for work today. I'm doing my best to cover for her, but they sent me up from Noble's and I don't know anything about anything up here."

"Kelly didn't come to work today?" Bessie repeated.

"Kelly? Is that the regular receptionist? I don't know. Whoever it is, she isn't here and I can't find patient records, the appointment book is just confusing, and the doctors are grumpy and rude. As I said, I'm trying to reschedule everything that isn't urgent since things are in such a mess. Can you come back tomorrow?"

"Do you know who Kelly spoke with when she rang in this morning?"

"As far as I know, she didn't speak with anyone. She just didn't turn up. Is she a friend of yours or something?"

"Or something," Bessie replied, suddenly very worried about the missing girl.

CHAPTER 11

"Did you want to reschedule, then?" the receptionist asked.

"Give me a minute," Bessie replied. She turned and walked into the empty waiting room. While she didn't usually like to use it, she had John's mobile number in her phone. This time she didn't hesitate to select it.

"John Rockwell."

"It's Bessie. I'm at the Ramsey hospital. Kelly Sutton didn't show up for work today. Today's the anniversary of her sister's death and I know she was worried about being too upset to work, but I spoke to her yesterday and she told me that she'd be here today."

"I'll see what I can find out," John promised.

Bessie slipped the phone into her pocket rather than dropping it back into her bag. For several minutes, she paced around the room, earning confused and concerned looks from the woman behind the desk.

"Is something wrong?" she finally asked when Bessie passed close to her.

"I'm worried about Kelly. I spoke to her yesterday and she told me that she'd see me this morning."

"Yes, well, I've rung her house but no one answered."

"I believe she lives with her parents. They may both be at work," Bessie replied thoughtfully. Cousin Arnold would be at work as well, which meant no one would be at home, unless Kelly was there, unwilling or unable to answer the phone.

Maybe she'd simply had car trouble on her way to work, Bessie told herself. And maybe her mobile phone needed to be charged, so she couldn't let anyone know. And maybe something awful has happened, a little voice in her head whispered.

"You seem awfully worried about her. I mean, as far as I know, she's always been reliable, but people do sometimes oversleep or forget to ring in when they're sick."

Bessie nodded. "I'm going to have to ring you to reschedule. I'm too distracted right now to think clearly."

Before the woman could reply, Bessie turned and walked out of the room. Outside, she hesitated. Should she head for home, or was there somewhere else she could go that might be useful? Her mobile rang before she'd reached a decision.

"I just spoke to Kelly's mother. Apparently, Kelly and Jake had a fight last night over dinner. Kelly came home, threw some things into a bag, and told her mother that she was going to a hotel for the night. Beverly wasn't worried until I rang, but she tried Kelly's mobile and didn't get an answer. I have two constables ringing around the various Douglas hotels, trying to track Kelly down."

"Why would she go to a hotel?" Bessie asked.

"She told her mother that she wanted to be alone. Beverly is angry with herself now that she let Kelly go, but at the time it seemed to make sense. Jake rang the house several times, wanting to talk to Kelly, even after Beverly told him that she'd left."

"Have you spoken to him today?"

"No, not yet. He's on my list."

"I'll let you go and get back to your list, then. Please keep me informed."

"I will do."

Bessie pushed the button to end the call and then frowned at her phone. It rang again almost immediately.

"Hello?"

"Miss Cubbon? It's Beverly Sutton. I was just ringing to see if you knew anything about where Kelly might be. She told me that she was going to ring you last night, you see."

"Did she? I've no idea where she is. I'm actually at the Ramsey hospital. When I got here and Kelly wasn't here, I rang John Rockwell. I understand that he rang you."

"He did, but he didn't mention that you were the one who'd discovered that she was missing. But where could she be?"

"John said you told him that she'd gone to stay in a hotel overnight. Maybe she simply overslept."

"I suppose that's one possibility, although it seems unlikely. Kelly is very responsible. She was so anxious about the anniversary today, though, that maybe she did forget about work."

"When did she tell you that she was going to ring me?"

"It was after her dinner with Jake, maybe eight o'clock last night. She was very upset when she got back to the house. I'm not sure what she and Jake fought about, but whatever it was, she didn't want to talk to him again in a hurry. I told her that she'd probably feel differently in a few days, but she didn't want to hear that, not last night."

"Why move to a hotel?"

"She said that she knew that Jake would ring. He actually rang twice while she was packing her bags. Kelly wanted me to be able to tell him that she wasn't home, so that he'd stop ringing. She knew I'd never lie to him."

"And did he stop ringing?"

"Eventually, but not until several hours later."

"That must have been annoying for you."

"Oh, I quite like Jake. We had a couple of lovely chats, actually. He kept apologising for ringing, but he was rather desperate. I never heard Kelly's side of the story, of course, but he told me that the entire argument had simply been a big misunderstanding and that if he could talk to Kelly for five minutes, he could clear everything up."

"But she wasn't even home by that point, was she?"

"Well, no, but I didn't want to tell him that she'd gone out, not right away. I didn't want him to think that she'd overreacted so badly. I know that everything that happened with Kara is preying on Kelly's mind right now, and she's far quicker to anger than normal. I was afraid if Jake knew how upset Kelly really was, he might decide to end things with her."

"Maybe she had a good reason for being angry with Jake."

"Maybe, but mostly it sounded as if she was just angry with the whole world and she was taking it out on Jake. I don't know. Last night it seemed like much ado about nothing, but now I'm so worried about Kelly that I can't even think straight."

"Where would she have gone? Did she have a favourite hotel on the island?"

"We live on the island. She's never stayed in a hotel here. Why would she? She used to talk about wanting to stay at the Seaview in Ramsey one day, but it's terribly expensive there. I can't imagine that she'd have driven all the way to Ramsey, either, in the state she was in."

Except that the Seaview isn't far from the hospital, which would have been convenient for this morning, Bessie thought. "I know John is doing everything he can to track her down. Maybe you could try ringing her friends to see if she told any of them where she was going."

"Maybe, although I can't imagine that she told anyone anything. She wanted to be alone, after all."

Bessie heard a click. "Hello?" Clearly Beverly had decided that the conversation was over, Bessie thought as she put her phone back in her pocket. A taxi pulled up and let an elderly man out of the back. Bessie rushed forward and jumped inside.

"The Seaview," she said impulsively, feeling a small pang of guilt when she remembered that the hospital was turning everyone away at the moment. The poor man would be coming back out in moments, only to find that his taxi had driven away.

The driver dropped her off at the luxury hotel a few minutes later. Bessie paid him and then climbed out. She exchanged polite greetings with the doorman and then asked the assistant at reception if she could see Jasper Coventry, the hotel's owner.

"Mr. Coventry is a very busy man," she was told.

"Tell him Bessie Cubbon is here. I'm sure he'll want to see me."

He looked doubtful, but he picked up the phone on the desk and pushed a button. "There's a Bessie Cubbon here to see you," he said a moment later.

Bessie grinned at the surprised look that flashed over the desk clerk's face. A moment later his bland expression was back as he put the phone down. "Mr. Coventry will be right with you," he said flatly.

The words were barely out of his mouth before Bessie found herself being pulled into a tight hug.

"Bessie, my dear, how lovely to see you," Jasper said. "What brings you here today? I do hope you're going to let me buy you lunch."

After a glance at the desk clerk, who was clearly listening to their every word, Bessie took Jasper's arm and led him across the room. "I'm looking for someone," she said in a low voice. "A friend of mine may have checked in last night. She didn't turn up for work today and I'm a bit worried about her."

"We're incredibly quiet this time of year. We only had one guest check in all of yesterday. It was a young woman who insisted on paying cash and wouldn't give her name. The man on the desk made me come and approve her stay, because that's quite unusual."

"That may well be her," Bessie said excitedly. "Is she still here?"

Jasper shrugged. "Checkout time is eleven, although we're flexible when we're mostly empty. I don't know if she's checked out yet or not."

"We need to check on her. She may not be well," Bessie said.

Jasper frowned. "We may not even be talking about the same person. I'd hate to disturb a paying guest who may just be having a lazy start."

"We can just knock on the door. If she answers and it's the wrong woman, I'll apologise," Bessie said as she dragged Jasper towards the lifts, getting him to describe the woman as they went. His description sounded very like Kelly to Bessie.

"I'm not sure what you think may have happened to her," Jasper said as they waited for the lift to arrive.

"I have no idea what happened to her. She simply didn't show up for work today, which is quite unlike her."

"If she has a job on the island, she must live here. Why was she staying with us last night?"

"She had a fight with her boyfriend and wanted to get away for a short while," Bessie explained. "Today is the first anniversary of her sister's death, and she's been having a difficult time dealing with that."

"Oh, dear," Jasper exclaimed. "She didn't seem suicidal when she arrived. She was clearly upset, but she seemed more angry than anything else."

"I don't think she was suicidal," Bessie said quickly.

The lift seemed to take hours to rise two floors. Bessie followed Jasper a short distance down the corridor. A "Do Not Disturb" sign was hanging on the door. Jasper frowned at it.

"She'll never stay with us again," he muttered before he knocked loudly.

After a full minute, he knocked a second time.

"You have a master key, don't you?" Bessie asked.

"I'll have to go down to the desk to get one. I don't usually carry one around with me."

While he was gone, Bessie rang John.

"I think I know where Kelly is," she told him. "I'm at the Seaview. They had a woman who matches Kelly's description check in last night. She isn't answering her door. Jasper has gone to get the master key."

"I'm on my way," he said. "I'm going to send the nearest constable and an ambulance, too."

Bessie put her phone away and began to pace up and down the corridor. Jasper was taking forever with that key and she was increasingly certain that something terrible had happened to Kelly. A moment later, a door further down the hall opened.

Jasper walked out of the stairwell, panting slightly. "The lift seemed to be taking ages, so I walked up," he told Bessie. "I need to stop eating in our dining room so often, though." He patted his rounded tummy and then sighed. "Maybe she went out," he said as he slid the key into the lock.

"I certainly hope so," Bessie muttered.

"Hello? Hotel security," Jasper called as he turned the door's handle. "This is security, performing a welfare check. Hello? Is anyone in the room?"

Jasper pushed the door open. The room was dark, the blackout curtains pulled tightly across the windows along one wall. When Jasper switched on the lights, Bessie gasped.

Kelly was lying on the bed. She was wearing a red dress and high-heeled shoes, probably the outfit she'd worn for her evening out with Jake. An empty wine bottle was sitting on the bedside table alongside an empty wine glass. Jasper crossed the room to the bed. Bessie felt tears welling up as he checked for a pulse.

"She's still alive," he said eventually. "Her pulse is very slow and erratic, but it's there. We need an ambulance."

"There's already one on the way," Bessie replied.

A moment later a police constable and the ambulance crew arrived together. Bessie and Jasper stood to one side as they worked on the unconscious woman. Eventually, she was loaded onto a stretcher and taken away. John arrived as they left the room.

"Sorry, Jasper, but this room is now a crime scene. I'm going to have people working here for a few days at the very least," he said as a greeting.

"It's not a problem. We're very quiet this time of year. I don't believe we have any other guests even staying on this level. When we only have a handful of guests, we try to spread them out so that they don't disturb one another," Jasper replied.

"Is there a room I can use as a command centre, then?" John asked.

"You can have your choice," Jasper told him. "The room next door is connected, if that helps."

"It does, actually." John watched as Jasper unlocked the connecting door and pulled it open.

"I'll just go and unlock it from the other side, too," Jasper told him.

As he headed for the door, John turned to Bessie. "Well done," he said.

She shrugged. "Kelly's mother suggested that this might be where Kelly had gone. I was only two minutes away, so I thought I'd check for myself."

"We were working through the hotels in Douglas first. Beverly didn't suggest the Seaview to me."

"But is Kelly going to be okay?"

"We hope so. It may be some time before she'll be able to answer questions, though."

"She left a note," Bessie said softly. The note, written on the hotel's stationery, had been on the pillow next to Kelly. It had simply read, "I want to be with Kara."

"Did she seem suicidal to you?" John asked.

Bessie hesitated and then shook her head. "No, not at all. In fact, having seen firsthand what Kara's death has done to those who were left behind, I can't imagine her doing any such thing."

John nodded. "If it wasn't suicide, could it have been accidental?"

"I'm assuming she overdosed on something," Bessie said. "Again, after what happened to her sister, I can't see her taking drugs of any kind."

"Which leaves attempted murder," John said. "Any thoughts on that?"

"I can't imagine why anyone would want to hurt Kelly."

"She was poking her nose into Kara's death."

"That would suggest that Kara was murdered and that Kelly was getting close to finding the killer."

"Maybe she was simply worrying the killer. Maybe the killer decided that it would be best to get rid of her before she actually managed to get the police to reopen the investigation."

"If I were you, I'd take a good look at Jake," Bessie said. "They had a fight last night. Maybe he was more angry than Kelly realised."

"He's first on my list of people to question," John assured her. "But he isn't last, by any means."

"If I can do anything to help, please let me know."

"I'll probably ring you later. In the meantime, I do need a formal statement from both you and Jasper. I'm going to have one of the constables take your statement so that I can talk to Jasper."

"He was here last night when Kelly arrived. He didn't think she seemed suicidal," Bessie told John.

John nodded. A handful of men and women in white suits walked into the room. John crossed to them and spoke to one of the women before gesturing towards the connecting door. She nodded and then turned to the others as John walked back to Bessie.

"I'm going to send you back to the Laxey station with one of the constables," he told her. "He'll take your statement there and then take you home."

"Maybe he could just take me home and I could give him my statement over tea and biscuits," Bessie countered.

"If you were anyone else, I'd say no, but why not?" John replied. "It will be a treat for Constable Stone. He's new to the island and to Laxey. I'm sure he's heard about Aunt Bessie, but I don't believe you've ever met him."

"I was hoping Hugh might be around," Bessie said.

John frowned. "It's his day off today. I did try to ring him to see if he wanted to come in for some overtime, but he didn't answer his mobile."

"That's unusual."

John shrugged. "Maybe the baby has been keeping him up at night. He and Grace might be having a lie-in since Hugh's not working today."

Bessie nodded. Now wasn't the time to bring up her concerns about Hugh. John had a crime scene to investigate.

Constable Stone was a pleasant young man in his mid-twenties. He appeared younger to Bessie in spite of his rather impressive beard and moustache. His brown eyes twinkled when John introduced the pair.

"I've heard so much about you," he told Bessie. "I've been wondering how long it would be before I finally got to meet you. All of the stories I've heard have made me quite sad that I didn't grow up in Laxey."

"I'd like you to take Bessie home and take her statement, please," John told the man. "If she gives you tea and biscuits, make sure you do the washing-up after."

The man grinned. "I think I can manage that."

Bessie had to give the constable careful directions to her cottage. As he followed the winding road down to the beach, he sighed. "I've been down here before," he told her. "This is the road to the holiday cottages. We've had several calls about them since I've been here."

"Oh, dear, have you?"

"The owners put some sort of security system into one of them, but it seemed to malfunction quite regularly. I was sent down to check on the cottages at least half a dozen times, but I never found anything amiss."

"Well, my cottage is the very first one," Bessie told him, directing him into the small parking area next to Treoghe Bwaane.

"I didn't realise that this cottage was occupied," he exclaimed. His face turned bright red as he turned to Bessie. "I didn't mean that the way it sounded."

"It is a bit older than the holiday cottages, but it's still a very snug and cosy home for me," Bessie replied.

She climbed out of the car and led the constable to her front door. He stopped right inside the kitchen.

"This is wonderful," he exclaimed. "It reminds me of my grandmother's cottage in Wales. As you say, it's very cosy."

"Tea or coffee?" she asked.

"Oh, whatever you're having is fine."

Bessie put the kettle on and then found some nice chocolate biscuits that she'd been saving for a special occasion. They seemed an appropriate way to welcome the young man to the island.

Half an hour later, he had her statement, and he'd eaten nearly half of the box of biscuits. "Thank you so much," he said as he shut his notebook. "I'll just take care of the washing-up, shall I?"

"There's no need. It's only a few plates and cups. They can wait until later in the day when I've a few more things to go with them," Bessie told him. "Thank you for offering, though."

"The inspector did say that I was to do them," he pointed out.

Bessie laughed. "Never mind. You can tell him that I wouldn't let you. You can even tell him that you did do them, if you'd rather. I won't tell him otherwise."

The constable grinned. "Now I know why everyone at the station speaks so highly of you. I've really enjoyed talking with you."

"And now you know where I am, so you can visit anytime you need to talk," Bessie told him.

He looked thoughtful for a minute. "I may take you up on that," he said eventually. "I've a few things on my mind, you see."

"As I said, you know where to find me."

Bessie walked him to the door, well aware that if she pushed him a little bit, he'd probably tell her everything that was bothering him. He was meant to be working, though, and she was far more interested in learning what had happened to Kelly than she was in hearing about Constable Stone's problems at the moment.

"Thank you again," he said in the doorway.

She watched him walk to his car, only shutting the door as he drove away. There were a dozen messages on her answering machine, and Bessie deleted them, one after another. They'd nearly all been nosy questions about Kelly, and Bessie wasn't in the mood to satisfy anyone's morbid curiosity. The last message was the only one that was at all interesting.

"Bessie? It's Beverly Sutton. I'm at Noble's with Kelly. They told me that you found her. What happened? How did you find her? What's going on?"

She called Beverly's mobile number, but Beverly didn't answer. No one answered the phone at the Suttons' residence either. Feeling a bit frustrated, Bessie found herself pacing around her kitchen again. Going out for a walk might have helped, but she wanted to stay by the phone in case Beverly rang again. It was time for lunch, but she felt full of chocolate biscuits and tea.

Eventually, she made herself a sandwich. She'd have something more substantial for dinner, she told herself as she ate.

The washing-up didn't take long, not even with the extra cups and plates from tea with Constable Stone. Feeling as if she had nothing better to do, Bessie dried all of the dishes and carefully put them away. With that job done, she found herself pacing around the kitchen again. The knock on her door was a welcome interruption.

"Beverly, hello," Bessie said to the woman on the doorstep.

"You're home," Beverly said. "We weren't certain that you would be."

She turned around and waved towards the car behind her. Bessie frowned as several doors opened at once. Karl, Jake, Kent, and Amelia all emerged from the car and headed for the cottage.

"We couldn't bother Arnold at work, but maybe he can come and talk to you later," Beverly said.

"Why?" Bessie asked.

Beverly looked surprised. "So that you can work out who tried to kill Kelly, of course."

Bessie shook her head. "That's a job for the police."

"But you were the one who found her," Beverly countered. "They were still ringing around the island, and you went and found her."

"You didn't suggest the Seaview to Inspector Rockwell," Bessie said.

Beverly shrugged. "I didn't think about it, really. When I talked to Inspector Rockwell, all I could think was that she'd have gone somewhere close to home. I never imagined that she'd go as far as Ramsey to get away."

"And it's all my fault," Jake said sadly.

Bessie wanted nothing more than to send them all away, but she was far too polite to do that. "Come in," she invited.

"We don't need tea or biscuits," Beverly announced as she sat down at the kitchen table. "Kent, go and get more chairs."

Bessie took Kent into the dining room, and he carried back two chairs, which were squeezed in around the small table. Everyone sat down except for Bessie, who was torn between a desire to get the conversation over with and a need to be polite and make them tea.

"We don't need tea," Karl barked. "What we need are answers."

Bessie slid into the only empty seat. "I wish I had some for you," she told him.

"She wasn't suicidal," Beverly said firmly.

"I'd have never left her if I'd thought she was going to do anything like that," Jake muttered.

"What did you fight about?" Bessie asked him.

He flushed and looked down at the table. "I don't even know how to answer that question. We fought about nothing, really. I was an idiot, basically. I knew that Kelly was upset about the anniversary today, but I insisted that we go out last night anyway. I thought I could take her mind off everything, but she wasn't paying any attention to me. I'm afraid I took that rather badly." He stopped and shook his head. "I'm embarrassed to admit that I got angry with her for being distracted."

Beverly leaned over and patted his arm. "It's okay. Kelly is completely obsessed with Kara. No one would blame you if you ended things with her after all of this."

Jake looked shocked. "I'm more worried that she'll want to end things with me. When I think that I might have driven her to try to end her life, I almost want to end my own."

"She didn't try to end her life," Beverly snapped.

"So what do you think happened?" Kent asked his mother.

Beverly shrugged. "Her doctor had given her some sleeping tablets, right after what happened with Kara. Maybe she simply took too many by accident."

"I don't believe it," Karl said. "Someone murdered Kara and now they tried to murder Kelly. It's the only explanation that makes sense."

"Except Kara was murdered in Manchester and Kelly's, um, incident happened here," Kent pointed out.

"So someone on the island went across and killed Kara, or someone from Manchester came here to kill Kelly," Beverly said. "That actually makes more sense. Someone from Manchester came here. Maybe that mystery man that everyone keeps talking about, the stalker one, maybe he found out that Kelly was trying to find him and he came over and killed her."

"If that's the case, the police may be able to find him when they check the flight and ferry records," Bessie said.

"Unless it was someone who came from Manchester earlier, like Pamela," Beverly said. "Kelly might have rung Pamela last night, once she got settled in her hotel room. Maybe she even invited her over for a chat."

"Why would Pamela have killed Kara?" Bessie asked.

"Jealousy," Beverly said flatly. "She secretly hated Kara and how beautiful and wonderful she was, so she killed her."

"Except she was in Glasgow when Kara died," Kent said.

"Maybe she mixed up all the drugs with the wine and then gave the bottle to Kara and told her to drink it when she felt lonely on the Saturday night," Beverly said. "It's possible."

"Maybe," Kent replied with a shrug.

"I'm sure the police will be taking a good look at where everyone involved was last night, including Pamela," Bessie told them.

"They should find out where the other two flatmates were, too," Beverly said. "One of them might have come over just to kill Kelly."

"I'm sure they'll coordinate their efforts with the Manchester police," Bessie assured her. "They'll check on everyone that they can find."

"Except they can't find the mystery man, the one that Kara called the Creepy Stalker," Amelia said with a shudder. "I'm starting to think that he's behind all of this."

"Him, or some other man that Kara met and went out with only once or twice," Kent said.

"I can't see Kelly letting some random stranger into her hotel room," Bessie said thoughtfully. "If the Creepy Stalker did come over to find her, how did he get her to let him into her room?"

"The police said she'd been drinking. Maybe she was too drunk to realise that she was in danger," Kent said.

"Did she often drink a lot?" Bessie asked.

"No," Beverly said.

"Occasionally," Jake countered. "She'd start talking about Kara and then she'd start drinking. I usually stopped her before she'd had too many, but if she was alone in a hotel room, I'm not sure what she might have done."

"She didn't drink much," Beverly insisted. "Not even when she was upset about Kara."

Jake looked as if he wanted to argue, but he simply sat back in his seat and gave Bessie a knowing look.

"This is pointless," Karl said sharply. "Bessie doesn't know anything more than we do, even though she found Kelly. This is a job for the police. We're wasting our time."

He got to his feet as he finished speaking. Before anyone could object, he stomped across the room to the door.

"I'm leaving. Anyone who wants to get back to Douglas should come now," he said.

As the others stood up, Beverly grabbed Bessie's hand. "Please, do whatever you can. Talk to John Rockwell. Talk to everyone. Find out what happened to my baby girl."

"I'll do what I can," Bessie found herself muttering.

Karl held the door as everyone left. Before he followed them, he turned to Bessie. "I still think you're nothing but a meddling old fool, but I do have to thank you for finding Kelly. The doctors told us that if you hadn't found her when you did, she probably would have been dead in another hour. Thank you."

Bessie was too surprised to reply immediately. The man slammed her door as he exited the cottage.

CHAPTER 12

When John rang an hour later, Bessie was trying to work her way through one of Onnee's letters.

"I hope I'm not interrupting anything important," he said.

"I'm wasting my time, trying to read difficult handwriting while my mind is elsewhere," she told him. "I've only managed to do three words in the last half hour, and I think one of them is wrong."

"Would it help if we got together tonight to discuss what happened to Kelly?"

"It wouldn't hurt. Her entire family showed up on my doorstep this afternoon."

"Did they? You'll have to tell me about the visit when I see you later."

"Will Hugh and Doona be coming, too?"

"Doona will. I'll be bringing her with me after we drop the children where they need to be. I'm not sure about Hugh. He's not at work today and he isn't answering his mobile."

"That's odd."

"He's not on call. He doesn't have to answer if he doesn't want to."

"I may ring him myself," Bessie said thoughtfully. "He's always at our gatherings."

"In that case, I'll bring enough food for six," John told her.

Bessie laughed. "That should be about right."

"We'll bring pudding, too. Amy has been baking every night this week. She's been making fairy cakes in every imaginable flavour. I'll bring a dozen or so."

"Should I be excited about them?"

"Some of them have been good. Others have been, well, interesting. I'll try to bring some of the better flavour combinations."

"Flavour combinations?" Bessie repeated, but it was too late. John had already ended the call. Wondering if she should throw together an apple crumble, just in case, Bessie put the phone down and then picked it up again immediately.

"Hello?"

"Grace, it's Bessie. May I speak to Hugh, please?"

There was a moment of silence before Grace replied. "He's at work, isn't he?" she asked, sounding confused.

"Oh, he may be," Bessie laughed, wincing at how forced it sounded. "I don't know why I was thinking he was off today. Don't mind me. I'll ring the station. I'm mostly trying to avoid Suzannah, really."

"I can understand that. If you can't find Hugh, please let me know. He's still behaving oddly. I keep telling myself that it's nothing, but I'm not sure that I believe me."

"There's been a development in a case we've been discussing. John and Doona are coming by tonight to talk about it. I was hoping that Hugh might join us, too," Bessie explained.

"If he does, can you let me know when he arrives and when he leaves?" Grace asked before sighing deeply. "I can't believe that I just asked you that. I'm making myself crazy. Just ignore me."

"I'll make sure that Hugh lets you know if he is going to join us tonight," Bessie said. And I'm going to have stern words with him after our gathering, as well, she added to herself. Whatever was going on, it was upsetting Grace, and that couldn't continue.

After a brief internal debate, Bessie tried Hugh's mobile number. The phone rang half a dozen times before it was answered.

"Hello?"

"Hugh? It's Bessie."

"Hello," he replied dully.

"There's going to be a gathering at my house tonight to talk about what happened to Kelly Sutton."

"Kelly Sutton? I thought the victim in the Manchester overdose was called Kara Sutton."

"She was. Kelly overdosed last night."

"She did?" Hugh sighed deeply. "I'm sorry. I'm a bit busy with something and I hadn't heard. John did ring me earlier, but I couldn't get to my phone."

"Really? Why not?"

"What time will everyone be there?"

"Six."

"I'll be there, too," Hugh told her. "Should I bring anything?"

"John and Doona are bringing both dinner and pudding."

"Great. I'll see you in a few hours."

Bessie put the phone down. "And you won't be able to evade my questions nearly as easily when you're here," she said.

She thought about ringing Grace back but decided against it. Surely Hugh would let her know what he had planned for the evening. The less she interfered with their marriage, the better.

Onnee's letters were still waiting for Bessie in her office, but she couldn't find any enthusiasm for tackling them. After some debate, she found a biography of Henry VIII and curled up to read about his convoluted life. She skipped much of his long marriage to Catherine of Aragon, choosing instead to read about his tumultuous relationship with Anne Boleyn. Jane Seymour had just appeared on the scene when someone knocked on Bessie's door.

"My goodness, is that the time?" she asked Doona as her friend walked into the cottage carrying a large box.

"John said that he told you we'd be here at six," Doona replied. "He ended up having to collect Thomas from one place to take him to another, so he'll be a few minutes late. I brought dinner, though, and pudding."

"I was reading about Henry VIII and his wives, and I completely lost track of time," Bessie explained. "I always end up feeling so sorry for all of them, the women who were unfortunate enough to attract his attention, that is."

"They are rather sad stories, the stories of his wives. I suppose Jane Seymour was the luckiest, dying after giving him a son and before he'd grown tired of her."

"Perhaps he wouldn't have grown tired of her, seeing that she had given him a son."

"Perhaps not, but he probably still would have had mistresses. Kings did in those days."

"And probably still do," Bessie sighed.

"Quite possibly."

Doona unpacked the box, piling takeaway containers on Bessie's counter.

"What did you bring?"

"Chinese," Doona said, making a face. "It wasn't really what I wanted, but it was the most convenient place to stop on the way here. I got lots. I hope Hugh is coming."

"He said he was, but he was acting oddly."

"Hugh was? In what way?"

"I'm not sure. Has he been himself at work?"

Doona shrugged. "I haven't been working much lately. John's only having me come in one or two days a week at the moment. I don't need the hours, and it's helpful if I can run the kids where they need to go. I'll probably be quitting sooner or later, but for now there isn't anyone to fully take my place. Suzannah is definitely moving to Castletown in the next month."

"I won't miss her a bit."

"She's doing somewhat better now, and she's been seeing one of the constables, so she's flirting less with the others, too. I won't miss her, really, but I'm not looking forward to going back to working five days a week, either."

"Maybe John will find a replacement soon."

"I hope so, but he has a lot on his plate right now."

Another knock on the door prevented Bessie from asking any

more questions. She let Hugh in and then stopped and watched as John pulled his car into the parking area next to Doona's.

"I'm sorry I'm late," he said in the doorway. "Thomas was supposed to be going one place and then, once he got there, they all decided it would be better to do something else altogether. I ended up having to take four boys all the way into Ramsey. The good news is that one of the other parents is going to bring them all back again."

"That is good news," Doona laughed.

"I'm starving," John said. "Let's get food before we talk."

Everyone filled plates. Bessie watched closely as Hugh took small helpings of just a few dishes. There was definitely something wrong with the man, she concluded as she passed around drinks.

"I rang Noble's before I left the office. Kelly is still unconscious, but they're cautiously optimistic about her chances for recovery," John said after his first bite.

"Then she'll be able to tell you what happened to her," Bessie said.

"Maybe. The doctors have told me not to expect much, especially in the short term. When she does wake up, she may well not remember anything about the night of her overdose. It's also possible that she'll never remember what actually happened."

"What do you think happened?" Bessie demanded.

John sighed. "It was set up to look as if it had been a suicide attempt."

"But you don't think she tried to kill herself," Bessie said firmly.

"Nothing anyone has said about her suggests that she was suicidal. She was upset about the anniversary of her sister's death, but she was excited that the police had some new angles to investigate."

"Could it have been an accident?" Doona asked.

"I can't see how anyone could take what she'd taken accidentally," John replied. "She had an odd mixture of drugs in her system, actually, some legal and some illegal. None of the legal ones were anything that she'd ever been prescribed."

"Her mother said something about her having been given sleeping tablets right after Kara's death," Bessie said.

"She was, but she didn't have any of those tablets in her system when she was found," John replied.

"If it wasn't an accident and it wasn't a suicide attempt, then someone tried to kill her," Bessie concluded.

"That's my working hypothesis, anyway," John replied.

"Who?" Doona asked.

"It has to have been whoever killed her sister," Bessie said. "That's the only thing that makes sense. I can't imagine why anyone would want to kill her otherwise."

"People get murdered every day for all sorts of odd reasons," John countered. "Having said that, I'm inclined to agree that what happened to Kelly is tied to Kara's death in some way."

"Which means the most likely suspect must be Pamela Ford, even though she was out of the country when Kara died," Bessie said.

"She could have given Kara the drugged bottle of wine before she left," John said. "She may have done the same with Kelly, actually. We've no idea if Kelly was alone in that hotel room last night or not."

"What about the cameras in the Seaview?" Bessie asked.

"The cameras only cover the lobby areas and some sections of the car park. There are several other doors into the building that someone could have used to get inside."

"They should put in more cameras," Doona said.

"They're expensive and generally unnecessary," John replied. "The other doors are all locked from the inside. That's meant to control access, but there's nothing to stop guests from letting friends or even strangers in through one of the other doors."

"I can't see Kelly letting someone into the hotel and into her room in that way," Bessie said thoughtfully. "Whom would she have agreed to let in through a side door?"

"We're trying to work that out," John said.

"What about calls or texts on her mobile?" Doona asked.

John frowned. "This doesn't leave this room, but her mobile is missing."

Bessie sat back, feeling stunned. "That proves that someone was in the room with her, doesn't it? Someone took her phone."

"Not necessarily. She might have decided to throw it away when she decided to end her life," John replied. "Or she may have simply lost it somewhere. We're doing our best to track it down, though."

"The person who tried to kill her took it because he or she had rung her or texted her to arrange to meet her at the Seaview," Bessie said.

"That's one possibility," John admitted.

"Where was Jake last night?" Bessie asked.

"As far as we know, he was at home. He rang Beverly from his mobile every half hour for several hours," John replied.

"But if he was ringing from his mobile, he could have been anywhere," Bessie said thoughtfully. "Maybe he kept ringing so that Beverly wouldn't realise that he knew exactly where Kelly was."

"Why would he want to kill her?" Doona asked. "He didn't even know Kara, did he?"

"What if he did, though?" Bessie said. "What if he was one of the men who went out with Kara once when she was living in Manchester?"

"We're checking his background," John told her. "He did live in Manchester for a while, but it seems that he'd moved on before Kara relocated there."

Bessie nodded, but there was something nagging her about the man. "What about the flatmates? Where were they last night?"

"We're having some trouble tracking down Rachel," John told her. "Brooke was in Manchester and has several dozen witnesses to her alibi."

"Unless she sent Kelly a bottle of wine in the post, something to drown her sorrows in on the anniversary of her sister's death, maybe," Doona suggested.

"Beverly was questioned about post and packages, and she doesn't recall Kelly getting anything recently aside from the usual bills and junk mail," John replied.

"What about Kelly's family?" Bessie asked. "I'd hate to think that her parents would do anything to hurt either of their daughters, but it isn't impossible."

173

"Kelly would have let either of them into her room last night," Doona said.

"The same is probably true for her brother and his wife, Amelia," Bessie added.

"We're checking alibis, but due to the nature of what happened, even if someone has an unbreakable alibi for the evening, that doesn't mean that he or she didn't provide the drugs that put Kelly in hospital," John explained.

Bessie sighed. "What about means? Where would perfectly ordinary people get their hands on a collection of different drugs?"

"Such things are probably not that difficult to find in Manchester," John replied. "Actually, they probably aren't that difficult to find on the island, either, although I hate to admit it. Nothing she'd taken would have been lethal on its own. It was the combination, and the alcohol, that nearly killed her."

"So the motive for the attempt on Kelly's life was probably that she was sticking her nose into the investigation into Kara's death. Who had a reason to kill Kara, though?" Doona asked.

"My first instinct is that it was someone with whom she'd been involved, however briefly. The man that she called the Creepy Stalker seems a likely candidate, although he was just one of several men with whom she only went out a single time, according to her friends and family," John replied.

"You think someone began to stalk her, but she didn't realise it?" Doona asked.

"She did tell her friends that she saw the man she'd called Creepy Stalker several more times," Bessie interjected. "He spent a lot of time in the local bookshop and they even had coffee together one afternoon. Apparently Kara was trying to find a nice girl for him."

"So she couldn't have been worried about him," Doona said.

"No, but maybe she badly misjudged him," Bessie countered.

"As far as we know, she went out with him in December, right?" John asked.

"Yes, although we aren't certain if he was the man that Kara told her father she was going to the Christmas party with or not," Bessie said. "I can't see that it really matters, though."

"No, me neither," John agreed. "The man may well have been harmless, but the Manchester police are anxious to track him down anyway."

"But if he was behind what happened to Kara, how did he get to Kelly?" Bessie asked.

"Maybe he disguised himself as a waiter at the hotel and dropped off a bottle of wine with the management's compliments," Doona suggested.

Bessie frowned. "It's a possibility, certainly. If he was stalking Kara and she didn't notice, he may have been following Kelly when she left home last night."

"You can check the ferry and flight records to see who is visiting the island right now, can't you?" Doona asked John.

"It's a huge job, but yes, we can. We've started checking flights already, actually. You'd be amazed how many young men fly into the island every day," he told her.

"How would he even know that Kelly was trying to get the case reopened?" Bessie asked.

"The police in Manchester have been asking questions around the bookshop. Maybe he stopped in to look at books and someone warned him that the police were looking for him," John suggested.

"We're overcomplicating this," Bessie said. "I think you should take a much closer look at Jake."

"As I said, we are doing so, but thus far we've nothing to connect him with Kara," John replied.

"So maybe he had nothing to do with her death but he did try to kill Kelly," Bessie suggested. She held up a hand. "I know, it's very obvious that I don't like the man. I want to know what he and Kelly fought about last night and I want to know if he gave her anything to eat or drink when they were together."

"He's been very cooperative with us thus far," John told her.

"He told me that their fight was just a stupid misunderstanding, that he wasn't being sensitive enough to how upset Kelly was about the anniversary of Kara's death. I don't believe him. They had their fight in a restaurant, didn't they? Surely there were witnesses."

John made a note. "That's a good point, actually. I need to find out where they went for dinner, although, according to Jake, they didn't actually eat or drink anything. They were already fighting when they arrived at the restaurant and they hadn't even ordered drinks yet when Kelly stormed out."

"Have the Manchester police tracked down the two men who went out with Kara more than once?" Bessie asked.

John flipped through his notebook. "They're working on it. Neither is still living in the same place as he was a year ago, but that isn't unusual for young people in the city."

"Would Kelly have agreed to meet either of them?" Doona asked.

"Maybe, if one of them rang her and said that he knew something about what had happened to Kara," Bessie said. "She was desperate for information."

"Desperate enough to end up alone in a hotel room with someone who was essentially a stranger?" Doona asked.

Bessie shrugged. "I don't know."

"Is there anyone else on the short list of suspects?" Doona asked after a minute.

John shrugged. "From everything we've heard about Kara, she probably went out with a dozen or more men while she was in Manchester. Any one of them could have been behind what happened to her. Why they'd come after Kelly is another matter."

"Time for pudding," Doona said, getting to her feet and starting to clear the table.

Bessie looked down at her empty plate. She didn't remember eating anything at all, but she must have eaten whatever she'd taken. She didn't really remember filling her plate, either, but no one had commented on it, so she must have done that, too. Hugh's plate was still half-full of food. He pushed it away and then stood up and carried it to the bin.

Doona took it from him with a raised eyebrow. "You didn't like it?"

"It was fine," Hugh shrugged. "I think I may be brewing something."

Doona and Bessie exchanged glances before Doona began to run hot water for the washing-up. John put a plate full of fairy cakes in the middle of the table.

"They look, um, interesting," Bessie said.

"They are," John replied dryly. "Amy found a website full of American recipes and she tried to recreate some of them. She wasn't always clear on what the various ingredients were, though. Some things have different names than we use here."

Bessie nodded. "Next time, have her ring me. I can translate American recipes. I've had years of experience because my sister used to send me recipes for her favourite things."

"The ones with the brown icing are the best," Doona said from the sink. "It's chocolate buttercream and it's yummy. The cake isn't as good, but the buttercream makes up for a lot."

Feeling slightly nervous, Bessie took one of the cakes with brown icing. She took a small bite and frowned. "What is the sponge meant to be?" she asked.

John shrugged. "Orange, I think."

A large bite confirmed it. "It is orange, and it's rather bitter," Bessie said.

"I think she put orange zest into the batter," Doona explained. "She may have zested the orange a bit too enthusiastically."

"It's not terrible, because the icing is very sweet," Bessie told her.

"You should try one," Doona told Hugh.

He shook his head. "I was watching Aunt Bessie's face. I don't think I want to try one."

"The ones with the white icing are okay," Doona said as she sat back down. "The cake is better, but the icing isn't sweet enough."

"I think one fairy cake is pudding enough," Bessie said, wiping her face and her fingers. "Hugh, you'll have to take the extras home with you."

"Thank you, but they should go back home with John. His children will appreciate them," Hugh said quickly.

"No, they won't," John laughed. "I'm not taking them back to my house. They can stay here or they can go in the bin. I'll never tell Amy that no one wanted them."

"I'm sure she tried her best," Bessie said.

"She did, but she's not much of a baker, really. I'm afraid I don't know much about baking, either. Her mother used to bake cakes for birthdays and Christmas, but Amy was never interested in helping her. Now I think she's sorry she didn't," John explained.

"And I'm no help," Doona sighed. "I can't bake to save my life."

"Send her to me on a Saturday or Sunday afternoon," Bessie suggested. "I can teach her everything she needs to know in just a few hours. Baking isn't complicated, it's just about following the recipe. It helps if you know what the ingredients are, of course."

"I may take you up on that," John said.

"I hope you do," Bessie replied.

"Was there anything else about the case, then?" Hugh asked.

John shrugged. "At this point, we're still just starting our investigation. We're really hoping that Kelly will be able to help as she recovers, too."

"I hope she's under police guard," Bessie said.

"She is. We've convinced her doctors to refuse to allow any visitors for now, not even her parents. I don't know that we'll be able to keep that up for long, but we're going to try," John said. "Pete is in charge down there."

"I hope he can keep everyone away from her until she can recover enough to tell you what happened," Bessie said.

"If she recovers enough to do that," he said grimly.

"I should be going," Hugh said, getting to his feet.

"Before you rush off, I need a small favour," Bessie said. "John, I'll ring you if I talk to any of the suspects."

John looked surprised, and then took his cue and got to his feet. "Doona, the kids will be out for another hour. Want to go back to my house and enjoy the peace and quiet for sixty wonderful minutes?" he asked.

Doona laughed as she stood up. "I know you don't mean it. You miss them terribly when they aren't around."

John nodded. "Yes, but maybe I could tidy an entire room in an hour."

"Ah, so that's why you're inviting me over. You want me to help tidy up," Doona sighed as she walked with John to the door.

John gave her a sheepish grin. "Think how much we could get done if we worked together," he teased.

Bessie watched as they walked out to their cars together. John pulled Doona into a kiss that suggested that they weren't going back to his house to tidy anything, and then they both got into their respective cars and drove away. After pushing the door shut, Bessie turned to Hugh, who was on his feet.

"I really have to go," he said. "Grace will be getting worried."

"Sit," Bessie told him.

He looked surprised and then slowly sank back into his seat.

"Tell me what's going on and don't try to lie to me," she demanded.

"I don't know what you mean," he said, staring at the table.

"Grace thinks you're having an affair."

Hugh looked up with a stunned expression on his face. "She what?"

"She thinks you're having an affair," Bessie repeated. Then she held up a hand. "That isn't exactly true. She wants to trust you, but she's worried. You aren't behaving at all normally. You didn't go straight home after our last gathering. You had the day off at work today but Grace didn't know it. There's something going on. You don't have to tell me what it is, but your wife, the mother of your child, deserves an explanation."

Hugh flushed and then looked back down at the table. "You know how I'm going to be taking college classes soon?" he asked her. "I'm supposed to start in June."

"Yes, I know. We're all very excited for you."

"I failed the entrance exam," he muttered.

"Oh, Hugh, I'm so sorry," Bessie exclaimed.

He shrugged. "It was maths that caught me out. I was never any good at maths, and the exam had a long section of algebra. I couldn't remember anything that I did at school. I could barely remember how to add and subtract."

Bessie nodded. She remembered helping young Hugh with his homework over the years. He'd been adamant that he'd never need algebra in the real world. Unfortunately, it seemed that he'd been mistaken.

"That doesn't explain your recent behaviour," she said after a moment.

"I've been having tutoring," he said sheepishly. "One of the other constables has been helping me in his spare time. He's really good with maths but he hates writing reports. I've been writing his reports in exchange for tutoring, but both of those things take time."

"Why not tell Grace?"

"She'll think I'm stupid. I have until the end of May to take the maths part of the exam again. If I can pass this time, Grace will never have to know."

"Except she's already noticed that you're sneaking around behind her back. Tell her what's happened. She's a teacher. Maybe she can help you with the maths you need."

"I can't tell her."

"You'd rather she keeps worrying that you're cheating on her?"

"No, of course not. I'll be more careful. I'll make sure I tell her that I'm working late whenever I have a tutoring session."

"Don't lie to her. I know you're doing it for what you think is a good reason, but you shouldn't lie to her. She loves you just the way you are. Tell her the truth and let her help you."

"I'll think about it," Hugh said.

Bessie put her hand on his arm and waited until he was looking at her before she spoke again. "I can tell her for you, if you'd like."

He shook his head. "I need to think about what I'm going to tell her. I love her so much. I don't want her to think that Aalish's daddy is dumb."

"No one thinks that you're dumb. I know you're a very smart young man. You didn't really apply yourself in school, and now that's come back to haunt you. There's no doubt in my mind that you can learn what you need and pass that exam the next time. But you'll do better if you have Grace's support along the way."

Hugh nodded, but he didn't look convinced. "I'll think about it," he said as he got to his feet.

"Do you want to think about taking those fairy cakes home, too?" Bessie asked.

Hugh laughed. "I don't need to think about that. I definitely don't want them."

Bessie walked him to the door and gave him a hug. "Grace loves you, and she won't think any less of you if you tell her," she said.

"I know you're right, but I still don't want her to know. I'm supposed to go and see Mike tonight for another session, but I'm going to cancel. I'm going home to my wife and my daughter and make sure that Grace knows that I love her, even if I don't tell her about the test results."

Bessie wanted to argue further, but she decided not to push him any more tonight. If he still hadn't told Grace in another day or two, she could try again to change his mind. She suspected that, once he'd given the matter some thought, he'd realise that he needed to share his secret with Grace. Her support would go a long way towards helping him through his exam troubles.

She let Hugh out and then took herself off to bed. It was a long night, full of bad dreams about bottles of wine and unconscious women. When she opened her eyes at six, Bessie was happy to be awake, even though she was still tired.

Going down to the kitchen to start a pot of coffee before she even took her shower was unusual for Bessie, but it seemed necessary that morning. After her first cup, she went out for her walk. Turning around at Thie yn Traie, she was back at her cottage before seven. What she really wanted to do next was find out how Kelly was doing, but the police wouldn't be releasing that information.

Pacing around her cottage did nothing to improve her mood. Finally, she decided that she needed to go into Douglas and find out what was happening for herself.

CHAPTER 13

She rang for a taxi and then paced around her kitchen, wondering why she was bothering. No one was going to tell her anything. Weirdly, she knew she'd feel better once she'd seen the police guard outside of Kelly's room. If she was honest with herself, she'd have admitted that she was hoping she might see a few of the suspects at Noble's while she was there. It might be interesting to talk to one or two of them individually, rather than in a group.

"Noble's? This isn't for your arm, is it?" Dave, her favourite driver, asked when Bessie told him where she wanted to go.

"No, my arm is fine," she replied. "I'm going to visit a friend."

"I hope your friend will soon be on the mend."

Bessie asked Dave about his wife, and they had a lovely chat about his holiday plans on the drive into Douglas.

"Do you want me to wait for you?" he asked as he pulled up in front of the building.

"I've no idea how long I'll be here. I may go into town after I'm done, as well. Thank you for offering, but you'd better get on with your day and leave me to sort out my own way home."

Dave looked as if he wanted to argue, but after a moment, he nodded. Bessie knew that he'd stay where he was until she was safely in the building. As the doors opened in front of her, she gave him a small wave and then continued inside.

"Can you tell me which ward Kelly Sutton is on, please?" she asked the woman at the information desk.

"I'm afraid I can't find any record of a patient by that name. Are you quite certain you have the right name?" was the reply.

"I'm quite certain," Bessie said. "Never mind, though. Maybe she's gone home."

"If she'd gone home in the last forty-eight hours, I'd have a record of her in our system," the woman said. "You must have the name wrong."

Bessie bit her tongue and then took a step backwards.

"Miss Cubbon," a voice said behind her.

Bessie spun around and smiled at Amelia Sutton.

"I thought that was you, but I wasn't sure," Amelia said. "I wasn't expecting to see you here."

"I came down to see if I could visit Kelly, but I was told she isn't here," Bessie replied.

Amelia glanced at the woman behind the information desk and then took Bessie by the arm. When they were several paces away, she stopped. "The police are trying to keep Kelly's stay here as quiet as possible. Officially, she isn't even here," she whispered.

Bessie nodded. "That makes sense. I suppose no one is being allowed to visit her, then."

"No one, not even her parents, which is making Beverly quite cross. She isn't as cross as Jake, though."

"Oh?"

"He's furious. He's desperate to apologise to her, even though the doctors have assured him that she isn't capable of understanding him at the moment." Amelia shrugged. "I think he's being rather unreasonable, but I've never cared for him."

"Really? Why not?"

"I wish I knew. I…" she trailed off and then waved to someone across the room. Kent joined them a moment later.

"There you are," he said. "Miss Cubbon? What brings you here?"

"I was hoping to see Kelly, actually," Bessie replied. "I'm worried about her."

"We're all worried about her, but no one is being permitted to see her at the moment. The doctors want to give her time to recover before she has to face visitors. As I understand it, she hasn't regained consciousness yet anyway."

"So she hasn't been able to tell the police what happened," Bessie sighed.

"No, she hasn't, although I believe they have several people standing by, ready to talk to her, the moment she shows any signs of waking up," Kent said.

Bessie nodded while she tried to think of a way to get rid of Kent. She really wanted to finish her conversation with Amelia.

"Darling, I'm going up to sit with Mother for an hour. Can you pop to the coffee shop and get us something for breakfast?" he asked his wife.

"Of course," she replied. "I'll be up with coffee and pastries in a little while."

Kent made a face. "There's no rush. Get yourself something first, if you'd like. Time seems to stand still in that little room upstairs."

Amelia nodded and then gave her husband a quick hug. "I know, it's awful. I'm sorry."

He shrugged. "I just hope Kelly recovers. I don't know if I can stand losing her, not after everything else that's happened." He rested his head on top of his wife's for a moment while she rubbed his back. Then he straightened. "Must get back to my mother. Jake is with her and he's done nothing but complain about the police since he arrived. I'm sure Mum is tired of listening to him."

"He should go to work and leave Kelly alone," Amelia said.

"I think he believes that she actually tried to kill herself and that it's his fault," Kent replied. "I don't know what they fought about, but it must have been a pretty terrible fight."

"There's every chance that Kelly won't want to see him when she wakes up. Tell him that we'll let him know if she does," Amelia suggested.

"I tried that. He won't hear of leaving, and Mum is encouraging him to stay. She's convinced that he and Kelly belong together."

Amelia shrugged. "I'll be up soon," she said.

Kent nodded and then glanced at Bessie. "I'll tell Mum that you were here," he told her. "I'm sure she'll appreciate it."

"Thank you," Bessie said.

She and Amelia watched the man walk away.

"Can I buy you some breakfast, then?" Bessie asked Amelia as Kent disappeared onto one of the lifts.

"It will have to be a quick breakfast. I really don't want to leave Kent with his mother and Jake, not for too long."

The coffee shop was only a few steps away. Bessie got a cup of coffee and a toasted teacake and Amelia followed suit. They found a table in the corner.

"You were saying something about Jake when Kent interrupted," Bessie reminded her.

"Oh, it was nothing."

"Really? You don't care for him. Why?"

Amelia flushed. "There's just something about him that bothers me. He and Kelly had only gone out a few times when she first introduced us. Apparently he insisted on meeting everyone, her parents and the rest of her family, almost immediately. It just seemed odd to me."

"That does seem a bit unusual."

"Kent and I were almost engaged before I met his family. Once I'd met his sisters, I was a bit cross about it, really, because I loved them both and I don't have any sisters myself. Kara and I were close before she moved across, and Kelly and I do a lot of shopping together and things like that, or we did before Jake arrived on the scene."

"Now Kelly would rather spend time with Jake?"

"I don't know if she'd rather spend time with him or if she feels as if she has to spend time with him," Amelia said. "I sometimes think that he's smothering her a little bit, being too attentive and taking up too much of her time. I haven't said anything to her, though. She seems happy enough and I do remember what it was like, falling in love and wanting to spend every second with that person."

"And you think Kelly is falling in love with Jake?"

"I thought she was, a few months ago. Now I'm not so sure. She seems less enamoured of him, although some of that could just be because they've been together for a while now." Amelia sighed. "I don't know what I'm saying. Kara's death was incredibly difficult, and we were all dreading the anniversary. Kelly's, um, incident has made things even worse. Some of my hostility towards Jake is probably because of everything else that's going on around us."

"What do you think happened to Kelly?" Bessie asked after a moment.

"I don't know what to think. I never would have suspected that she was suicidal, but she was very upset about Kara's death. If ever she were going to try to end things, it probably would have been on the anniversary date or on Kara's birthday. Maybe the fight with Jake simply drove her over the edge."

"Could it have been an accident? Can you see her taking drugs simply to numb the pain she was feeling?"

"A year ago I would have said no, definitely, but Kelly has changed a lot since Kara died. As much as I hate to admit it, I can see her being desperate enough to take something. She was given sleeping tablets right after Kara died, but she told me she never took them. If she still had them, maybe she took a few on Sunday night, just to try to help her get to sleep or something."

Bessie nodded. She knew that Kelly hadn't taken those sleeping tablets, but she couldn't share that with Amelia. "Can you imagine any reason why anyone would want to kill Kelly?"

Amelia shook her head. "I know you said it must be related to Kara's death, but I can't see any connection. Maybe whatever happened to Kelly is completely separate from what happened to Kara."

"So what happened to Kelly, then"

"That's the problem, isn't it? Kelly is a perfectly ordinary woman, doing an ordinary job and living an ordinary life. I can't imagine anyone trying to kill her. Murder is extraordinary."

"It isn't, though," Bessie told her. "I've been involved in many murder investigations and nearly all of the victims have been ordinary people who were killed for rather mundane reasons."

"Maybe her fight with Jake was really serious and he decided to get rid of her."

"Do you mean that?"

"I don't know. I don't care for the man, but murder is a big step up from just being a bit too intense. He seems to be devoted to Kelly."

"If he is, and she'd ended things with him, can you see him trying to kill her?"

"I simply don't know. Murder is unfathomable to me. We're talking about people that I've known for a long time, my family and my friends. In some ways, it's easier to believe that Kelly accidentally overdosed because, as impossible as that is, it still seems more likely than murder."

Amelia finished her coffee and then got to her feet. "I have to take breakfast up to my husband and his mother. It was nice seeing you again."

Bessie watched as the woman bought coffee and some pastries and then left the café. Feeling slightly frustrated by the entire conversation, she got to her feet and headed for the door.

"Bessie? What a lovely surprise," a voice said as she crossed the hospital's lobby.

Bessie turned around and was pulled into a hug by a dear friend. "Helen, hello," she said.

Helen Baxter was a nurse and an amateur historian. She and Bessie had been friends for years, having met while Helen was doing some research at the Manx Museum. They'd been caught up in a murder investigation together, and that investigation had been where Helen had met police inspector Peter Corkill. Bessie and John Rockwell had been the witnesses to their subsequent marriage, and Bessie had been thrilled to learn that the pair were expecting their first child together later in the year.

"I hope you aren't here because of your arm," Helen said, looking concerned.

"Not at all. I came down to see Kelly Sutton, actually, even though I'd heard she wasn't being allowed visitors."

"She isn't. I'm working in that ward at the moment, actually. Pete requested that I be put there, as he seems to trust me."

Bessie laughed. "I should hope so."

"I'm just having a coffee break, although I'm not drinking coffee at the moment. It seems to make my morning sickness worse."

"How are you feeling?"

"Miserable but very happy, which I think is pretty normal. The morning sickness is quite bad, and it seems to last all day, too, but my doctor insists that that is perfectly normal, especially for an older first-time mother."

"Isn't it meant to get better as the pregnancy progresses?"

"It is, yes. We'll see. Right now I'm taking it a day at a time and counting it as a victory if I manage to keep much of anything down."

"Oh, dear."

"I may be exaggerating slightly, as I've already put on five pounds," Helen admitted. "But how are you?"

The pair chatted for several minutes until Helen looked at her watch. "And now I must get back to the ward. Things are interesting up there. Everyone wants to see Kelly and no one seems to understand why they can't."

"I've been told her boyfriend is being difficult."

"He is, although you didn't hear that from me. Apparently, they'd had a fight and he's blaming himself for Kelly's overdose. I've seen it all before."

"Really?"

"We see everything here," Helen told her.

A dozen questions sprang into Bessie's mind, but before she could ask any of them, Helen dashed away, heading back to work. Making a mental note to ring the woman later in the day, Bessie headed for the door again.

"Pardon me, but it's Miss Cubbon, isn't it?" a voice said.

Bessie stopped. "Jake Holt, right? You're Kelly's boyfriend."

The man winced. "I certainly hope so, although no one here is treating me as if I am."

Bessie raised an eyebrow. "I'm not sure I understand what you mean."

Jake shrugged. "Most of Kelly's family seem angry with me. I understand why. They blame me for what happened to Kelly. I blame myself, too."

"Let's get a cuppa and chat," Bessie suggested.

Jake hesitated and then nodded. "I'd like that."

Back in the café, Bessie ordered a slice of shortbread to go with her second cup of tea. After a moment of hesitation, Jake did the same.

"I should probably have something more substantial," he said as he sat down across from Bessie at a table near the door. "I don't remember when I last ate anything."

"You need to look after yourself," Bessie scolded.

He nodded. "It's just so difficult. I feel responsible for what happened and I want more than anything to tell Kelly how sorry I am. The doctors won't tell me anything because I'm not family."

"Won't Beverly tell you what's happening?"

"She just keeps saying that no one is telling her anything, either," Jake sighed. "There's a police guard on Kelly's door, too, which makes no sense at all."

"That rather depends on what happened to her."

"What do you mean? It's rather obvious what happened to her."

"What do you think happened, then?"

"She was upset about the anniversary of her sister's death. We'd had a fight. I should have realised that our fight had pushed her over the edge, but I didn't. I should have recognised the signs, seen that she was thinking of ending things, but it never even crossed my mind that she was that unhappy."

"You think she attempted suicide," Bessie said.

"What other options are there?" Jake asked.

"Maybe she overdosed accidentally."

"Maybe. I like that idea a lot better, actually. As far as I know, she never took drugs. I know her doctor gave her something at some point to help her sleep, but she never took the tablets. Maybe she decided to take a few, but misjudged how many to take."

Jake sat back in his seat, smiling. Clearly the idea of an accidental overdose had pleased him.

"The police also have to consider the possibility that someone tried to kill Kelly, of course," Bessie said.

The man looked stunned. "That's not possible," he said firmly. "No one had any reason to want to hurt Kelly. It's a crazy idea."

"Perhaps, but until Kelly recovers and can tell the police what happened, they have to treat it as a possibility."

"Why would anyone want to kill Kelly?" he demanded.

"Maybe because she knows something about what really happened to Kara."

"What do you mean, what really happened to Kara? She died of an accidental overdose. Don't tell me you really think she was murdered? I know Kelly wants to believe that, but I've never really taken the idea seriously."

"It's a possibility. I'd suggest that it seems more likely now, after what's happened to Kelly."

"I'd suggest that you're adding two and two and getting five," Jake muttered under his breath. "Kara's death was a tragedy, but no one actually thinks she was murdered."

"Kelly does."

"Kelly can't accept the idea that Kara was anything less than perfect. She doesn't want to believe that Kara might have been taking drugs. The idea that she was murdered is almost as crazy as the idea that someone tried to kill Kelly."

"Tell me what happened Sunday night," Bessie suggested. "You and Kelly were supposed to have dinner together, weren't you?"

"Yes, but when I went to collect Kelly at home, she told me she'd changed her mind about going out. She wanted to be alone, she said. I pointed out that she still had to eat and that she could be alone after dinner if that was what she really wanted. It took me several minutes to talk her into going, but she finally agreed."

"Where did you go?"

"We went to that little Italian place on the promenade, but we argued all the way there. She said she didn't want to go anywhere that might be busy, that she wasn't up to seeing a lot of people. When we got there, it was fairly quiet, but then she argued about which table we were given. She really wasn't herself, now that I think back. Maybe she'd already taken something."

Or maybe she really didn't want to be dragged out of the house, Bessie thought. Jake should have respected her wishes and left her home alone.

"She didn't stay for dinner, then?"

"We never even ordered," Jake sighed. "We'd barely sat down when she decided that it was too much for her. She told me that she'd get a taxi home and she left."

"And did she get a taxi home?"

"No, of course not. I followed her out of the restaurant and then drove her home. She didn't speak to me for the entire drive, even though I kept trying to talk to her." He took a sip of his tea and then put his head in his hands.

"Are you okay?" Bessie asked.

"When we got back to her house, I walked her to her door. I told her that I didn't think she should be alone, not that night. She insisted that she'd be okay, that her parents were at home and that they'd be there for one another." He stopped and then shook his head. "I pushed her too hard."

"What do you mean?"

"I tried to insist that she come home with me, that she'd be better off at my flat than she would be at home. She, well, she told me that she thought it might be best if we ended our relationship. I knew I'd pushed too hard, but she wouldn't listen when I tried to apologise. I begged her to forgive me, to give me another chance. I tried to tell her how much I loved her and how I couldn't live without her, but she wouldn't listen. After a few minutes, she went inside and shut the door in my face."

I wouldn't have waited a few minutes, Bessie thought. "What did you do next?"

"I went back to my car and tried to ring her mobile. She didn't answer. I sat there for a while, maybe half an hour, trying her mobile every few minutes. Then I realised that I wasn't going to get anywhere doing that, so I started texting. I told her how sorry I was and begged her to reply, but she didn't. Eventually I drove myself home."

"So you didn't talk to her again?"

"No, I didn't. I'm sure you can see why I'm so desperate to talk to her now. Once I got home, I rang her house and spoke to Beverly. She told me that Kelly was fine and that I should give her a day or two to calm down before I rang again. I agreed, but I simply couldn't do it. I rang again a short while later, feeling that talking to Beverly was better than nothing." He gave Bessie a sheepish grin. "I probably rang her more than I should have."

"How many times did you ring?"

Jake shrugged. "I didn't count, but I kept ringing. I'd talk to Beverly and try to explain. She was very sympathetic, by the way. We'd talk for a few minutes and I'd calm down, but then, after the call was over, I'd start to think about Kelly and get worried again. So I'd ring back and beg Beverly to put Kelly on. And she'd calm me down again. It was a vicious cycle that I'm embarrassed about now, but at the time I couldn't seem to stop myself."

"At some point, did Beverly tell you that Kelly had gone to a hotel?"

"She did, which upset me even more. I wanted to know where she'd gone and I didn't believe Beverly when she said that Kelly hadn't told her. I still don't believe that Beverly didn't know, actually."

"If she had known, she would have sent the police to the Seaview as soon as Kelly didn't show up for work," Bessie pointed out.

"I suppose so. Whatever, I kept ringing and bothering poor Beverly until two or three in the morning. That was when she finally convinced me to get some sleep. She told me that she'd do everything she could to persuade Kelly to talk to me the next day. I never imagined that Kelly was trying to kill herself while her mother and I were talking."

"Unless it was an accident."

"I hope it was an accident. I'd hate to think that our fight distressed her that badly. I mean, I hope that she loves me enough to die for me, but I don't actually want her to die."

Bessie stared at him. His words rang all sorts of alarm bells. "Let's hope she makes a full recovery."

"I need to see her," he said. "You know people with the police. Surely you can help me."

"I'm sorry, but the police and the doctors know what's best. If they don't think she should have visitors, then I agree with them."

"I'm not just a visitor, though, I'm the man who loves her. I want her to understand how I feel. I need to tell her that I'm sorry and give her a reason to fight to survive."

Bessie frowned at the intensity of Jake's words. She had to hope that Kelly would refuse to see him when she did wake up. There was something disturbing about the man. "Once Kelly wakes up, it will be up to her whom she sees," she said.

"And she'll still be mad at me, which means she won't want to see me," Jake replied. "I'll have to wait until she's out of hospital to visit her at home."

"Give her time," Bessie suggested. "She's going to need time to recover from what happened to her. You're going to have to be patient."

"I'm not very good at being patient," he told her.

"I'm afraid you don't have any choice this time. If you truly love Kelly, you're going to have to wait for her to recover and then ask to see you."

Jake nodded, but he was staring past her, out into the building's lobby. "There's Karl. I wonder if I can persuade him to tell me how Kelly is doing," he said. He jumped up from the table and rushed out of the café.

Bessie sat back in her chair. Jake seemed unstable to her, weirdly obsessed with Kelly. Was it possible that he was behind her overdose? The police hadn't yet found any connection between Jake and Kara. But maybe Kara's death and Kelly's overdose weren't connected.

Feeling as if her head were spinning, Bessie finished her tea and got to her feet. There was a single car at the taxi rank, and Bessie climbed into it gratefully. The driver knew the island well, which let Bessie sit back and think on the journey back to Laxey.

"Thank you," she told him as she got out of the car.

"You're very welcome," he replied, nodding and then slowly driving away.

Bessie walked back into Treoghe Bwaane as her phone began to ring.

"Hello?"

"It's John. I was just wondering why you were at Noble's this morning."

"I wanted to see the people involved in the case," Bessie explained. "It's all very worrying and I thought maybe, if I could talk to a few of them, I might start to understand what's going on."

"And did it help?"

"I saw Amelia and Jake, and I had a nice chat with Helen as well."

"You'd better tell me everything," John said.

Bessie did her best to repeat the conversations she'd had with everyone. "Jake worries me," she said when she was done. "He seems unstable and I think he's obsessed with Kelly. I hope Pete keeps him well away from her until she's able to tell him exactly what happened."

"He's keeping everyone away from her for right now," John told her. "He let her mother have a brief visit, but only with two constables in the room. He's not taking any chances."

"He thinks it was a murder attempt, then."

"Mostly because of the missing mobile phone, but yes, he's treating it as a murder attempt."

"It must be related to Kara's death."

"We think so, but we can't be sure. We've found the man Kara called the Creepy Stalker, by the way."

"You have? Tell me more."

"His name is Gary Woods, and as far as we can tell, he's perfectly harmless. He was in Madrid the weekend that Kara died and he's never been to the Isle of Man."

"And you're sure he's the right man?"

"Pretty sure. The Manchester police talked to the manager at the bookshop and she gave him the man's name. He's a regular when he's in the area, but he often travels for work. He was interviewed and he admitted to having taken Kara out for a meal once. According to his statement, he wanted to go out again, but she turned him down. He did volunteer that he saw her a few times after that at the bookshop, and that she was trying to find him a single friend."

"So the Manchester police have ruled him out?"

"Yes, although they've given me his contact details. I may ring him for a chat, if only to try to better understand Kara."

"They went out for a meal?" Bessie asked.

"That's what he said."

"They didn't go to a Christmas party?"

"He didn't mention a Christmas party. Let me double-check the notes I took when I was talking to my colleague in Manchester."

Bessie paced back and forth next to the phone. There was something about that Christmas party that was bothering her. For some reason, it seemed significant.

"According to his statement, they went out for a meal. He wasn't certain of the date, but he thought it was probably around the middle of November."

"So he wasn't the man that Karl remembered Kara mentioning," Bessie said.

"Apparently not, but I can't see that it matters."

"It probably doesn't," Bessie agreed. "There's just something about the Christmas party that's bothering me."

"If you work out what it is, let me know. You often pick up on things that end up being significant."

"I just want to get to the bottom of all of this," Bessie sighed. "I keep hoping that Kelly will wake up and tell someone what happened to her."

"Pete spoke to her doctors about an hour ago. They don't expect her to wake up for another twenty-four hours or more. They've also warned him that she'll probably struggle to remember what happened the night of her overdose."

Bessie put the phone down but kept pacing. She didn't like Jake, but maybe she was letting her feelings influence her thinking. Everything was muddled up in her head. What she needed to do was think about things logically.

Searching for some paper and a pen reminded Bessie that she'd already started a timeline for Kara's life in Manchester. Where had she put that sheet of paper? she wondered. As she started to look for it, someone knocked on her door.

"Pamela? This is a surprise."

"I heard about what happened to Kelly. I was hoping you might know more," she replied.

"I don't know anything," Bessie admitted. "But why don't you come in? I'm trying to work through everything that happened to both Kara and Kelly. Maybe you can help fill in some information about Kara's time in Manchester."

"If you think it will help, I'll tell you everything I can remember," Pamela replied.

Bessie filled the kettle. It was really time for lunch, but after two trips to the café at Noble's, she wasn't really hungry. "I can make sandwiches or just put out biscuits," she told her guest.

"Biscuits are fine."

Bessie filled a plate and made tea. While she worked, she remembered where she'd put the timeline, so she dug that out before she sat down opposite Pamela.

CHAPTER 14

"Kelly wasn't suicidal," Pamela said as Bessie took a sip of tea.

"You sound very certain of that."

"I am certain. We talked about suicide, just the two of us, once. It was not long after I'd moved back to the island. We were talking about what had happened to Kara. I told her that I didn't think Kara had committed suicide, that she wasn't the type. Kelly agreed and then we talked for a long time about why people might want to die. It was one of those conversations that got really intense very quickly, and we ended up promising one another that if either of us ever felt as if we couldn't go on, we'd ring the other. I know Kelly was upset about the anniversary and I know she'd had a fight with the man she's been seeing, but she would have rung me, I know she would have."

"And she didn't."

"She didn't. I was home all night, and I had my mobile with me because I was texting a friend. I never heard from Kelly."

"When did you last speak to her?"

"Just a few days ago. We talked about the anniversary coming up and I reminded her that she should ring me if she started to feel too overwhelmed. She told me that she was sad, but not depressed, and that she was feeling very hopeful that your involvement was going to actually help her finally get some answers."

"What do you think happened to her, then?"

"I wish I knew. I can't imagine anyone trying to kill her. Why would they? But she wouldn't have overdosed accidentally. She knew better than to touch drugs. That was another thing we talked about a few days ago. She told me that her doctor had given her sleeping tablets, but that she wasn't going to take them. She said she didn't want to feel numb. She wanted to remember Kara and grieve."

"Let's talk about Kara," Bessie said. "I was working on a timeline for the months she was living in Manchester. Maybe you can help me fill it in."

"I can try. I've been thinking about her a lot since we talked the first time. I've been remembering more, too."

Bessie unfolded the sheet and stared at it. "Kara went out with a man that she nicknamed the Creepy Stalker. Do you remember anything about him?"

"I do, actually. I should have told you about him before. He hung out at the bookshop. Kara actually introduced me to him. She didn't really think he was a stalker, just that he seemed the type to get intense too quickly. She loved giving men nicknames, but most of them were exaggerations. They were her shorthand for why she didn't want to see that particular man again, that's all."

"Kara introduced you to the Creepy Stalker?"

"She did. He was called Gary or Grant or something similar. He was nice enough, but not my type. I think Kara was hoping I might like him. She was eager to find him a nice woman, for some reason."

"You didn't think he might have been stalking her, though?"

"No way. She wouldn't have introduced me to him if she thought he was genuinely a stalker. Like I said, it was just a silly nickname."

"Do you remember when she introduced you to him?"

"Let me think," Pamela answered. She picked up a biscuit and ate her way through it with a frown on her face. "I think it was in early December, right in the middle of the madness at work. I had an odd hour off and Kara and I went to the bookshop for a quick cuppa before I had to go back to the office."

Bessie added a line to her timeline. "So she must have met the man sometime before December."

"I think she'd met him a few weeks before we bumped into him in the bookshop. It wasn't much earlier than that, anyway."

"So mid-November," Bessie said. She wrote that on the timeline, too. As she worked, she noticed that she'd written "Christmas party date?" on the bottom of the page. Kelly's father had dated that to sometime in December.

"I wish someone could remember more about that Christmas party date," she said as she copied what she'd written at the bottom into December on her timeline.

"I've been trying to recall December more clearly, but work was really demanding at that point. It may have been that same day, actually, the day she introduced me to Gary or Grant, whatever his name was." Pamela shook her head. "I hope the poor man never finds out what she called him. He'd be very upset."

"What might have been the same day?" Bessie asked.

Pamela blinked. "Oh, she might have gone out to a Christmas party with someone that same night. I remember we went for a cuppa and she said something about having to get all dressed up for the evening, more so than for just a normal night out, anyway."

"Interesting," Bessie said. She wondered if the Manchester police had asked Gary Woods about Kara's Christmas party date. If it had been the same evening that he'd seen her, maybe she'd said something to him about her plans.

The pair talked for several more minutes, and Bessie filled in more details on her timeline. Pamela had vague recollections of two other men who'd taken Kara to dinner, one in January and a second in March.

"None of this is getting us anywhere," Pamela complained eventually. "The police are never going to be able to track down random men who once took Kara to dinner."

"The question is whether any of the random men have subsequently come to the island," Bessie said.

"You think one of them attacked Kelly?"

"It's a possibility. You said she didn't try to kill herself and that she didn't overdose accidentally. That leaves attempted murder."

"And you think the attempt is connected to Kara's death?"

"Can you think of any reason why anyone would try to kill Kelly?"

Pamela frowned and looked at the table. "I don't much like her boyfriend, Jake. I'm not accusing him of murder, but, well, I don't like him."

"I don't like him, either."

Pamela nodded. "I heard they'd had a fight. Maybe she told him she didn't want to see him any longer and he decided that if he couldn't have her, no one could."

"What a horrible thought."

"I know, but it does happen."

"Yes, it does," Bessie agreed.

"I know he's been giving Kelly a hard time about the investigation."

"What do you mean?"

"When we spoke the other day, Kelly said that Jake kept reminding her that Kara's death had been ruled an accident. He kept telling her that she was wasting her time and wasting valuable police resources by going over and over the case again and again. He didn't think she was going to learn anything new because he didn't think there was anything new to learn."

"Poor Kelly. That was the last thing she'd have wanted to hear," Bessie said. "He said much the same thing when he was here, though. Kelly brought her family to see me, and he turned up uninvited. He was pretty insistent then that she was wasting my time."

Bessie thought back, remembering Jake laughing when Kelly had told him about the Christmas party date. He'd said something about it not being possible that there was a connection between Kara's death and a man she'd gone out with once in early December.

"You look as if you've just remembered something important," Pamela said.

"Jake said something about Kara going out with her Christmas party date just once in early December," Bessie replied thoughtfully.

"So? That's right, isn't it?"

"Yes, at least, I think so, but how did Jake know that Kara only went out with him once? And how did he know that it was in early December?"

"Did he see your timeline?"

"Yes, but I'd written the Christmas party date on the bottom of the page, not under December," Bessie replied slowly. "I wish I could remember the conversation better. I can't remember when he arrived, so I'm not sure what he might have heard or not heard."

"Maybe I should ring him," Pamela said. "I can tell him that I just remembered Kara telling me that she was going to a Christmas party with a man called Jake. It might be interesting to see how he reacts to that."

"It might, but it will be safer if we let the police handle it," Bessie said firmly. "I'm going to ring John Rockwell now. At the very least, he can try to find out where Jake was in early December. He's been looking into Jake's past anyway."

"Ring your inspector friend, by all means, but tell him that I'm going to confront Jake. That will be faster than waiting for the police to research his past, and I'll have the satisfaction of seeing his face when he learns that his lies are crashing down around him."

"If he did kill Kara and try to kill Kelly, then he's dangerous," Bessie pointed out as she picked up the phone.

"He's a coward who drugs women. He isn't going to be able to do anything to me."

Not wanting to talk to Suzannah, Bessie rang John's mobile number. "I'm sorry to bother you, but Pamela is here and we've been talking about Jake and that Christmas party date that Kara mentioned to her father. Jake seemed to know more about it than he should have when I spoke to him. I didn't notice it at the time, and now I'm kicking myself because if I had, I might have prevented what happened to Kelly."

"Slow down," John said. "Start at the beginning."

As Bessie began to talk, Pamela stood up. "I'm just going to go," she mouthed to Bessie.

"Wait," Bessie exclaimed.

"Who's there?" John asked.

"Pamela. She wants to confront Jake."

"I'll be there in five minutes," John said. "Keep her there until I arrive. I want to hear what she has to say before I go and talk to Jake."

"Inspector Rockwell is on his way here. He wants to hear everything you can remember about the night of the Christmas party before he goes to talk to Jake," Bessie told Pamela.

"I'm going to go and talk to Jake," Pamela countered. "Then I can tell him everything Jake said when I confronted him with what I know."

Bessie sighed. "Please don't do this. Jake could be dangerous."

"As I said, I'll be careful. I'm not afraid of him."

"You should be."

A knock on the door interrupted Pamela's reply. Bessie crossed the room, grateful that John had arrived so quickly. She pulled open the door and then gasped.

"Jake? What are you doing here?" she demanded.

He shrugged. "I was driving around, thinking about Kelly, and I realised that I was quite close to your cottage. I thought maybe we could talk some more. Talking to you made me feel much better this morning."

Bessie opened her mouth to tell him to leave, but Pamela was already at the door.

"Jake? What a surprise. Come in and have a cuppa with us," she said.

He frowned. "Pamela? I wasn't expecting to find you here."

"No? I was visiting Bessie. I'd just remembered something and I wanted to share it with her," Pamela replied.

"What did you remember?" Jake asked.

Bessie thought he looked incredibly nervous. "Let's have tea, shall we?" she asked.

The last thing Bessie wanted to do was make tea, but it seemed to be the best way to waste a bit of time. John was on his way. He'd probably be there before the kettle boiled, Bessie told herself as she filled the kettle and got down another teacup.

"I'll put out some more biscuits," Pamela offered.

Bessie handed her a packet and then focussed on making tea. The kettle seemed to boil much more quickly than normal. A few moments later, the trio were gathered around the table together.

"This is nice," Pamela said with a small smile.

Bessie bit into a biscuit before she could disagree.

Jake frowned. "Maybe I should come back another time," he said hesitantly. "I didn't mean to interrupt anything."

"You're fine. You're more than welcome, really," Pamela told him. "Bessie and I were just talking about you, actually."

"Talking about me? Why?" he demanded.

"We were talking about all of the men that Kara went out with," Pamela replied. "She used to go out with a different man nearly every night, you know."

"I didn't know. I never met her," Jake said flatly.

"She had silly nicknames for the men that she went out with, too," Pamela continued.

"That I did know," Jake said. "Kelly was convinced that the one Kara called her Creepy Stalker was behind her death."

"That's old news," Pamela said, waving a hand. "I know the man in question and he had nothing to do with what happened to Kara."

"You know him?" Jake echoed.

"Yup. He's lovely, actually, although I do understand where his nickname came from. Kara was being a bit unkind, really. She often was when it came to the men with whom she spent her time."

"Really?" Jake looked bored.

Bessie jumped when someone knocked on the door.

"John, hello," she said brightly as she opened the door wide. "Come in."

John looked at the pair at the kitchen table and frowned. "I didn't know you had company," he said.

"Pamela came to talk to me about Kelly and then Jake just arrived for a chat," Bessie explained.

"I was just telling Jake a few things," Pamela added. "You should sit down and listen. They might be of interest to you."

John raised an eyebrow and then took a seat at the table. It only took Bessie a moment to get him his own cup of tea.

"Where were we?" Pamela asked with a smirk as Bessie sat back down.

"I was just leaving," Jake said. "I have better things to do with my time."

"Don't rush off," Pamela replied. "Things are just about to get interesting."

"I hardly think so," Jake told her.

"Kara always told me about the men in her life," Pamela said. "Sometimes she even woke me up when she got home and told me all about her evening. I wasn't always in bed, though. Some nights she got home as I was coming in from work, especially in December, when I was working a lot of extra hours. The night of the Christmas party was one of those nights."

Bessie frowned. Pamela was going to spoil everything by making up too many details.

Jake chuckled. "That Christmas party is rapidly becoming the stuff of legend. Kelly seemed to think that it was the key to whatever happened to Kara. As I said when I first heard about it, I can't imagine what a single night out in early December could possibly have to do with Kara's death many months later."

"Except no one ever told you that it was a single night out or that it took place in early December," Pamela said in a conversational tone.

Jake looked startled and then shrugged. "Kelly tells me everything."

"Except Kelly was here when her father remembered about that evening. She didn't get to speak to you about it before you made that statement," Bessie said.

"I'm not sure what you're suggesting," Jake said. "She told me that Kara had gone to a Christmas party. I suppose I simply assumed it was in early December. Isn't that when most of those things happen? As for only seeing the man once, well, that was Kara, wasn't it? That's how Kelly always describes her, anyway."

John frowned at Bessie. This wasn't the way he wanted to conduct his investigation, that was clear.

Pamela wasn't deterred, though. "Here's the thing," she said to Jake. "When I first met you, I thought you looked awfully familiar."

Jake raised an eyebrow. "Let me guess, you now think I'm one of the men who once went out with Kara. Somehow, even though I was living in Coventry when she died, I managed to go out with her in Manchester."

"I don't think anything," Pamela replied. "I know you were one of the men who went out with Kara in Manchester. You took her to a Christmas party. She told me all about it when she got back. You'd told her you were this big important bank executive, but when you got to the party, no one knew who you were. Kara told me you were embarrassed, but that you just made it worse by strutting around and acting as if you were more important than you clearly were."

Jake turned bright red. "I hope you're taking notes," he said to John, sounding as if he were struggling to contain his anger. "There must be laws against lying about someone when it comes to a murder investigation."

"Kara said that she told you that she had a migraine and needed to leave. You brought her home, and I was just getting in. You were sitting outside in your car and you didn't leave for a very long time. I didn't get a good look at you, but I know it was you."

"Fascinating. Next you'll be accusing me of actually murdering Kara," Jake said.

Bessie watched as a nerve twitched in Jake's face. He was only just keeping his emotions in check.

"I think we should continue this conversation in my office," John said, getting to his feet.

"I do hope you're talking to Pamela," Jake said. "She's the one making wild accusations. I'm totally innocent."

"I'm going to need to talk to both of you," John replied.

Jake shook his head. "I'm tired. I want to go home and get some rest. The last few days have been very difficult for me."

"I can't imagine how disappointed you must have been when Kelly didn't die," Pamela said.

"What a horrible thing to say," Jake snapped. "Kelly is the love of my life. Of course, I'm delighted that she survived her suicide attempt."

"It wasn't a suicide attempt, though," Pamela argued. "You tried to kill her, just as you killed Kara."

"I don't have to listen to this nonsense," Jake said. He stood up.

John put a hand on his arm. "We can continue this conversation at the station."

"I've nothing further to say. Pamela is making up all sorts of crazy lies. I can't believe you're taking her seriously."

"It will be easy enough to find out if she's telling the truth," Bessie said. "If you did take Kara to a party for your work, then you must have been seen together by dozens of people. Surely some of them will remember."

Jake inhaled sharply. "I won't have you questioning my work colleagues. It's inappropriate. Besides, who knows what they'll say? Some of them might think it's funny to try to get me into trouble with the police."

"I don't think that's a concern," John said.

"They can start by looking at your travel history," Pamela added. "They'll be able to find out exactly when you were in Manchester and how often you came back after that night out with Kara, too. I'm sure it wasn't easy, stalking her from Coventry. No doubt you flew back and forth fairly regularly. You could have driven, I suppose. It probably would only take what, two, two and a half hours each direction? You'd better hope you never got a speeding ticket along the way. Or a parking ticket, either."

Jake's face turned bright red again. "This is insane," he said tightly.

"Let's go," John told him. He started to walk towards the door, still holding Jake's arm.

Jake shook himself free and then surprised them all by punching

John in the face. As John fell to the floor, Jake turned and ran towards the door at the back of the cottage. Pamela stepped in front of him, and when he charged straight at her, she laughed.

Bessie watched in awe as the woman sidestepped and then deftly swept the man's legs out from under him. She grabbed his arm and twisted it behind his back as he cried out in pain.

"I can hold him for a minute or two," she told Bessie. "But maybe you should ring for an ambulance for your friend."

Hugh was the first constable on the scene. By the time he'd arrived, John was sitting up, with a bag of frozen peas on his jaw and a second one on the back of his head. Pamela had tied Jake's arms behind his back, and he was sitting, staring sullenly straight ahead, when Hugh walked into the cottage.

"Arrest this woman for assault," Jake snapped, nodding at Pamela.

Hugh raised an eyebrow and then looked at John.

"Arrest Jake for assaulting a senior police officer," John said, wincing as he spoke. "We also want to discuss murder and attempted murder with him, but we'll start with the easy charges."

Hugh was reaching for his handcuffs when Constable Harrison arrived a moment later. He flushed when he looked at Pamela.

"What happened here?" he asked.

"That woman assaulted me," Jake snapped, giving Pamela an angry look.

"I've been training in Tae Kwon Do since I was five," Pamela replied. "All I did was a basic self-defense technique to get him to the ground and keep him there."

Harry looked at Hugh and laughed. "Remember the amazing new woman I was telling you I'd met? Apparently I'm going to have to be very careful around her."

Hugh grinned. "You're a braver man than I am," he told Harry.

A loud knock on the door interrupted the conversation. Bessie opened it to a very concerned-looking Doona.

"Is he okay? Are you okay?" she asked, rushing to John's side.

John shrugged. "He punched me, and I hit my head on the floor when I landed. I'm not sure which blow knocked me out."

"There's an ambulance coming, right?" she asked Bessie.

"I rang the police. John didn't want an ambulance."

"John's an idiot. He could have a concussion. He was knocked out. He needs to see a doctor," Doona said.

"I'm not going to argue," John told her. "Maybe you could take me, though. I'd rather not go in an ambulance."

Doona looked as if she wanted to argue, but after a moment she nodded. "You need to be more careful," she said softly. "I was really worried about you."

"I'm fine," John told her.

"I'm not," Jake interrupted loudly. "Remember me? I was the one who was falsely accused of things and then assaulted by a madwoman."

"You hit a police officer," Pamela reminded him. "I was just trying to protect myself and Bessie."

Jake scowled at her. "I just wanted to leave, that's all. You were throwing out all sorts of wild accusations."

"Which will be investigated properly by the police," John said as he slowly rose to his feet. Doona did her best to help, but as far as Bessie could tell she was mostly in the way.

"There's nothing to investigate. Even if I did once take Kara out, it was only the once and has nothing to do with anything."

"So you admit it," Pamela said with a satisfied smile.

Jake shrugged. "As someone said earlier, there will be witnesses. I took her to a Christmas party. We had a nice time. I took her home. I decided that I didn't want to see her again. Maybe there were hard feelings on her part. That may be why she told you so many unpleasant lies about me. I don't know."

"You never told Kelly that you'd been involved with her sister," Pamela said.

"I didn't realise they were sisters at first," Jake replied. "Once I'd worked it out, it would have been too awkward to try to explain."

"Didn't Kara tell you about her sister?" Bessie asked.

He shrugged. "She may have mentioned her. As I keep saying, we only went out the one time. We didn't have time to share every detail of our lives with one another."

"Let's continue this conversation at the station," John said.

"Look, I'm really sorry that I hit you," Jake replied. "I wanted to get away because I've nothing to tell you. I barely knew Kara and I know nothing about what happened to her. I'm sure you're eager to get to a doctor to get your head checked out. Why don't I come and talk to you tomorrow, maybe around one o'clock? Would that suit you?"

John stared at Jake for a full minute before he spoke. "I am eager to get my head checked out, yes, but I'm also eager to speak to you. I'm fairly certain that you know a good deal more about Kara Sutton than you're willing to let on. I'm also fairly certain that you had something to do with Kelly Sutton's overdose. My men are going to take you down to the station now and they'll make sure that you stay there until I'm ready to speak with you. If that isn't until tomorrow, well, we have a holding cell at the station."

"A holding cell?" Jake repeated, the colour leaving his face. "That isn't necessary. I can answer all of your questions here. What do you want to know?"

"Hugh, Harry, take him down to the station," John said, sounding tired. "I don't want to hear another word out of him for now."

Hugh fastened his handcuffs around Jake's wrists and then untied the rope that Pamela had used. He handed it back to Bessie with a wink.

"I may be a bit late for our dinner tonight," Harry told Pamela in an apologetic tone.

"What time is dinner?" John asked.

"He's supposed to be at my flat at six," Pamela replied.

"I'll make sure he's finished at the station in plenty of time," John told her.

She laughed. "Excellent. I'm going to make something special tonight."

Harry grinned, and then he and Hugh walked out the door with Jake. They'd only gone a few yards when Bessie heard one of them shout. Everyone in the cottage rushed to the front door.

Bessie tried not to laugh as she watched Jake running down the beach. His hands were cuffed behind him, which seemed to be throwing off his balance. The thick sand probably didn't help, and Bessie thought it was a bit of poetic justice when he tripped over a large piece of driftwood and fell heavily into the water.

Hugh dragged him out and then looked over at Harry. "He's dripping wet. Put him in your car," he suggested.

"I brought a patrol car, so you may as well," Harry replied.

The pair marched Jake back down the beach and loaded him into the back of the marked police car.

"Take him to Ramsey," John told them. "There will be several constables there ready to help you escort him inside. They have better holding facilities than we have in Laxey. I have a feeling we're going to be keeping Mr. Holt with us for some time."

"He did seem awfully desperate to get away," Bessie remarked.

They all watched the patrol car drive away, closely followed by Hugh in his own car.

"We need to get you to hospital," Doona said to John as the cars disappeared from view.

"I'm sure I'm fine," John countered.

"What if it had been Thomas who'd been knocked out?" Doona asked.

"Then I'd make him see a doctor," John sighed.

"Exactly. Let's go," Doona said firmly.

"I hope you don't mind if I leave my car here for a short while," John said to Bessie. "I don't think Doona is going to let me drive myself anywhere right now."

Doona just rolled her eyes at him.

Bessie laughed. "Your car can stay here as long as necessary. I don't need the parking space."

John nodded and then followed Doona to her car. She gave Bessie a wave as they drove away.

"That was an interesting afternoon," Pamela said as she followed Bessie into Treoghe Bwaane.

"That's one word for it."

"What I told Jake about the Christmas party, that was all true. Kara told me many stories about the men she'd been out with. None of them really stuck with me at the time, but once we were really talking about it, it all came back to me."

"Did she ever mention seeing him again?"

"No, but he worked for the bank where she did her banking. That was how they'd met in the first place. He worked in lending, I believe, and she had her mortgage on the flat there. She may have seen him in the bank occasionally but never bothered to mention it to me."

"I have to believe that he was stalking her for months," Bessie said.

"That's creepy, but what's worse is that he came over here and started seeing Kelly."

"That is odd and rather scary. If he did kill Kara, why would he then start pursuing her sister?"

"That's a question for his psychiatrist," Pamela suggested.

Bessie nodded. "He's clearly mentally unbalanced."

"Beverly is going to get a shock," Pamela said.

"I just hope the police can find the evidence they need to lock Jake up for a very long time."

Pamela nodded. "And now I must get home and start cooking. I want to make something special for Harry. I just thought he was handsome and looked good in a uniform, but he's actually quite interesting and intelligent. He might have real potential."

"Good luck to you both," Bessie said. "Let me know if I should buy a hat."

Pamela laughed. "It's far too soon for that, but if it ever does get to that point, you'll be the guest of honour. I never would have met him if it hadn't been for you."

Bessie let her out and then sat down at the table, feeling overwhelmed by events. It seemed likely that Jake had killed Kara and tried to kill Kelly, even though his motives were unclear. If he had been stalking Kara, it seemed as if she had been completely unaware of it. Bessie could only hope that things would make more sense once Kelly had recovered enough to talk to the police. She refused to consider that Kelly might not pull through.

CHAPTER 15

*B*essie felt out of sorts for the next two days. John would only confirm that the police were still questioning Jake and that the Manchester police were also involved. As she got out of bed on the third morning after the dramatic scene at her cottage, Bessie vowed to put the whole thing out of her mind. What she really needed was a nice long walk, past Thie yn Traie and the new houses to the stretch of beach where they were planning to build even more houses. She hadn't been that far in some time.

The sign advertising the new homes was now partially covered with a sticker that read "Only Two Plots Remaining." Bessie stood on the beach for several minutes, staring out at the sea. Before long the area would become a construction site. It was just as well that she rarely walked this far.

As she turned for home, Bessie suddenly felt tired. Her arm was aching again, something it seemed to do when she felt fatigued. Feeling as if she'd been foolish to walk so far, Bessie could only sigh as a light rain began to fall. Of course, she'd left her umbrella at home. When the new houses came into view, she felt slightly better.

"Bessie? Come in out of the rain," Grace called from her house.

"I'll get everything wet," Bessie protested.

"It's fine," Grace assured her. "Come in. I'll grab you a towel."

Moments later, Bessie was wrapped in a warm and fluffy towel, sitting comfortably in Grace's kitchen. Grace put the kettle on and then put out a plate of biscuits.

"Where's the baby?" Bessie asked as she glanced around the room.

"Shhh," Grace laughed. "She's still asleep. I know it won't last long, but I'm enjoying a few minutes of peace and quiet. If it gets to ten minutes, I might even start to remember my own name."

Bessie grinned. "She's hard work, then?"

'Yes, but so very worth it. I've been saying that since she arrived, but I'm actually starting to believe it now. She's starting to gurgle and interact more, and every time she smiles at me my heart melts."

The kettle snapped off and Grace made tea. As she was pouring, strange noises began to come from somewhere.

"What's that?" Bessie asked, looking around, confused.

"It's the baby monitor," Grace explained, pointing to the small white box on the counter. "Aalish is awake and she isn't very happy."

Bessie sipped her tea while Grace rushed upstairs to get the baby. She had time to eat her way through two biscuits before Grace returned with Aalish in her arms.

"She needed changing, and it was a bit of a mess, so I had to change her clothes, too," Grace explained. "But she's all clean and happy now, aren't you?"

Aalish gave her mother a toothless grin and then babbled something at her.

"Would you like a cuddle?" Grace asked Bessie.

Feeling as if it would have been rude to say no, Bessie took the baby and held her close. "Hello," she said softly.

Aalish seemed to study her for a minute before she closed her eyes.

"I think she's gone back to sleep," Bessie said a minute later.

Grace shrugged. "She gets to sleep whenever she wants. I'm incredibly jealous, actually."

"You don't want me to wake her?"

"No, not at all. I want to enjoy my tea and biscuits. She was up half the night, so she probably needs the sleep now."

Bessie stared at the baby, watching her little chest rise and fall. She hadn't had much experience with babies, really, but Aalish was lovely.

"I was going to ring you later," Grace said after she'd eaten a few biscuits. "I wanted to thank you for talking some sense into my husband."

"Oh?"

"He finally admitted why he's been sneaking around. I can't believe he thought I'd be disappointed in him for failing the maths part of his exam. He's such an idiot sometimes."

"When does he have to retake the test?"

"He has until May, but he'll be ready long before that. We've been working together every night and he's a very quick study."

"That's good to hear. I told him you would be able to help."

"Mike was doing a good job with him, but Hugh prefers my methods," Grace laughed. "I give him kisses for every right answer, and if he gets an entire section right, I let him off one nappy change. He's very motivated."

Bessie laughed. "What does he get if he passes the exam, or shouldn't I ask?"

Grace blushed. "I promised to cook him one of his favourite meals, with pudding. He's having trouble choosing what he wants, though. He has a lot of favourite meals."

This time when Bessie laughed, it woke the baby. Aalish took one look at Bessie and began to cry.

"I'd better take her," Grace sighed. "Thank you for the small break, anyway."

"I'll do the washing-up before I go," Bessie replied.

They hugged at the door before Bessie, feeling refreshed, continued back to Treoghe Bwaane. The light on her answering machine was flashing as she let herself into the cottage.

"Bessie? It's Beverly Sutton. Kelly is awake and she'd like to see you."

Bessie rang for a taxi before dashing up the stairs to comb her wind-tangled hair. She powdered her nose and added a bit of lipstick to her lips before going back down to pace anxiously while she waited for her car.

She'd rung Beverly back to let her know she was on her way, and Beverly was waiting for her in the lobby at Noble's.

"Thank you for coming," she said stiffly.

"I'm just happy to hear that she's awake," Bessie replied.

Beverly nodded and then led Bessie through the building to one of the wards. Bessie waved at Helen Baxter along the way. The police constable at the door to Kelly's room checked Bessie's name against his list.

"You're cleared," he said, stepping back to let Bessie enter.

"She can only have one visitor at a time," Beverly said. "I'll wait out here."

Bessie was shocked at how pale and unwell the woman on the bed looked. She did her best to hide her surprise as she crossed the small room. "Kelly?" she said softly.

Kelly opened her eyes and smiled. "I'm doing better than I look," she said softly.

"That's good to hear."

"The doctors are cautiously optimistic that I'll make a full recovery."

"Wonderful."

"They told me that if you hadn't found me when you did, I probably would have died."

Bessie shrugged. "I was lucky that I found you."

"I should have told someone where I was going. I wasn't thinking clearly."

"Do you want to tell me about it?"

Kelly sighed. "No, but I will anyway. I told the police and then I had to tell my parents. Mum was very upset. She thought Jake was wonderful."

Bessie pulled a chair up next to the bed and sat down. "You don't have to tell me anything," she said politely.

"You deserve to hear the whole story, though. It all starts with

Kara. Jake worked for the bank where she had her mortgage. He was there one day when she went in to make a payment. According to his version of events, their eyes met and they both fell madly in love on the spot."

"Did they speak?"

"Not that day. He was working in Coventry. The way he told it, he kept coming back to see Kara, but I don't think she even knew he existed at that point. It was a month or more later when he finally asked her to go to the bank's Christmas party with him. He'd been invited because he'd been working in Manchester for much of the year, apparently. I'm not really clear on all of that."

Bessie nodded. "Maybe someone at the bank will be able to explain it."

"Anyway, they went to the party. I don't know what happened, but Jake was clearly angry when he told me about it. I suspect that Kara told him she didn't want to see him again, but he didn't give up."

"Poor Kara."

"I can't imagine that she even realised that he was stalking her, but he definitely was. He drove from Coventry to Manchester just about every weekend so that he could see her. From what he said, he mostly just sat in his car and watched her going in and out, but once in a while he'd see her at the bookshop or elsewhere and they'd chat for a bit. I'm sure Kara was polite, just not interested."

"But she didn't guess what was really happening?"

"I'm sure she would have told me if she'd suspected anything. After a while, he decided that he needed to declare his love. He drove down early on a Friday, with a bottle of wine and flowers. When he got to the flat, Kara's flatmates were all leaving with suitcases. He was afraid she might be going with them, but then, a few hours later, she came home from work. For whatever reason, he decided to wait another day, coming back on the Saturday afternoon with his gifts. Kara let him in. She probably felt as if she knew him, since she saw him regularly. She might have been feeling a bit lonely, too. I don't know."

"As you say, she probably felt as if she knew him. He worked for her bank, after all."

"He told me that they had a drink together and that he told her how much he loved her. He was shocked when she said she didn't feel the same way. He didn't mean to kill her, of course. He simply misjudged what he gave her."

"He admitted to drugging her?"

"Oh, yes. He said he could see that she'd been working too hard and that he wanted to help her relax. He was very careful not to drink the wine himself, of course."

"So he drugged the wine, and then watched her drink it and left her to die?"

"Something like that," Kelly said, tears streaming down her face.

"And did he do the same with you?"

"More or less. We had a terrible fight in the restaurant. I just wanted to be alone, and he kept insisting that we should be together. In the end, I demanded that he take me home, and then I went to the Seaview. I don't know how he found me there, but he did. He begged me to just let him apologise and I was dumb enough to agree. I knew after the first few sips of wine that it was drugged, but he kept making me drink more and more. I was too weak to stop him as he poured the stuff down my throat."

Bessie shuddered. "How awful for you."

"He kept talking, too, about how much he loved me, but he kept calling me Kara. He told me how he'd come to the island especially to find me, because Kara had told him so much about me. I don't know if that's true, though."

"It doesn't sound as if Kara really spent much time with him."

"No, but I can see her talking about me with him. She may have struggled to find other things to discuss, actually."

"So he came to the island to find you?"

"'To find me and to win my heart,' he said. He even broke his wrist deliberately, just so he'd have an excuse to come to hospital."

Bessie gasped. "That's crazy."

Kelly nodded. "He told me that he wanted to marry me and spend forever with me, but that I'd made him angry. He didn't want to hurt me. He just wanted to help me get through losing Kara. He told me that I'd sleep for many hours, and that when I woke up I'd feel much better."

"He never would have confessed to killing Kara if he'd expected you to recover."

"I know. I knew that at the time, but I didn't know what to do. He kept making me drink more and more and I was so very tired. I just kept thinking that if I could just sleep, everything would be okay."

Bessie patted Kelly's arm. "And it is now."

Kelly nodded. "The police are pretty sure that Jake will be locked up for a long time. He isn't admitting to anything yet, but the evidence is mounting. Now that they know where to look, apparently they're finding a lot."

"That's good to know."

Kelly nodded and then yawned. "I'm still very tired," she said apologetically.

"I'll let you get some sleep, then," Bessie said, getting to her feet.

"Thank you for everything," the woman murmured before she shut her eyes.

Bessie slid the chair back into the corner and then quietly let herself out of the room. Karl was standing in the corridor just outside the room.

He looked at Bessie and then shrugged. "I owe you an apology," he said gruffly.

"Not at all," Bessie protested.

"No, I do. You were right about the significance of that night out in December and you were able to work out what happened to Kara. And you saved my baby girl's life. I'm sorry that I ever doubted your abilities and that I was rude to you the night we met."

"I'm just glad that Kelly is going to be okay and that Jake is behind bars. Nothing else matters."

Karl nodded. "You're right about that, too. As a family, we're forever in your debt, but I hope you'll understand if I say that I hope none of us ever sees you again."

Bessie felt a bit hurt, but she also understood. No doubt she would bring back nothing but bad memories for all of them. She nodded and then walked away, happy to have helped and relieved that it was all over.

GLOSSARY OF TERMS

House Names – Manx to English

- **Thie yn Traie** — Beach House
- **Treoghe Bwaane** — Widow's Cottage

English to American Terms

    advocate —Manx title for a lawyer (solicitor)

    aye — yes

    bin — garbage can

    biscuits — cookies

    bonnet (car) — hood

    boot (car) — trunk

    brewing something — catching something (a cold or flu)

    car park — parking lot

    chemist — pharmacist

    chips — french fries

    cuppa — cup of tea (informally)

    dear — expensive

    estate agent — real estate agent (realtor)

    fairy cakes — cupcakes

fancy dress — costume
fizzy drink — soda (pop)
flat — apartment
holiday — vacation
jumper — sweater
lie in — sleep late
lift — elevator
midday — noon
pavement — sidewalk
plait (hair) — braid
primary school — elementary school
pudding — dessert
skeet — gossip
skirting boards — baseboards
starters — appetizers
supply teacher — substitute teacher
telly — television
thick — stupid
torch — flashlight
trolley — shopping cart
windscreen — windshield

OTHER NOTES

The emergency number in the UK and the Isle of Man is 999, not 911.

CID is the Criminal Investigation Department of the Isle of Man Constabulary (Police Force).

When talking about time, the English say, for example, "half seven" to mean "seven-thirty."

With regard to Bessie's age: UK (and IOM) residents get a free bus pass at the age of 60. Bessie is somewhere between that age and the age at which she will get a birthday card from the Queen. British citizens used to receive telegrams from the ruling monarch on the occasion of their one-hundredth birthday. Cards replaced the telegrams in 1982, but the special greeting is still widely referred to as a telegram.

When island residents talk about someone being from "across," they mean that the person is from somewhere in the United Kingdom (across the water).

Traditionally British women wore hats to weddings, often using them as an excuse to purchase something new. The phrase "buy a hat" became short hand for talking about someone planning a wedding in the future. (Do I need to buy a hat, therefore, means: Should I be expecting a wedding invitation soon?)

ACKNOWLEDGMENTS

Thank you to my wonderful editor, Denise, who cleans up my mistakes on book after book.

Thank you to Kevin for the beautiful pictures that I use for my covers.

And thank you, readers, for continuing to enjoy Bessie's stories.

Aunt Bessie Yearns
An Isle of Man Cozy Mystery
Release Date: July 17, 2020

Aunt Bessie yearns for a typical walk on the beach.

It's been exactly two years since Elizabeth Cubbon, Aunt Bessie to nearly everyone, found a dead body on Laxey Beach. Since then, finding murder victims has been something of an unfortunate habit for her.

Aunt Bessie yearns for a quiet life where she never finds dead bodies.

Unfortunately for Bessie, she once again stumbles over a murdered man on her morning walk. Harrison Parker was a newspaper reporter for a London paper, but he used to work on the Isle of Man.

Aunt Bessie yearns to understand why the police are so certain that Harrison's death is tied to someone at Thie yn Traie, the beachfront mansion near Bessie's cottage.

Thie yn Traie's owner, George Quayle, has four guests staying with him at the moment. They all seem to have secrets, but are any of them worth killing for? With the mansion's regular butler off the island, Bessie is missing one of her best sources of inside information.

Can the temporary butler, Geoffrey Scott, be persuaded to tell Bessie everything he knows? Which of the four men has a secret he's prepared to kill to keep? Can Bessie help the police solve the case, and finally get the peaceful life for which she yearns?

ALSO BY DIANA XARISSA

The Isle of Man Cozy Mysteries

Aunt Bessie Assumes

Aunt Bessie Believes

Aunt Bessie Considers

Aunt Bessie Decides

Aunt Bessie Enjoys

Aunt Bessie Finds

Aunt Bessie Goes

Aunt Bessie's Holiday

Aunt Bessie Invites

Aunt Bessie Joins

Aunt Bessie Knows

Aunt Bessie Likes

Aunt Bessie Meets

Aunt Bessie Needs

Aunt Bessie Observes

Aunt Bessie Provides

Aunt Bessie Questions

Aunt Bessie Remembers

Aunt Bessie Solves

Aunt Bessie Tries

Aunt Bessie Understands

Aunt Bessie Volunteers

Aunt Bessie Wonders

Aunt Bessie's X-Ray

Aunt Bessie Yearns

The Isle of Man Ghostly Cozy Mysteries

Arrivals and Arrests

Boats and Bad Guys

Cars and Cold Cases

Dogs and Danger

Encounters and Enemies

Friends and Frauds

Guests and Guilt

Hop-tu-Naa and Homicide

Invitations and Investigations

Joy and Jealousy

Kittens and Killers

Letters and Lawsuits

Marsupials and Murder

Neighbors and Nightmares

The Markham Sisters Cozy Mystery Novellas

The Appleton Case

The Bennett Case

The Chalmers Case

The Donaldson Case

The Ellsworth Case

The Fenton Case

The Green Case

The Hampton Case

The Irwin Case

The Jackson Case

The Kingston Case

The Lawley Case

The Moody Case

The Norman Case

The Osborne Case

The Patrone Case

The Quinton Case

The Rhodes Case

The Somerset Case

The Tanner Case

The Underwood Case

The Vernon Case

The Isle of Man Romance Series

Island Escape

Island Inheritance

Island Heritage

Island Christmas

The Later in Life Love Stories

Second Chances

Second Act

ABOUT THE AUTHOR

Diana Xarissa lived on the Isle of Man for more than ten years before returning to the United States with her family. Now living near Buffalo, New York, she enjoys having the opportunity to write about the island that she loves so much. It truly is a special place.

Diana also writes mystery/thrillers set in the not-too-distant future under the pen name "Diana X. Dunn" and fantasy/adventure books for middle grade readers under the pen name "D.X. Dunn."

She would be delighted to know what you think of her work and can be contacted through snail mail at:

Diana Xarissa Dunn

PO Box 72

Clarence, NY 14031.

You can sign up for her monthly newsletter on the website and be among the first to know about new releases, as well as find out about contests and giveaways and see the answers to the questions she gets asked the most.

Find Diana at:
www.dianaxarissa.com
diana@dianaxarissa.com

Made in United States
North Haven, CT
06 November 2023

43689071R00134